Starlight Dunes

A Pelican Pointe Novel

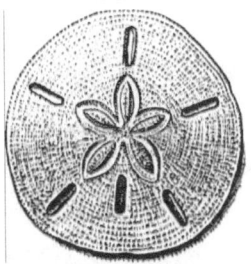

VICKIE McKEEHAN

beachdevils
PRESS

Starlight Dunes
A Pelican Pointe Novel
Copyright © 2013 Vickie McKeehan

beachdevils
PRESS
ISBN-10: 0615941826
ISBN-13: 978-0615941820
Printed in the USA

Cover design by Vanessa Mendozzi
Pelican Pointe map designed by Jess Johnson

Visit the author at:
www.vickiemckeehan.com
www.facebook.com/VickieMcKeehan
http://vickiemckeehan.wordpress.com/
www.twitter.com/VickieMcKeehan

The Indigo Brothers Trilogy
INDIGO FIRE
INDIGO HEAT
INDIGO JUSTICE
INDIGO BROTHERS TRILOGY BOXED SET

Coyote Wells Mysteries
MYSTIC FALLS
SHADOW CANYON
SPIRIT LAKE (2018)

For Kevin with the tender heart and the best father I

know

To see the complete **Cast of Character** list go to my
website:
www.vickiemckeehan.com
under the **Pelican Pointe Series** tab.

Acknowledgements

Thousands of years before the Spanish arrived in California, a Native American people called the Chumash, or "shell people" lived and thrived along the state's rugged coastline, canoeing back and forth among the Channel Islands, specifically Santa Cruz Island. For years these native people fascinated me so much so that I wanted to bring a Chumash descendant to life in a contemporary setting. To do that in a creative way, there's a lot of research and support involved. My thanks to Nakia Zavalla, Cultural Director of the Santa Ynez Band of Chumash Indians for providing me with translations, and to the Santa Barbara Museum of Natural History.

And a softness came from the starlight and filled me full to the bone.
William Butler Yeats

Starlight Dunes

A Pelican Pointe Novel

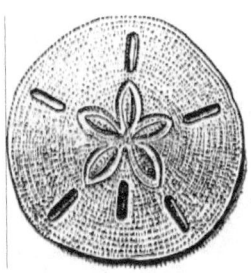

by

VICKIE McKEEHAN

Welcome to Pelican Pointe

Prologue

Three weeks earlier
Santa Cruz, California

A storm churned out at sea. He could smell the rain on its way in. He might not possess the same psychic ability as his brother, Ethan, the now full-time mystery writer, but Brent Cody recognized a good Pacific squall when he saw one forming on the horizon.

He'd grown up around the ocean, not five miles from the spot where he now walked. Except for the fifteen years he'd given to the military, he'd made this coastal town his home. Now as he left work and crossed the dark parking lot to his truck, he stared up at the ugly-looking, purple clouds moving inland. The heavy low-hanging marine layer had blacked out the stars and more than likely meant before nightfall they'd get wind gusts and rain.

His mother's garden could use a good soaking, Brent decided as he climbed into his Dodge Ram pickup to head for home. He placed his briefcase on the passenger side of the bench seat, and started up the engine.

After putting in a fourteen-hour day Brent was more than ready to kick back in front of the flat-screen. He was pretty sure the pre-season San Jose Sharks were on the road tonight in Detroit hitting the ice against the Red Wings. Of course, he'd already missed the first two periods. Good thing he'd remembered to DVR the game.

He could already taste a cold Anchor Steam to go with the leftover pizza he'd ordered from the night before. All he had to do was toss it into the microwave, zap it, and he had dinner. With the comfort of cheese, pepperoni and beer, he'd be set to catch the last of the hockey game.

With his mind on slap shots, he scanned the secure lot out of habit before exiting onto the deserted side street. He hadn't been a member of law enforcement for the better part of a decade not to key in on his surroundings this time of night.

Since the people of Santa Cruz had elected him county sheriff six years earlier, most of his days were like today, long and exhausting. He didn't like to admit how much time he spent sitting on his butt plopped in front of his laptop, handling paperwork these days. Because of it he did whatever it took to stay in shape.

Since he'd celebrated his fortieth birthday over the summer, he was mindful his body wasn't the same as it used to be. Even though he'd once been able to throw a ninety-five mile per hour fastball for his high school baseball team, he knew those days were long gone. Though he did play softball on Sunday afternoons on a team with his co-workers, the long days were one of the reasons he made sure he jogged at least five miles three times a week. Whenever his schedule permitted, he also tried to hit the state-of-the-art gym down the street from the office to lift weights or work up a cardio sweat on the elliptical. Plus, he'd gotten into the habit of limiting his bacon and egg consumption to a measly two times a week. For all his efforts he still weighed the same as the day he'd landed in Iraq.

Bottom line, it sucked getting older, he thought now as he made the four-mile drive to his house. When fat drops of rain began to splat on the windshield, he turned on the wipers and listened as the blades began an annoying back-and-forth, rubber-on-glass screech. He countered the whap, whap, whap sound by turning up the volume on the Pearl Jam CD already in the player.

Glancing at his reflection in the rearview mirror, he caught the shadow of a man with Native American features, the straight nose, the strong chin, deep-set eyes so brown they were almost black. He audibly sighed at the makings of crow's feet at the corners and the fact that his raven black hair was starting to turn a little gray at the temples. Something his father, Markus Cody, teased him about.

It was hell turning forty, he decided as he drove the streets of the neighborhood where he'd essentially grown up. On impulse he pushed the button to roll down the window several inches on the driver's side in spite of the mist so he could breathe in the cool night air. If there was a benefit to living next to the sea, this was it. The fresh, salty air always made for a good night's sleep.

Once he'd gotten his bad marriage behind him, he'd finally taken the plunge and bought a little Spanish bungalow with a pretty view of the water. The place wasn't large, no more than twelve-hundred-square-feet, but it suited a single guy who had no plans to ever make a family. That's why when he got home tonight, there would be no one waiting for him, no woman, no girlfriend, not even a dog.

It was best that way, he thought, even if he did on occasion dip his toe into the shallow end of the dating pool. After all, he was anything but a loner. He was social enough when the occasion called for it. His mother saw to that because she seemed hell-bent on fixing him up with...someone. Especially since his little brother had settled down in wedded bliss a couple of years back with Hayden and they now had a son.

Since Ethan's marriage, Lindeen seemed more determined than ever to get her oldest to follow in Ethan's footsteps. Hell, she wasn't even subtle about it anymore.

He could laugh about it—most of the time. Mainly because the woman thought she was so damn clever whenever she invited him over to supper—as if he hadn't caught on years earlier to her interfering ways when it came to his social life.

But what kind of social life did he really have when he was married to his job? He supposed he needed to put his foot down and take a stand with her one of these days, tell her to knock it off. Yeah, like that was ever going to happen. Lindeen Cody had invented stubborn and patented the formula.

But the truth was without his mother's meddling, he rarely bothered doing anything on his own about it. For one, the long hours made it damn near impossible to sustain a relationship. In his experience women required assurances they were in it for the long-term. The one time he'd walked down the aisle to say 'I do' had been a disaster. While he'd promised to love and cherish, his bride had been the unfaithful one who'd had a hard time remaining steadfast for one damn tour of duty in Iraq.

But that was ancient history. He'd gotten past the cheating Cindy and never looked back.

Didn't his mother realize that the only women he met on a regular basis worked for him in some capacity or another? And Brent Cody refused to cross that line at work mingling anything personal at the office. Been there. Done that before, too—and it hadn't worked out any better. In his experience office affairs *never* worked out.

But if Lindeen Cody came across an attractive medical assistant at the doctor's office who she thought might interest her eldest son—or a cute saleswoman she happened to run into at the mall who looked like future daughter-in-law material—Brent would hear about it. Then he'd inevitably give in and meet her through his mother.

Which meant Brent went on a lot of first dates—or met up with women over coffee on Saturday or Sunday mornings—to talk. If the two of them happened to click, they might plan a couple of movies or dinner dates before they'd tumble into the sheets. They might text during that time—hot and heavy. They might even resort to calling each other for a little phone flirting. It might last three weeks or three months. But it never led to anything more permanent or more serious than that.

Brent was aware that at his age it was plenty embarrassing to leave it to his mother to hook up with the opposite sex. But on fourteen-hour days like today, he didn't really see much hope that Mrs. Brent Cody was out there somewhere, waiting in the wings. And at this stage of his life, he didn't dwell on it.

He made the turn onto his street, a nice residential area where young families made children. On automatic, he reached up to hit the remote to open the garage door. The rain picked up as he pulled into his driveway. Slowly, he inched the big Dodge inside the narrow garage opening. Grabbing his briefcase, he crawled out of the pickup, absent-mindedly wondering whether or not the Sharks were adding a win to their column.

When his stomach rumbled craving the leftover pepperoni and cheese, he remembered he hadn't eaten lunch until four that afternoon and it was now well past eleven. Maybe he'd forego heating up the greasy pie and opt for a quick bowl of Cheerios instead.

Before he reached the door going into his house, however, he held the clicker for the remote over his shoulder and hit the button to close the garage door. With that one push, the door blew. The force of the explosion blasted him through the air, knocking him back into the wall.

Brent never even had time to reach for his .45 still in its holster strapped to his shoulder. It wouldn't have done any good anyway. The ensuing fire had him trapped.

For a span of several seconds, he couldn't feel his body, didn't remember how he'd slid onto the concrete floor. The blinding light of what seemed like a thousand stars impaired his vision. But then just as quickly, the bright white color leveled out and speared to blazing red. He struggled to move, to lift his arm to dial the cell phone he still gripped in his other hand. He realized then and there he could only move one arm.

Brent heard sirens in the distance. At least he thought he did. It sounded as if two dozen freight trains were roaring through his head all at once. He fought to stay conscious. When his eyes did finally clear enough, he zeroed in on all the blood covering his hands. He realized then how badly he was bleeding. As his strength faded, the blazing hue of red came back threefold.

And then, there was nothing but blackness.

Chapter One

Present Day
Pelican Pointe, California

Brent Cody's physical injuries were healing. Gradually, a little more each day, he made progress. After three weeks, he could hobble across the street to the pier if he felt like it, even though he still walked with a noticeable limp and the aid of a cane.

Yesterday he'd even walked down to Main Street and back again. It had taken him damn near an hour and a half to do it but he'd managed to work the slight hill at the top and stay upright.

The blast had dislocated his shoulder and wrenched his back out when he'd been thrown against the garage wall. He'd suffered cuts from flying glass, numerous contusions and abrasions. He'd suffered burns, a concussion, which had kept him unconscious for close to five days. The pain was still with him every single day. He did his best not to rely on the Demerol the doctors had prescribed him. Instead of the opiate, he popped naproxen like they were M&M's.

Thanks to his father Marcus Cody, twice a week he took the trip into Santa Cruz for PT, his physical therapy. There he worked like a dog on getting his legs to move the way they once had and his body to loosen up. The doctors had convinced him his back would get better. It would take time but if he stuck with the routine he would begin to see results.

Bottom line. Brent was grateful he still had all his limbs. That fact alone made him very aware he was damned lucky to be alive.

But his mental state was a lot more undefined and shaky. He'd decided not to mention that little fact to his family or his friends. His mind kept going back to that night, replaying the explosion and what he could have done differently.

He no longer had his little house. It was in shambles, pieces here and there strewn about like toothpicks. His totaled, mangled pickup truck had no doubt saved his life. The ten-thousand-pound mass of metal and steel had somehow shielded him from the full impact of the bomb. Something the person who had placed it there hadn't counted on.

It hadn't taken all that long for investigators to determine that an explosive device with a sophisticated timing mechanism put together to make sure he was in that closed up space of a garage, would detonate the *second* time he pressed his remote-controlled garage door opener. Experts in matters like this were impressed with the workings of the device. Whoever had been responsible for making it possessed a decent knowledge of detonation, specifically experience with radio control. It didn't take a genius to figure out that the bomber first had to get Brent into the confined garage for greater impact. It meant the detonator couldn't go off with the first click but had to ignite the switch the second time Brent pressed down on the remote.

Someone wanted him dead. And they were willing to go to extreme measures to see it happen. Added to that, they were still out there.

With all his years in law enforcement, the list of suspects could be long and varied. Any number of people—from drug dealers with friends in low places—to murderers he'd help put behind bars. Maybe they had family on the outside willing to take the grudge to the next level.

He didn't think it had anything to do with the serial killer, Carl Knudsen, he'd put away months ago. Since the pharmacist's arrest, the man's wife had been so humiliated she'd sold the business to a family from Portland, Oregon. It hadn't taken Elaine Knudsen long for her to file for divorce and move away to parts unknown. Ten days ago, the Knudsen's sign had come down. The new owners, Jill and Ross Campbell, had renamed the place, Coastal Pharmacy. A name change meant things were finally headed in the right direction there.

Brent for one, like many residents in Pelican Pointe, felt it was a welcome sight, even if it had put an end to an era. It was time for a new beginning. Most were glad to see the drug store change hands. A few old-timers though still grumbled that it had always been Knudsen's as far back as they could remember and always would be. But in time, Brent believed they would come around to accepting the latest arrivals.

He had no doubt that townspeople like Nick and Jordan, Ethan and Hayden, Keegan and Cord, Logan and Kinsey, would see to it the Campbells were made to feel at home here.

But simple issues, like watching the newcomers settle in, didn't have him waking up at three a.m., unable to get back to sleep.

Like a baseball coach before a big game, Brent's mind seemed to choose that time of the night to go over his lineup of who wanted him dead.

The FBI had already ruled out most of the drug dealers in Santa Cruz. Much to his dismay, they'd already cleared his top suspects. No doubt the whole thing had him stressed out and waking up in a cold sweat ticking off suspects. Trying to figure out who wanted him dead was always there nagging at him.

His deputies had canvassed the neighbors. The neighbors hadn't seen a thing. No strangers in the area. No reports of unusual cars. Which meant, so far, the bomber's identity remained unknown.

It bugged him.

To make matter worse, over the past three weeks, there'd been a lot of back and forth within his own department about the best course of action to take. A few of his advisers thought it best to "pretend" the perpetrator had succeeded in killing him. There had been talk about his faking his own death. But that hadn't made a lot of sense to Brent Cody. He'd nixed that idea before it had time to take hold.

In the hospital room, Brent had done some major soul-searching. He'd awakened to find his worried parents, his brother, and several of his closest friends standing watch, waiting for him to come out of the coma. Since he'd spent the last three weeks in recovery mode, a little downtime had made him realize the enormous pressures of his job. The prospect of not knowing who wanted him dead was merely part of it. He wasn't happy about being placed on medical disability even though his body had yet to regain its full mobility. With all that, he had to dig deep to remember why he'd gotten into law enforcement in the first place.

By the time he'd turned twenty-one he'd been an MP in the army. It meant he didn't know how to make a living doing anything else. If his career ended at forty, he wasn't sure how he was supposed to handle that.

Even now, he knew there were politics at play in getting back to his job. Those twice a week PT visits to Santa Cruz weren't just for medical reasons. They also included mandatory trips to a shrink, paid for by the department. Brent had decided after the second visit, he might need to watch what he admitted—he wasn't sure the sessions were completely privileged information. Even if he needed to address a few issues, like the daily grind of his job, it was best to remember to keep certain aspects of his life—private. So far, he'd managed to maintain the focus on getting his body working and his life back to the way it had been before.

While he'd been out of it, his friends and family had gone through what remained of his home and possessions. They'd tried to salvage whatever they could from the debris. It hadn't been a lot. Before he'd regained consciousness, his optimistic father had even leased him a truck to use. The Chevy Silverado, a model father and son had admired on the showroom floor together, had been waiting in the hospital parking lot for Ethan to chauffer him over to Pelican Pointe.

After he'd said goodbye to his hospital bed, he'd moved into Autumn Lassiter's house. The same house his brother, Ethan and wife, Hayden, had occupied up until six weeks ago when they'd purchased a larger place on Landings Bay.

Brent would have preferred to stay in Santa Cruz. But as soon as his mother started a campaign to get him to move in with her, he'd opted for his late grandmother's little bungalow on Ocean Street. It made the most sense. Even though it meant he'd have to hobble around on his own, fix meals on his own, even though the cottage didn't have all that much furniture left inside, he needed and wanted his solitude.

That's why before his release, his mother and Hayden had furnished the rooms with a few odds and ends people had donated. The rest they'd picked up at thrift stores in Santa Cruz and San Sebastian and had hauled over for him.

Brent found the gesture incredibly generous, especially since Hayden had her own house to fix up. For the last couple of months, she and Ethan had been involved in major renovations on the home they'd bought, the much-larger one that had once belonged to Sissy Carr, the one-time banker's daughter and embezzler.

The couple had wisely put the history of the Carr house behind them. Good thing too because with an eight-month-old baby, no family needed the extra space more than the

Codys did. His nephew, Nate, was sprouting up faster than a weed in spring.

As Brent wobbled along Ocean Street toward the beach, he glanced over at his brother walking beside him, pushing a stroller. He couldn't believe fatherhood had taken Ethan Cody full circle.

"Sorry, Nate, I know you love to go faster but your uncle here is having trouble keeping up."

"Kiss my ass," Brent muttered.

"Hey, is that anyway to talk in front of my baby boy?"

Brent looked over to see Nate sound asleep. "I doubt I could get in position anyway. Funny thing happened to me last night though."

"If this is about your sordid sex life I'm all ears."

"I don't have a sordid sex life."

"That's just sad, bro. You're a single guy with no strings and no significant other in your life. And no prospects on the horizon either—at least none that I know anything about."

"Not unless you count the cute brunette who kept sticking a bedpan under my ass the entire time I spent flat on my back and couldn't make it to the bathroom on my own."

Ethan shook his head. "If that's all the action you've gotten lately, I'll say it again. That's just pathetic. So what happened last night?"

"You know that rumor about Scott Phillips?"

"You mean the fact that he's a ghost? Yeah. It's no rumor. Ask Hayden next time you see her. Hell, for that matter ask Cord Bennett or Logan Donnelly. You saw him? Where? In Autumn's house?"

"No, not in the house. I saw something. Someone."

"Scott's all over this town, Brent. Has been for years now, ever since he didn't come back from Iraq. Scott paid you a visit?"

"Not really. Last night I nuked some chicken in the microwave, cooked it way too long and ended up having to stuff it down the garbage disposal. I had to settle for a ham and cheese sandwich. Anyway, the smell stunk up the house so much though that I had to open the front door to let in some fresh air. When I did, I saw this guy standing across the street on the wharf looking out to sea."

"That's not so unusual. People stand there all the time, especially tourists. It's a pretty view."

"It is. But that's not the unusual part. This guy was just standing there staring up at the lighthouse." Brent stopped walking to bob his head in the direction of the cliffs. "And there, up ahead, the area that collapsed during the storm three weeks back."

Ethan nodded. "The night you almost died." Ethan tapped his brother gingerly on his injured back. "I'm glad you didn't. Not sure I said that to you in the hospital but I'm saying it now."

"I'm pretty happy about that, too."

The night Brent's house exploded, a Pacific disturbance had rolled in hitting the coast hard. It had brought power outages and flooding to the area. For two days the massive wind and rain had battered the cliffs. Once it had passed, the top of the bluffs near Smuggler's Bay had given way to a series of mudslides. The shift in the earth along with the erosion had given up a Chumash encampment beneath the surface sand and grit.

Brent knew for scientists it amounted to hitting the lottery. For the local tribe it caused them a headache, an immediate uneasy fear that sharks of the two-legged variety would descend in droves and start removing Chumash relics from the past. Although the so-called experts might shed light on how the tribe had lived, it didn't mean there was a happy medium, at least not yet.

"So what happened after you saw Scott Phillips?" Ethan wanted to know.

"He vanished into thin air right in front of me. Seriously. One minute he's standing there big as life, the next he's gone. I swear to God it was so weird that I thought my pain had crossed over into hallucinations. But before I flushed my meds down the john, I remembered a conversation you and Dad were having one afternoon about ghosts, specifically Scott Phillips."

Ethan sighed. "We were talking about it because Scott's often done that to me, and quite a few others. Locals say it isn't unusual to see him strolling around town with Megan Donnelly."

Brent scratched his chin at that and shook his head. "Megan Donnelly? Logan's sister, the one murdered by the serial killer, Carl Knudsen, when she was seventeen? That Megan Donnelly?"

"Yep, one and the same."

"This town's a virtual lure for the weird these days."

"I can't disagree with that statement. And Wade Hawkins certainly wouldn't. He's finally published his own book after two years of research on the subject. He let me read the manuscript. I have to say, Wade did a decent job with the topic."

"Wade specifically wrote about Scott?"

"He didn't name names, no. But he did illuminate a few intriguing details about him."

"Like what?"

"For one, lately whenever Scott's seen with Megan he's around seventeen. Other times people have reported seeing a boy of around ten years old fishing down at the cove. He's even been seen swimming off Treasure Island at the ripe old age of fourteen. Of course, he vanishes before anyone can approach him. Then there's the ghost of the soldier who died in Iraq, a man in his mid-thirties, usually seen wearing a pair of khaki shorts and T-shirts that vary like he changes clothes. Probably the same image you saw standing on the pier though. Dad seems to think Scott is one of the most powerful spiritwalkers he's ever encountered, one with a strong, unbreakable bridge between his world and this place. You know the legends as well as I do."

"Sure, I know the stories, grew up with them. But seeing it right outside my front door is another matter. I know what I saw last night but I'd be hard pressed to admit it to anyone else but you."

Glancing at his brother, Ethan said, "As I recall, you and Scott used to hang around together quite a bit as kids, didn't you?"

"Despite the age difference, yeah we did."

"But it's only two years. Dad believes Scott appears to people who are troubled about something. If you're depressed, Brent, it's okay to admit it."

"Don't try to psychoanalyze me," Brent snapped. "I have a departmental shrink who does that on a regular basis. It pisses me off."

"I can see that. But all I'm saying is someone tries to kill you, it messes with your head, messing with your head you start to show a little anxiety from time to time."

Brent decided they needed a change of subject. "What do you know about this archaeological find on the dunes everyone's talking about? I've been a little busy to pay much attention to it. According to Dad, the Southwest Tribal Foundation already sent someone out to head the dig. It's all over town she's checked into the B & B, looks to be here a while. Dad's not too happy about it."

"Just what he's mentioned in the last week or so and the grumblings I've heard from the other elders. None of them are too keen on unearthing our ancestors so a bunch of scientific studies can be done on them."

"I didn't hear they'd found remains. In fact, I didn't even know they'd started to dig."

"They haven't. Yet. But if it turns out this is a settlement, there's a good chance human remains are down there somewhere. We all need to prepare for that eventuality. I told Dad the same thing. There's been some talk around town about how this discovery will likely put Pelican Pointe on the map. Half want the exposure. The other half would rather the whole thing just go away. It's split the town down the middle."

"Like we needed that to happen," Brent said, looking up at the uneven crags as the waves splashed up against the rocks. Two days ago the park rangers had finally showed up to rope off the area and post signs warning the public about the now unstable side of the one-hundred-foot drop off. In spite of that, beachgoers were out sunning themselves at the base and enjoying a perfect fall day with temperatures expected in the high seventies.

"We always knew it could happen," Ethan went on. "We always knew one bad squall could cause a collapse. Who knew we might find evidence of a settlement belonging to our ancestors underneath the sand right here in town though?"

That's one reason Brent wasn't sure he understood why his father was so upset about the whole thing. "Now that you mention it, I guess it was just a matter of time before something like this happened. Since our forefathers lived all up and down this same coastline for thousands of years I'm surprised it took this long. Think about it."

"All I know is I haven't seen Dad this excited since he found that little missing girl in Oregon. Not sure he trusts this archaeologist the center brought in though. He's afraid this will turn the ruins into nothing more than a tourist attraction just like a lot of the other Native sites in North America. He doesn't want that and neither do the elders."

"Can't say I blame them. Once the vultures begin to circle they'll likely hang around for whatever they can scrounge and put up for sale on eBay."

"They did that with Hohokam artifacts found in Arizona."

"I know. Well, the council delegated the job to Dad so he's stuck with it."

"Hey, it isn't the first time he's ended up the liaison between the elders and the center."

"From what I hear he's already at odds with this woman and she hasn't even been in town a week."

"I wouldn't say *at odds* so much as establishing a trust between the two. River Amandez is her name," Ethan revealed.

"You're kidding? River? What kind of name is that?"

Ethan grinned and repeated, "River. She's Pueblo Indian. And she's a smart one all right. Has enough degrees to rival Keegan Fanning. Well, Bennett, now. Nick says this River seems to be settling in just fine at the B & B despite the fact she's a hotshot archaeologist who's been all over the world, excavated digs in the deserts from Texas to Mongolia."

That brought a chuckle out of Brent. "With that kind of background, River Amandez will get bored with our little neck of the woods real quick. Wanna bet she'll be ready to hightail it out of here first chance she gets?"

Chapter Two

Brent Cody couldn't have been more wrong.

River Amandez was in her element. She stood on the sandy shore between Smuggler's Bay and the cliffs staring at the aftermath of the mudslides. Goose bumps formed along her arms at the idea of getting her hands in the dirt, particularly this dirt, this site.

As the lead archaeologist on the project, River studied the Chumash ruins winking back at her from the glistening sand. Mother Nature might've done her damage and moved on—but sometimes she left treasures in her wake.

Now, thanks to low tide, an exposed base of the bluff opened up enough where one could peer inside an open crater. She could make out the first object, a canoe that had more than likely been stuck in the sludge for centuries. She itched to touch, to run her hands along the wood. A mass of shards from pots and cooking utensils and other remnants of village life also remained lodged in the mud. A string of what she'd already deemed were animal bones, most likely used in some decorative manner, drew her in and had her wondering how these people had lived.

Standing among the dunes and sandbanks, she tried to imagine what the Spanish explorer Juan Rodriguez Cabrillo might have seen in the sixteenth century from the bow of his ship as it sailed past the bay heading northward.

River had already learned the Chumash Indians had thrived along the Pacific Coast for hundreds of years. She could picture their villages, the gatherer-hunters paddling out to catch supper, and then maybe bargaining to exchange the fish for the bead money they used to make from olivella shells.

River knew the cave-in would yield more, a lot more. Her instincts told her what she saw now was tip of the iceberg stuff, including the canoe. She tried to picture what might be farther down in the sandy muck.

Among waist-high beach grass, sand and rock, the dunes and bluffs had probably protected this site since before Cabrillo had ever set foot on California soil.

From the minute her phone had chimed with the news that an ancient Native American campsite had been discovered in Pelican Pointe, California, the Southwest Tribal Foundation had reassigned her.

Her boss, Emilio Matias, had split up his staff and taken her off the Coushatta project in the swamplands of Alabama to come here to head her own excavation. It had taken her less than seventy-two hours to pack up her stuff, hop into her ancient Jeep Wagoneer to drive across the flat prairie grasslands of the Southwest to California.

It was a place she'd never been before, a new adventure that would keep her busy without a lot of time on her hands to dwell on anything personal. She took it as a sign, an opportunity to redirect her thoughts, even for the duration of a dig was welcome.

By concentrating on her job, River would stay sane. She liked to think that by digging up artifacts and what had once been a thriving village hidden under all the silt, she could bring to light the people who had inhabited this area. As an expert in pre-Columbian settlements, River had lobbied to get here, to be part of it all.

She knew the representative from the Santa Ynez Indian tribe didn't completely trust her—at least not yet— it wouldn't be the first time she'd had to work to build up a bond from the ground up. That's why she intended to do whatever it took. No one could accuse River Amandez of the unwillingness to wade through bureaucrats determined to prevent her from accomplishing her goal.

The research center had found a descendant of the Chumash who would act as the go-to guy on her project. Because of that, she knew it was way too early to make waves. So she would rein in her frustration and play the game. She really had no choice in the matter anyway.

Since the Native American Graves Protection and Repatriation Act required federal agencies, like the research center, to consult with all Native tribes in the excavation of any human remains, or sacred objects, or any cultural entitlements found at a dig, she was prepared to deal with whatever the spokesperson the tribe deemed necessary. She had to convince Marcus Cody, the representative for the Santa Ynez Band of Chumash Indians, that anything dug up would be handled with the utmost care to preservation. She'd already tried several times to assure him of that.

After all, she worked with an excellent team of experts who were top in their field. Her two assistants, Julian Gustave and Laura Angleton, would be here by week's end, along with a couple of interns Emilio had wrangled into committing to the dig for the duration.

Julian and Laura were gold at what they did. She knew because she'd worked with Julian since they'd both started out together. She'd trained Laura from lowly intern to one of the most trusted anthropologists around.

While Laura might be a little better at describing and cataloguing, Julian excelled at analyzing and recognizing artifacts still embedded in the earth. River didn't know how the man did it, only that he could study an item layered in muck and mire and give it a best guess as to how it would come back after the carbon dating was done. That guess usually turned out to be right.

She'd already emailed Julian and Laura photos from the site. They were chomping at the bit to get here and get started on extracting the canoe. If it came down to removing human remains—and River believed it would—no one was better or more meticulous at it than her team.

River had done her best to assure Marcus that her crew knew what they were doing. But even from the very first day she'd stepped onto the dunes, she'd sensed the man's anxiety and his fear. Fear because he didn't want hordes of people descending on the town and in the process disrupt ground his people now considered sacred.

Being Pueblo Indian, she understood that. But it didn't mean she wouldn't fight tooth and nail to be the one who documented the Pelican Pointe Project. Native or not, she was first and foremost a scientist who studied previous civilizations—and she was good at it.

Once she'd checked into the only available lodging in the area, an enormous B & B north of town called Promise Cove, she'd spent every waking minute of the day she could spare on research. She'd even managed to nail down the timeframe of what she'd seen here, at least ball-park it anyway. What was left of the village might easily date back to the twelfth century, maybe even earlier. She'd know more when she could get her hands in the dirt. So far, she'd only been allowed to photograph the discovery from six feet away.

She would wait on Marcus to give the go-ahead for more. According to him, the tribal council hadn't yet voted to give them clearance. River didn't doubt for a minute they would. Waiting for the red tape to wind its way through the system had never been her strong suit though. Even when she knew it would happen eventually, she had trouble chilling her jets for a week, which meant she was already getting antsy.

She'd gone over charts and maps of the area. She'd consulted with Marcus on numerous occasions. The man had even taken the time to show her a number of other landmarks in the area once occupied by his ancestors. After looking at that firsthand, River had to admit she was intrigued by what her project might give up.

She'd never had a guide quite like Marcus before. The sixtyish man seemed to know everything there was to know about the Chumash and then some. Of course, he'd lived around the area all his life.

Not only that but his wife's mother, Autumn Lassiter, had been born and raised in and around Pelican Pointe. River found it fascinating that Autumn could trace her family roots back to seventeenth-century Chumash descendants. But because Autumn had died a couple of years before, it meant she was stuck with Marcus as her go-to guy.

She wasn't really complaining. The man even spoke the dialect which she had yet to master. Having an expert handy was like having access to a walking Chumash encyclopedia. River intended to use his knowledge to her fullest advantage.

She'd already learned that less than two hundred and fifty miles from this very spot near Santa Barbara was a true Chumash treasure. Painted Cave State Park had yielded a small sandstone cave with rock art dating back a thousand years or more. Marcus and his wife had even played tour guide, taking River there to see it for herself.

River was convinced that when her team got to dig, there was an excellent chance they might uncover the same type of pictographs here in Pelican Pointe. The possibilities were endless. At least she hoped to be a part of that kind of find.

On any given day, River Amandez could be dedicated, motivated, focused and persistent. At thirty-three she'd paid her dues at dig sites along the way since the day she'd turned eighteen. That meant she had fifteen years of field work under her belt. She'd earned a master's degree at twenty-four, her doctorate at twenty-six.

To her credit, River had made only one major mistake in judgment, not a career one mind you, but a personal one. Marrying the lying, bastard Wes Patton capped what otherwise could be called a decent history of judging character, not stellar maybe, just decent.

She'd wasted two messy years with the verbally abusive Wes. And then at thirty her life had completely gone off the rails. It had taken her almost a year to get back on track. Even after two years, there was still one huge missing element to her life. The biggest hole of all she hadn't been able to fill no matter how hard she tried, or what project she took on, or how far she roamed across the four corners of the country to do it.

There were times her arms ached to hold, to cuddle what was gone. A part of her was missing, and nothing could repair that hole in her heart.

That's why these days she made sure she kept stateside, just in case there was any word. She no longer made herself available for overseas assignments in places like Egypt or Ireland. If she ever stumbled upon a viable lead that might possibly turn everything around, she didn't dare risk being out of the country when it happened.

River tried not to dwell on anything pessimistic because if she did it tended to make her crazy with worry and guilt—which might mean checking into a padded cell where she'd settle in for good and never come out. That wouldn't help anyone.

Not a day went by that it didn't nag at her to the point she couldn't concentrate. No matter how stubborn her resolve seemed to be, there had yet to be a resolution. She refused to accept defeat. These days she had only one purpose. Her single-mindedness began every morning and ended every night the same way.

River Amandez refused to give up. She would find her son if it took the last breath in her body.

It was true her life was a nomadic existence as she went from dig to dig. To this day, her home base was where she'd grown up. She kept an apartment in Santa Fe, New Mexico. But she was rarely there. If she went back at all, it was to check on her mother. Sad to say, her mom hadn't recognized her in over two years. Stage-6 Alzheimer's had robbed Malinda Amandez of almost every memory she had left. The last time River had seen her, she'd watched as the fifty-six-year-old woman spent most of the visit rocking back and forth wringing her hands. Frequent phone calls to the staff at the nursing home were the only way she had to keep up with the progression of her mother's condition and day-to-day care.

What with her mother's deteriorating condition and her driving obsession, most times doing field work was the only thing that kept her grounded. She had no room in her life for anything else. For the last two and a half years, staying busy kept her from thinking about what-ifs or failed personal relationships, or blame.

Shaking off those thoughts so she could work, River adjusted her lens to get a better picture.

As boats bobbed up and down in the harbor, as a slight breeze brushed her cheek, she stepped farther into the shallow inlet, her worn Timberland hiking boots getting soaked in the process. While waves crashed up against the rocks around her, on instinct, she brought the camera into focus to capture the condition of the canoe.

There were benefits to working outside at her own pace. But it had been a good long time since she'd landed in such a pretty little town. Because of that, on impulse, she aimed the lens toward the scenic bluffs and the picturesque lighthouse high above her head.

After taking several shots, she gingerly inched closer to aim the Nikon at the six-foot-wide opening and the exposed ruins.

Bending at the waist, she angled her body over the muck as close as she could get without crossing the rope barrier. Zooming in, she began snapping the photos she needed.

All Brent Cody saw when he rounded the ridge was the sexy way the raven-haired beauty wiggled her butt to get the best shot.

Ethan saw it, too. They both tilted their heads in the way of brothers, taking in the woman's long, lean tanned legs, the slender build, the athletic way she moved. Tall, at least five-nine in the hiking boots she had on, she wore olive-green shorts and a white button-down shirt. Her cinnamon skin caught Brent's attention and held.

Ethan elbowed him in a tender rib and said, "Whatcha lookin' at there, bro?"

"Same thing you are. You didn't mention the body or the hair. You said she was smart. I thought—"

Ethan laughed. "I know what you thought. She's hot all right. Apparently Dad didn't mention it either. Or Mom, which is unusual. Like what you see, do you? Good. That means you aren't dead below the waist."

"The equipment works just fine, thanks."

"Glad to hear it," Ethan said, tapping Brent again on his sore shoulder. Then all at once with a gleam in his eye, Ethan pivoted the stroller on two wheels, heading in the opposite direction. Without warning, he put his fingers between his teeth. Before Brent could stop him, Ethan let go a loud wolf-whistle the entire beach crowd had no trouble hearing over the sound of the surf.

Brent rolled his eyes. "Do you ever intend to grow up? Do I need to remind you that you're married?"

"Hey, it's not for me. I got a woman. That's how I got the kid. I'm just trying to light a fire under my big brother here in the romance department. And you're a little slow. Besides, four's a crowd," Ethan shouted over his shoulder as he ducked around the nearest sand dune and started hot footing it away, knowing full well Brent couldn't keep up if he wanted to.

With his injury Brent was left standing there to take the heat. And he didn't have to wait long.

By this time, the female above him with the dark hair and great body glanced down from her perch to find him staring up at her.

Like any damned fool, Brent leaned on his cane and did the only thing he could.

He stuck his hand in the air and waved to River Amandez.

Chapter Three

At the sound of the loud two-note whistle, River's head snapped up. She glared at the tall man standing below her on the stingy strip of concrete causeway. River eyed his bronze skin, the black hair, the unmistakable Native American heritage. His lanky frame leaned on a cane that he clutched like a lifeline. It looked as though he'd hobbled to this point. The sheen of sweat on his brow told her the effort had taken a lot out of him.

Good-looking aside, this wasn't the first gawker she'd had to shoo off from her dig before it ever got started. So she would nip it in the bud now.

Backing away from the rocky ground she inched down the side of the embankment a little at a time, ducked under the security rope to where he stood. All the while the ocean air between them pulsed with an equal measure of curiosity and mutual interest.

"I'm River Amandez. I'm in charge of this site and you really shouldn't be hanging around here. The cliffs are unstable and off-limits for the next few months," she explained, looping the strap over her head so the camera dangled around her neck. "See the barrier? It's there for a reason."

Gutsy, Brent decided as he cocked his head to peruse her from head to toe. "Beautiful name. River. Suits you. I hear you're Pueblo from somewhere in the Southwest, right?" When she looked slightly puzzled, he added, "It's a small town. Word spreads like wildfire about any newcomer," he said, extending his hand. "Brent Cody."

The name sunk in. "Cody? Ah. Then you're Marcus and Lindeen's oldest." Before he could answer, she grinned and tossed back, "It's a small town. Plus, your parents and I shared a car driving down to Santa Barbara last weekend. You were a major topic of conversation."

Brent grimaced, shook his head. "Please don't tell me my mother hinted at getting us together."

"Ah, no. Actually Lindeen made it known several times you had your eye on an attractive first-grade teacher. I believe her name was Julianne or maybe it was Julie. I forget which."

Brent rolled his eyes and felt the rush of humiliation go straight to his cheeks. He shook his head. "Julianne, a neighbor of my mother's. She's been trying to hook either my brother or me up with Julianne Dickinson since they first got to know each other at a book club some years back. Ethan's off her radar now because he's married. She's the bane of my existence. My mother, not Julianne. She's made it her life's work to interfere and embarrass me with every woman she happens to come across."

"Your mother, not Julianne," River echoed with a grin.

"Exactly. And to think you drove hundreds of miles with her in a confined space with no way to escape. You should probably get an award for that."

River chuckled and studied his face, the stubble along his jawline and chin where he hadn't shaved. "Are you okay? Do you need to get off your feet or something? You look drained." Prepared to grab for the bottle of water in her pack around her waist, she kept her eyes locked on his, eyes so brown they were almost black.

He bristled at her concerned tone. "I'm fine."

River's lips curved, recognizing the prickly quills attached to male pride. She decided the topic of his mother was a lot safer. "So your mom loves to play matchmaker every chance she gets, huh? She does love to talk about her sons. According to your mother, your younger brother, Ethan, is the next Michael Connelly."

"See, that sounds like Mom. It was only last month Ethan released his second book. It's doing pretty well though."

"There's a bookstore in town, Hidden Moon Bay Books. I'll make sure I stop in to support the local author while I'm here."

"I'm sure he'd appreciate that. His wife, Hayden, owns the place."

"Ah. That small-town atmosphere again. Makes sense. What happened to you? Were you in a car accident?" She saw the irritation come into his eyes at the question. She found it strange that during a five-hundred-mile round trip, his parents had never once mentioned that their son had been injured.

"No."

"You might as well tell me," she prodded. "Otherwise I'll just ask Nick or Jordan when I get back to the B & B tonight. It's been my experience it's better to hear things from the source."

Reluctant to divulge his own troubles, he grumbled, "My house blew up."

Her mouth dropped open. "A gas explosion? That's rare."

"Not exactly."

Realization began to dawn. Cop. House going boom. "Someone tried to kill you? Here in Pelican Pointe?"

"Santa Cruz."

"Right. Do you know who's responsible yet?"

"Not a clue. So where does River call home?" Brent wondered, hoping to get the focus off him.

River spread her arms out. "For the next several months right here in Pelican Pointe will do just fine. For me, right this minute that means Promise Cove is home."

Brent wrinkled a brow. "No, I mean where do you call home? Where is your home base when you aren't in the field? Where were you born? Where do you vote? That sort of thing."

Impatience crawled up her throat. Even for a cop the barrage was a little much for a get-to-know-you conversation. "Do you always insist on grilling every person you meet right upfront?" She didn't give him time to answer. Instead she put both hands on her hips and added, "I have no outstanding warrants, no unpaid traffic tickets, and I've never been to the West Coast before this trip. But if you must know, my driver's license was issued in New Mexico." Because she wasn't about to offer more, she added, "You savvy?"

He understood attitude, often displayed it himself but when it flared so fast in those chocolate eyes of hers it sucked him right in. Because he itched to reach out and touch her hair, he switched gears. "How are they treating you out at the B & B? Settling in okay?"

"No complaints. The accommodations are first-rate. Once my staff gets here on Monday though, I'll be moving out of the comfy surroundings and into the RV we always set up as our base for the duration of a dig."

"Really?" Brent turned his head to stare across Ocean Street. "There isn't really a good place to park an RV hereabouts. They make exceptions for parades and street fairs of course, but you'd have to have a special permit for anything longer than three days."

"Nick Harris, the owner of the B & B, gave us permission to use the farm next door to his place for as long as we're here."

"I think I might be able to arrange for you to use the empty lot over at the old newspaper office, the one across from the Fanning Marine Rescue Center. That way you'd be closer to the site."

"You mean the building where the side is painted with all the faces of the women, the mural? Sure. Thanks, that'd be great, I appreciate it."

"No problem."

"What's that about anyway, the mural?"

"I'm not sure a newcomer is ready to hear about the town's sordid past but since you're here... Last month we caught a serial killer."

"No kidding. In Pelican Pointe? Wait. If you're trying to scare me off, you'll have to do better than that. I'm not the type who responds to campfire stories about axe murderers and then goes running back to where I came from screaming like a girl."

Brent raised one brow. No, she didn't seem the type who frightened easily. "What's scarier than a serial killer who preyed on young women for two decades before he got caught? Those women you see depicted on the side of the building are his victims. The artist, Logan Donnelly, isn't finished with it yet though. His sister was one of Knudsen's earliest victims."

"Okay, so you aren't just saying that to put me off the area. Do you mean *the* Logan Donnelly? The sculptor is here in Pelican Pointe painting a mural on the side of an old building?"

"The case was all over the Internet. And Logan makes his home here now. He's married to Kinsey Wyatt, our resident attorney. He has workers remodeling the lighthouse, refurbishing the keeper's house." Brent nodded toward the bluff. "Have you seen it at night? Logan even replaced the old drum lens and installed a state-of-the-art aero beacon that beams out a white light every ten seconds. After so many years, we have ourselves a lighthouse that actually works now."

"I'll be damned. I did notice it, hard not to. I thought it was so cool in this day and time. Saw the busy workmen too as I drove by. I thought it might be a state project though, grant-funded, like the dig. Besides, I've been a little busy over the summer burrowing around through marshland and up to my ass in mosquitoes to keep up with serial killers and what's happening three thousand miles away."

She didn't intend to mention that most times back in Alabama getting on the Internet was a luxury she used for one specific purpose only. Instead she merely said, "Where we were we didn't always have cell service let alone access to the Internet."

"That must get annoying when you're trying to keep in touch with family. Most people these days can't go five hours without tapping into social media or texting."

"That's true but most locations where we dig are way out in the boonies, miles away from everything else. Pelican Pointe is unique that way. The dig's right here in town and Nick Harris sees to it that the B & B has high-speed Internet. I love it."

"Nick and Jordan aim to please. Look, there will obviously have to be security here at night. Have you thought of that? Otherwise you'll get looters willing to sell whatever they take away on the open market. Some bold ones even resort to using eBay."

"Sad but true. I wouldn't be offended if you put the word out that I'll press charges on anyone who dares remove relics or anything they find here—been on too many digs not to think about security—Marcus promised me he had it covered though."

Brent scratched the scruffy growth on his chin. "Huh. Wonder who the old man intends to rope into doing that?" But he had a sinking feeling he already knew the answer to that.

Chapter Four

River headed her Wagoneer along the driveway leading up to Promise Cove, all the while yearning for a hot shower. She'd been on the go since six that morning. Tired muscles were beginning to ache and need attention. Not only that, the moist ocean air tended to act like glue when you were out in it all day. The sand sticking to her skin was beginning to make her itch all over. She couldn't wait to scrub off several layers of grit and grime before sitting down to some of Jordan Harris's food.

She cruised past majestic cypress and tall feathery willows that stood like sentries guarding the stately old house from the road. The Victorian itself was impressive. A gabled roof with deep angles formed the massive eaves and triangles that rose up to meet the cloudless sky. The long pinewood porch caught her eye—she realized now the setting reminded her of Santa Fe. Not so much in style and design nor grand in size but the B & B was obviously a lively hub for family and social gatherings, just as her own had once been.

She longed to have what Malinda and Orlando Amandez had provided their daughter growing up—a warm, loving home environment. Maybe that was why the entire place gave off the same basic vibe as what she remembered from her childhood—that of hearth and home, of security, a place that symbolized the heart of a thriving family.

Regret speared through her. She should have provided that same type of atmosphere for her own. She wondered now why she hadn't. She'd tried but failed at it. While guilt wanted to pour through her, she stubbornly blocked it from taking hold. If she let it crawl in after a long, brutal day like today, she'd be done.

But blame would get her nowhere.

As she pulled the SUV to a stop next to a Ford Explorer, the archaeologist in her focused on how long the Victorian had stood on this very spot. She already knew that William Howard Taft had sat in the Oval Office when the builder had first poured the foundation. That fact alone was a tribute to its enduring beauty, its solid construction, holding up over generations.

Strong roots were meant to carry on. Origins were meant to be unearthed. Like the Chumash settlement in town, there was history here. And this place seemed to matter to the people living inside. It mattered to the town.

Outside the car, River drew in deep breaths of ocean air. The sound of children's laughter hit her coming from the end of the long, concrete drive. She spotted two toddlers playing with their daddy.

River's heart clutched and wanted to plummet. Before she could take a step, she had to steady her wobbly knees.

For more than two years now, she'd known despair. Being around kids was the toughest part. Little ones, like the Harris children, tended to make her yearn for what she no longer had. She was tempted to dart up the front steps to the porch to avoid the scene altogether. She could slip inside and be in her room without anyone seeing her. But she'd always met her troubles head on. Now was no different.

She forced back tears that wanted to trickle down her cheeks. She made certain to plaster a smile on her face. It wasn't that difficult to maintain a grin any time she got around the Harris kids because the two were adorable.

Why did fifteen-month-old baby Scott have to remind her so much, so often, of what she'd missed out on though?

As she approached Nick Harris, the owner of the inn, sitting across from his daughter at a play table painted bright pink, she forced out a laugh. The chairs were tiny compared to the grown man. She caught sight of the dainty tea cup Nick held in his huge hands and the multicolored dog of undetermined origin stretched out underneath his feet. The dog wore some type of pink frilly frock around his middle. Quake as he was called, seemed humiliated at the outfit but despite that waited for whatever attention he could get.

"Looks like I'm just in time for tea and cakes."

The little tow-headed Hutton shook her head as she reached out to take River's hand. "River! Hi! No cakes but um…we had cookies a long time ago. Mama says it's too close to supper to eat more now though. Um, did you dig up anything yet? Did you bring me anything?"

"Hutton!" Nick said. "You don't ask our guests that. We talked about this before, remember?"

River laughed. "It's okay. I didn't dig anything up yet. But I did find a pretty abalone shell and put it in my bag for you."

Hutton clapped her hands. "Yay! I love shells. I find them washed up down at the cove and keep them in my room."

About that time Scott toddled up to River. Despite her mood, she bent down to swing the little boy onto her hip. "And what exciting things did you two guys do today that I missed out on. I hope you didn't go pick flowers without me."

"Um, um, we helped Daddy catch a bunny," Hutton finally said, brushing her hair off her face.

"Bunny," Scott repeated, slapping his hands together like he'd seen his sister do.

"Well, let's see this bunny."

"Daddy said, um, he said we had to let him go back to his family 'cause he prolly missed all his brovers and sisters."

River shot a smile over at Nick who finally got to his feet with an amused look on his face. "Noting how much lettuce the entire bunny family devoured, they certainly had a *lot* of brothers and sisters."

River snickered. "Did they now? Good idea to let the bunny go back home though. Smart daddy."

Hutton bobbed her head at that. "We gots to catch the bunny 'cause he eats Mama's veggies all the time. That's why Daddy builded another fence."

"Rabbits, lettuce, the two go together," River pointed out.

"Yep. Can you show us how to dig and find stuff in the dirt?" Hutton persisted.

About that time, Jordan crossed the courtyard, a flower-lover's dream. Hardy golden chrysanthemums vied for space among delicate purple asters and blue daisies. But it was the white turtleheads snapping in the ocean breeze that had River realizing this was such a contrast to her native New Mexico.

"Hutton, you let our guest get settled before bombarding her with chatter. Let River take a breath and get inside first, she's worked hard all day," Jordan said.

"It's okay. Hutton's no bother at all."

"Are you sure? She can be a chatterbox sometimes, although a delightful one," Jordan said smiling down at her daughter before running her hand over Hutton's hair.

"She was telling me about the rabbit and how she let it go," River explained as they started making their way up to the back door.

"Yes, well, Nick had some persuading to do there I'm afraid. She wanted to keep it."

From behind them, Nick chimed in, "Let's be honest, Hutton wanted to put a dress on it just like the one she has on Quake now. There were a few tears after we had to let the furry thing hop away into the woods. Let's hope it stays there and not in Jordan's herb garden."

"I bet," River said beginning to realize her black mood had lifted just a bit as it had other times over the past week whenever she spent any time around the Harris tribe.

"Dinner will be in about an hour. That should give you time to shower and unwind."

Still carrying Scott, who nibbled on his finger, River walked through the back door and into a large, spotless kitchen. But a few toys were scattered here and there on the floor telling anyone who happened inside that children lived and played here.

It made her want for a life she might never have.

By the time River reached the living room, Scott wanted down so he could toddle off to follow his sister.

"Your home is amazing. I'm not sure how you two do it. But this might be the most unique, most comfortable place I've ever stayed for any length of time."

"Really? We certainly put a lot of work into it."

"I'm sure you did. The house reflects its owners, no doubt about that. But I wasn't really talking about the house itself, although it's a gorgeous, peaceful setting. I've never stayed anywhere that seems so...*alive* with energy. It's so different I've started documenting certain aspects of it for when I'm no longer here."

"Really?" Jordan said, sending River a quizzical look. "What kind of energy?"

"Oh, I don't know. It's a feeling I get each time I walk through the door. I've been here almost a week now and I think it's a house of old souls." When she noticed Jordan's continued stare, she added, "I know something about old souls. I've been on enough excavations where people settled in, raised families, put down roots. I recognize this place has a past, another life so to speak." She watched Jordan's face for a reaction, lifted a brow in understanding. "You've no doubt heard this before?"

"Have you seen any indication of that energy?" Nick wanted to know.

River sent him a sly grin. "Why don't you just ask me if I've seen *him*? I might be new in town but I have ears, eyes, and enough sense about such things to know the locals go on about seeing Scott Phillips around town. His name's on the sign out front. Throw in the fact that I come from a long line of people who believe in spiritwalkers— which contrary to popular belief are different than shamans—and you have the perfect venue for a terrific—" River stopped in mid-sentence, looked around for the kids to make sure they weren't listening. As soon as she noticed they weren't even in the room, she added, "Ghost story. You know as well as I do that Scott is becoming a local legend."

"Did he upset you in some way? He's good at that," Jordan added. "He doesn't mean anything by it."

River laughed. "Not since the second night here. He did give me a good jolt the first time though." She wasn't ready to mention that Scott had known things about her he had no way of knowing.

Nick rubbed at the tension forming at the base of his neck. "I wish I could tell you that he'll leave you alone if you tell him to go away."

"But he won't," River finished for him, rocking back on her heels. "Especially if he feels strongly about something. Look, I'd appreciate it if you'd keep this conversation between the three of us for now."

"No worries there," Jordan returned. "We're used to this."

River grinned again. "I bet you are. Look, I need to wash off some of this dirt before dinner. You don't have a full house this weekend do you?"

"We have rooms," Nick stated. "But why? I thought your friends were bringing an RV?"

"They are but after such a long cross-country trip, they want a night out of that tin can before the grind starts. They should roll in sometime this weekend," River explained, spreading her arms wide. "They'll love this place, not to mention a real bed and the fantastic spread you guys fix. I probably won't be able to pry them out of here without using a crowbar."

"We'll take care of them," Jordan assured her. "Any particular type of food they don't like?"

"Trust me. This crew will eat anything," River said before dashing up the stairs.

After she'd gone, Nick turned to his wife. "I know you told her we were used to this sort of thing with Scott but sometimes I don't think I'll ever be entirely comfortable with it, especially how he targets certain guests. He obviously has River in his sights now and won't let up."

"I said that for her benefit. I'm right there with you. So you noticed he'd already zeroed in on River? You know what I don't get."

"What's that?"

"Think about it. We get people coming and going here all the time. River's just one guest out of dozens over the summer. Why her? Why not the attractive blonde from Montana last month?"

Nick's eyes twinkled and his lips curved up. "You mean Piper Drake? Piper was hot."

Jordan playfully elbowed him in the ribs. "She was but that's beside the point. See, you remember Piper though. She stayed two weeks to complete her travel guide about Central California and while she was here Scott never once bothered with her. And then there was that attractive brunette from Seattle in July, Bonnie Butler."

"Bonnie came here to photograph the area for some online magazine article, stayed ten days. Scott left her alone, too."

"Exactly. Both women were here in town to do a job just like River. There's about as much chance of her sticking around this place after her work here is finished as there was for Piper or Bonnie—so why River Amandez and not Bonnie Butler or Piper Drake?"

"That's a good question." Nick scratched his head. "I don't know the answer. I stopped trying to figure out how this thing with Scott works a long time ago."

"I don't have the answers either but Scott has to know something about River that we don't, some trouble she's in like Hayden. Or the fact that she needs help in some way like Cord and Logan did."

"No argument there. But what?"

"I guess it'll come to light like it always does—in due time. Go see what the kids are up to, will you? I need to go check on dinner." But before she left she studied Nick's face and tossed out, "Are you okay?"

"I worry sometimes that one day Scott will cross the line with one of the guests. Give them a heart attack or something. I'm hoping he knows better."

"I wouldn't count on that," Jordan muttered as she headed off in the direction of the kitchen.

River found herself strolling through dense woodland laden with a carpet of fall foliage in colors of rust and orange. Fragrant starry clematis swayed in the breeze and peppered the landscape. She stepped around trees with big fat trunks wrapped in lush green vines. Ripe berries were there for the picking. But just as she leaned down to touch the fruit, she heard a baby cry. Her heart thudded faster at the sound, precious to a mother's ear so long denied. She recognized his cry. Because her son needed her, she quickened her pace.

The wind changed from the north. It hit her face sending chills straight through to her bones. The cold made her feel old in years. And if she was shivering, her child had to be doing the same. And probably hungry, her baby had to be starving. Her brown-eyed boy needed her. She had to get to her baby, her Luke.

Her feet moved through damp leaves that stuck to her legs. As she moved under the branches of the trees, they cracked and bent in the shadows at her back. But then she saw the fog take shape in front of her as it hugged the earth and began to surround her.

All the while the baby kept crying. Her stomach churned and knotted as she trekked on while the thick vapor turned to heavy clouds hovering overhead. Rain began to fall, fat drops splattered until it became a steady downpour.

With one purpose she kept her pace brisk, all the while the baby kept wailing even louder.

The sound drew her onward. Tears ran down her cheeks and mingled with the raindrops there. The thought of not reaching him in time had fear clutching at her throat, her heart. But she would not stop, she would not give up, she would never stop searching.

The wind battered her path, whipping her face with sharp stings and slashes. The rain came down harder. Thunder snapped. Lightning crackled overhead. It began to grow darker and darker still. Panic set in. Her teeth began to chatter as the temperature dropped to freezing cold.

She had to find her child before it was too late.

River spotted him then, her bright-eyed baby boy, sitting on a bed of damp leaves wearing nothing but his diaper, one finger tucked into his mouth, his chubby cheeks rosy red from all the crying. He looked the same as he had the last time she'd seen him, except that his baby-fine black hair was matted with dirt and his skin slick with rain. But he was alive. It would all be okay. Luke would be okay.

But as she reached to snatch him up and whisk him out of the elements, her fingers moved through air. One unsuccessful attempt after another, she kept trying to pick him up but every time she did, her hands slipped through nothingness.

River heard the wail, recognized her own screams as she clawed through the leaves and dirt to find her child.

She woke to someone beating on her bedroom door.

River ran a hand through her wet hair. She looked down at the way she was dressed and realized she had nothing on but the towel she'd grabbed after her shower. She remembered sitting down on the bed for a minute and must have fallen asleep.

"Are you okay?" Jordan shouted from the other side of the door. "River, if you don't answer me, I'll have to use the passkey to check on you myself."

River crawled off the bed, dazed and confused from the nightmare she'd had several other times before, the same dream, the same search, the same ending—in bitter disappointment.

She swallowed hard and went to the door, cracked it open. Her voice was rough and craggy. "I'm fine. I guess I must've fallen asleep and had a bad dream."

"River, you were screaming. We could hear you all the way downstairs. You scared us half to death."

"I'm sorry."

"It's fine." Jordan reached over and took River's hand in hers. "You're freezing and you've been crying. Is there anything I can do? Would you like me to fix you a tray, some hot tea maybe? I'll bring it to your room. You can eat in here."

"No, no, don't go to that kind of trouble. I'll be down to eat. Just give me a minute or so to get dressed," River said wiping the tears off her face.

"You take all the time you need."

By the time River got down to the dining room, she felt a little better. She'd splashed water on her face and put the dream where it belonged—locked away in that part of herself where hope lived.

She looked around the table at the kids, their cheery faces smeared with spaghetti sauce and ached for another chance. What mother wouldn't?

She caught the worried faces of her hosts.

"You okay?" Nick asked.

She nodded. "Thanks for checking on me."

"We were worried."

"I know." She took a seat across from the kids and did her best to dig into the huge plate of spaghetti and meatballs Jordan had fixed.

The couple didn't ask questions but River could tell the temptation was there to pry. Instead of offering an explanation, she decided to put them both at ease the only way she knew how. She picked up the conversation from earlier to explain what she'd meant about Scott. Since the kids were right there though, she thought it best to temper her words.

"Do you mind if I ask a few questions about our convo from earlier?"

"I suppose you've earned a few," Nick groused, glancing over at Hutton. "She's too young to understand all this so keep it low-key."

"I agree. And we can table this discussion for another time if you're uncomfortable talking about it in front of the kids. Because I totally understand if we put this on hold in front of them."

Jordan stared at her children, both preoccupied with stuffing their mouths with pasta and meat sauce. "Sometimes I wonder if they'll reach a point where they'll see him, too."

"And what we'll tell them when they do," Nick added, reaching across the linen tablecloth to take Jordan's fingers in his.

River nodded and lowered her voice. "I know this much, I don't think it's an 'if' situation but rather a 'when.' Scott prides himself on being a truly benevolent spirit, no aura surrounding him says otherwise. That makes what you have here a built-in, ready-made protector of sorts, a guardian. He obviously watches over what and who he cares about. And just so you know, I've seen Scott walking along the boardwalk a couple of times so it isn't as though he spends all his time here on the grounds or upstairs scaring the guests."

"Our Scott will always be here to look after what he loves. We know that," Jordan agreed.

"But how do you know so much about him in such a short amount of time? I mean, it's only been a week. It's accurate, but how could you tell all that so fast?" Nick wondered.

"The first night he could've scared the bejeezus out of me. He didn't. Instead he took the time to put me at ease right up front. At first, I was like, what the...? But then he said one word, like a code word, that calmed me down."

River noted Nick and Jordan exchange glances. It was Nick who reflected, "So he had personal knowledge about you that there's no way he should've known?"

"He did. And like I said earlier, I've encountered such things before just not one quite as vocal as yours or as strong in spirit."

"You have?" Jordan asked, wide-eyed. "You're so calm about it."

"About this, I guess I am." River sipped her glass of merlot, pondered whether or not to disclose anything of a personal nature. Since the couple appeared to have moved on from the episode upstairs, River decided to keep it about Scott. "I've been at sites where things got a little weird real quick when the spirits made it clear they didn't like the fact that we disturbed their abode, if you know what I mean. They aren't all friendly like Casper."

"I see. You mean when you dug up bones or artifacts belonging to them? Do you expect anything like that here in town once things get more—interesting?" Jordan asked.

"Who knows? I certainly didn't expect anything like Scott when I checked into your lovely B & B. But here we are. I've learned over the years that in my line of work it's best to keep an open mind about these things."

"But you're a scientist who deals with facts staring back at you. How is it you believe in...such things?" He'd almost used the G word, but changed it at the last minute in front of the kids.

But about that time Hutton and Scott decided they were finished eating and wanted down. While Nick stood up to mop messy faces and fold bibs, the discussion ground to a halt.

The minute the children scampered off to play in the other room, River went with intuition. "One of the things I wanted to ask, and you're under no obligation to answer this, but how do you know Hutton hasn't already seen him? He is, after all, her father."

Jordan's eyes went wide again. "Okay, how did you know that?"

River decided to keep it simple. "I was reminded earlier today that Pelican Pointe is a small town. People talk."

"Ah. So you weren't using your vast experience with these sorts of things to hone in on that?"

"Not yet," River said, smiling, keeping her skill close to the vest.

"That touches on all kinds of possibilities," Nick surmised. "That must be one of the reasons Scott's opened up to you already."

River let him think that for now without setting him straight. "Let me remind you that because I have Native blood running through my veins I grew up on myths and legends, some beautiful, some not so pretty. Some were downright scary. But scary isn't Scott."

"Scary? Not at all, but he does love to bug people sometimes. This all must relate in some way to why you're here and what you do for a living."

"I've thought of that. I made archaeology my life's work because most times I could come up with a reasonable hypothesis, an assessment if you will, about how a civilization lived at one time based in fact." She didn't share how because that would take another discussion.

"But some days I admit to blending the rational facts and figures I learn with what I know of my own ancestral beliefs. That isn't to say at the moment, I'm meshing Pueblo lifestyle with Chumash or Coushatta for that matter, quite the contrary. I deal in what I find in the ground, go from there. But sometimes there are other factors at play that can't be so easily explained. Throw in those elements and they tell me a lot about the people from the past."

Nick raised a brow. "You're not ready to divulge these other factors, are you?"

River smiled again. "Another night maybe."

"That's extremely candid for you to admit that digging up artifacts is so theoretical," Jordan said.

"It would be disingenuous of me otherwise. Don't get me wrong. Like other archeologists, I deal in facts and figures, what I find in the ground. I live by carbon dating just like others do, most of the time anyway. But I also take my Native heritage seriously. The part of me that grew up listening to magical tales about supernatural beings is in here." She tapped her chest. "I don't turn away from who I am or where I came from."

"But keeping an open mind is probably what brought Scott to your door."

"More like brought me here to his. But it's also why I'm the best person for this job here in Pelican Pointe. This is a different kind of site altogether for me. That's why I lobbied to get it. I'll have a successful dig site here because I'm thorough and I'm willing to give Marcus Cody his due. I want to learn as much from him about the Chumash people as I do by digging in the dirt."

"As soon as the cliffs collapsed and gave up that canoe, I started reading about carbon dating on the Internet," Nick admitted.

River nodded again. "A fascinating subject to have over dinner and my own personal favorite. Even though I liked working in the lab, it wasn't for me. Give me field work any day over sitting inside four walls. Plus, I love to get my hands dirty, merge what I take for fact about the area, any area where Native people lived and thrived."

"Will you take soil samples?"

"Sure. We'll take whatever we happen to come across down in that hole and send it to the lab for testing. I get the results back, I come up with a theory. I can sustain that theory because I believe it will more closely resemble the truth rather than some of these crackpots who go on and on about cannibalism and human sacrifices occurring in this part of North America."

"But the Aztecs did practice human sacrifice," Nick reminded her.

"And I concede there's proof of that but certainly not all tribes did, not the ones who lived along the coast, not the Chumash."

"You'd make a great host for one of those programs on the *National Geographic Channel*," Jordan decided.

River laughed at that. "I just love what I do. I want you guys to know I'm going to miss this place when I check out. You've made me feel incredibly welcome."

"That's the idea. I know your reservation is up Monday but we hoped you'd extend it," Jordan said. "We enjoy having you here."

"If only I could. I'd love nothing better than to do that but the budget won't allow it. Once Julian and Laura, my crew, get here and bring the RV to town, I'll have to give up the full-size shower and rough it. God, I'm going to miss that luxurious queen-sized bed and all the comforts of home like we're doing now, sitting around a regular table instead of that tiny thing in the RV. Having all these amenities are a little slice of heaven for me. Not to mention having to give up your cooking."

"Any time you or your team needs a place to stay, feel free to come back. We'd love to have you."

"Believe me, if I could work it into my budget, I'd prefer staying right here to sharing an RV with a couple of goofy lovebirds."

"Hmm. What if we dangled a better price in front of you?" Nick prompted. "We're approaching the off-season."

"Better price? Now you have my attention."

Nick threw out a figure.

"I could definitely work with that using my allowable per diem. Add in a little of my own money and I think it might work for me. We may have ourselves a deal, Mr. Harris, because living in that tin can gets old really fast. Besides that, I'm pretty sure I'm in love with Promise Cove. I'm pretty sure I understand why Scott is so reluctant to give it up."

"Is it true Marcus Cody isn't all that keen about this dig?" Jordan asked.

"You heard right. Marcus may not trust me yet but the rest of the family seems like a sure bet."

Chapter Five

At the Cody house in Santa Cruz, Marcus stood in the kitchen helping his wife of forty-three years load the dishwasher after supper. While he might not have been sure about River Amandez his wife, Lindeen, was showing the first signs of total adoration. She'd already talked the woman's ear off all the way down the 101 on the trip from Pelican Pointe to Santa Barbara. Lindeen liked what she'd learned from the pretty archaeologist.

And she wasn't above sharing how she felt with her husband. "They'd make a perfect couple. She's unattached. She seems sweet. And she's cute as a button. What could Brent find wrong with any of that?"

Marcus, however, remained stoic. At sixty-seven, the man still wore his long hair, albeit white, tied back in a ponytail. He'd been far less charmed with the vibe he'd gotten from River than Lindeen had been.

He calmly poured himself another glass of iced tea and stated flatly, "She's hiding something."

Lindeen fluffed her graying mane of black hair and waved him off. "So was Hayden and look how that turned out. We have our first grandchild and our youngest has never been happier."

But Marcus stood firm. "River isn't what she seems. Besides, you need to stay out of Brent's love life. I told you that already."

"That's why this time I'm playing it crafty. *This time* I'm not letting on that I like her. First mistake. Psychology. Reverse thinking," she said, tapping the side of her head. "If I push him her way, you and I both know he'll run the other direction for sure. You know your oldest son. This is the *one*, Marcus. She's Native. She's perfect for our Brent."

Marcus didn't reply right away. Instead he looked over at his petite wife. Glancing back down at the liquid he'd poured, he thought for a moment before he said, "Lindeen, River's from out of state. California isn't her home. Think about it long and hard before you push her on Brent. This woman travels the globe. What makes you think she'd be content giving all that up? Her heart's in her work. I sensed that about her right away. Have you thought about that at all? Do you want to see Brent up and leave the state, to uproot his life to follow River Amandez all over the world?"

"What on earth makes you think he'd do that? He's settled here. His home's here. Once the insurance company settles, he'll rebuild it."

"Be that as it may, I'm convinced she has problems of her own locked up inside. Brent doesn't need to be dragged into more drama at the moment."

"Why do you say that?"

"Other than someone wants him dead, you mean? In case you haven't noticed, our son is at a crossroads right now with his life, his career."

Lindeen paled at that. Then she thought about it for another minute. Like any good matchmaker though, she quickly rebounded and waved off her husband again. "If you mean the fact the county hasn't let him come back to work yet, that's just temporary. He's the sheriff. The people elected him. The county can't just dismiss that. He'll be back on the job in no time. You'll see. But that other stuff about River, I admit I hadn't considered any of it. She is rather dedicated to her work, isn't she?"

"She is. Not to mention there's something…off…about her. But first and foremost, why would a woman like that who travels for a living, put down roots here in California? There's no reason for her to do it, none at all. And if she and Brent should happen to get together *briefly*, I doubt it would last. I'm afraid your oldest son is a confirmed bachelor. After his disastrous marriage, I doubt he'll ever consider matrimony again at all. The sooner you accept it the better off you'll be."

"But you're planning on pushing this security detail on him, right? The two of them will be in close proximity for months. The setup's perfect, more so than any of mine have been."

"Indeed I plan on getting the council to hire him for security but not to fix him up with River Amandez. But because he's the best man for the job even with one bum leg," Marcus stated. "Fixing him up was never my objective. I have no intentions of making that trip into Pelican Pointe every day for the next two months. Fact is, Brent's already there. It makes sense. I just have to get him to see that."

Lindeen's shoulders slumped. "I really did think River would be perfect for him. But now I can see your point. I suppose I need to call Julianne and see if she's busy this weekend. I still have hope the two of them might connect that way. It's time I had her over to supper anyway. Do something nice to pay her back for running to the store for me all those times when my back was out."

Marcus gave his wife a disbelieving look. "Right. That story might fly with Julianne. It might even fly with Brent, but not me. I love you dearly, Lindeen. You've been the love of my life for forty-three years now. But you need to let Brent find his own woman. You need to give that boy some breathing space. He's right about that, you know. And if it never happens, if he never finds that special woman to share his life with, I'm telling you, you need to accept it and move on."

Lindeen harrumphed at that. "I'm only thinking of Brent. And after what happened to him, our boy almost died, Marcus. Brent needs someone in his life."

"I'm aware we almost lost our son, Lindeen. But at some point you have to respect Brent's privacy, his wishes. He's asked you to butt out. I know because I've heard him do it before. He's been patient about it so far, good-natured about it even, but since the explosion, I'm picking up changes in him."

"The disability thing again?"

"Brent's always been our adventurous one, seeking new undertakings at that. Remember when he up and joined the army and headed to Iraq. That's our Brent. Now Ethan, Ethan's always had a more creative side to him, less impulsive—and he's showing that in his writing now. But since that night Brent woke up in the hospital, he's having a tough time with something—something is troubling our boy, Lindeen. The medical disability is only part of it. He isn't dealing well with hobbling around and having to fight to get his job back. They haven't even given him the chance to return to work part-time, which is unusual."

"I think it's a political ploy by his replacement, that Jim Richardson."

"Brent thinks so, too. Because politics are entering into the equation, he's having difficulty accepting the whole downtime thing. I don't know how to help him other than get his mind on something else."

Lindeen stared at her husband. "Like the security job?"

"That's the goal. There are rumors that this Richardson fellow is making plans to challenge Brent at the polls if he decides to run for re-election next spring. To be honest, I think Brent's lost faith in the system. He gets injured and immediately his second-in-command starts a campaign to replace him—for good. I'm not sure Brent cares one way or the other though. In fact, he doesn't seem interested in much of anything these days. And that's what bothers me."

"Of course, he isn't interested in anything else. He was seriously injured. He has to concentrate on getting better, getting his body to heal from all the injuries. That's all it is." But then Lindeen narrowed her eyes, beginning to catch on. "That's the real reason you want to turn this security job over to him at this dig site, isn't it? You want to get his mind off the explosion, get him focused on something else, anything else, other than his job right now and all the political ramifications, even if it's a stupid rent-a-cop job."

"That's right. That's why I don't see your fixation with River working out. My advice is to stick closer to home, shift gears toward Julianne again. But I'd be wasting my breath to try to talk you into anything. I know better than that."

"There's no reason to take that tone with me, Marcus Cody. You know I only want what's best for my sons."

"I know. So why not see if Julianne's free for Saturday night. It's just a meal. And who knows? Maybe it'll work out this time."

"I really had my heart set on River though. Imagine what beautiful children they could make together."

Marcus shook his head. "Get over it. Right now we have bigger issues than dreaming about imaginary grandchildren. Brent needs something to take the focus off getting his job back. He needs some downtime, a breather."

"He needs to find out who did this to him."

"I know he does—and he will—but right now a mini vacation wouldn't hurt, away from the grind and pressure of what he's used to at the sheriff's office."

"The dig site will be a mini vacation? I'm not so sure about that. What should I do then?"

"If you invite Julianne, this time don't be so obvious about it. Ask Ethan and Hayden to join us."

Lindeen's eyes lit up, not really needing much more of a boost to get on board with the idea. "I'd get to spend time with Nate."

"There you go. Suggest they drag a reluctant Brent here along with them. Maybe then when he finds Julianne already sitting here, he won't be able to kick up a fuss in front of everyone. Plus, he'll be more open to asking her out himself."

"Good idea," mumbled Lindeen as she went to the kitchen phone on the wall and punched in Julianne Dickinson's number. "The local girl has to have the inside track, right?"

"They say the home team always has the advantage. Let's hope that's true."

Chapter Six

In sleep, Brent fought the feeling of being trapped in a fire. With every breath he took smoke burned his lungs. Caustic smells hung in the air making him sick to his stomach. He relived passing out, losing consciousness. He felt the pain all over again until his bones ached.

The ringing in his ears grew louder.

He came awake stretched out on the sofa. A minute went by before he realized someone kept on pushing the damned doorbell. On instinct, he reached for the .45 he'd slid under the couch then shook his head. No self-respecting bomber would ring the doorbell. Sitting up, he yelled in the direction of the front door. "Go away."

"It's me, Brent. Ethan. Open up."

Brent sighed and reached for his cane. Hobbling all the way to the door, he brought it back with a thud and a snarl. "I've seen you more in the past three weeks than I've seen you in three damned years."

"I love you, too," Ethan sang out as he moved past his brother into what used to be his own living room. It wasn't until he turned that he spotted the weapon still gripped in Brent's fist.

"I'd love to say you don't need that around here but I guess that's a ridiculous thing to suggest after almost getting blown to bits. You want to talk about it?"

"No," Brent growled as he limped over to hide the gun in between the seat cushions.

"Too bad. Mom wants you to come to dinner Saturday night."

"Why didn't she ask me herself?" But even as he got the words out, he knew the answer. "Please do not tell me she's fixed me up with someone."

"Okay, I won't tell you."

"Damn it," Brent said, running a hand through his disheveled hair. "Tell her you couldn't find me. No, on second thought, tell her you found me but I went to San Francisco for a fun weekend with a redhead. No, make that two redheads."

"If I'm going to go that route and lie, I might as well make it twins, barely legal," Ethan said with a wink.

"Nice touch. You know, I've been a good sport about this for way too long because it's my mother. But hey, I'm getting fed up with her meddling in my love life. It's none of her damn business."

"I hear ya."

"Want a beer?" Brent said making his way into the kitchen.

"Sure."

"Who is it this time?"

"Who do you think?"

Brent let out a sigh, handed Ethan a beer and got himself one out of the fridge. "Not Julianne again."

"'Fraid so. She's a nice person, pretty as a picture, too, but—"

Brent didn't let him finish. "Do you realize I've shared a meal with that woman more times than I have with Hayden over the years? And Hayden is my sister-in-law. That's not counting all the times Mom's begged Julianne to come over under the guise of hooking up. I even took her out to dinner once. We went to a movie afterward. We laughed. We talked until almost one in the morning. But there's not a damned bit of chemistry between us. Julianne knows it, too. And she's too polite to tell Lindeen Cody to buzz off."

"I thought it might be something like that. For what it's worth, I do have a suggestion, although it's pretty sneaky."

"Sneaky as in behind our mother's back? I like it."

"It wouldn't exactly be behind her back, more like, in-your-face or rather in-her-face. Not sure you're gonna like it though."

"If it sends Mom a message, I'm in. What do you have in mind?"

"How do you feel about asking River Amandez to a barbeque at the Cody house Saturday night?"

This time Brent groaned. "You have got to be kidding me."

"No, listen. It'll work."

"I doubt that."

"Look, do you want to spend another evening with Julianne where it gives Mom the slightest bit of hope you two might eventually get together?"

"Not really."

"Then bringing River along might just send a message to Mom that you're in charge of your own love life once and for all."

"I barely know the woman. We've had one conversation."

"Make it two. She's already met the parents. She has a working relationship with Dad. It's an inroad into why you're bringing her to a family event."

Brent eyed his brother with open suspicion. "What do you know exactly? I want the truth."

"I didn't want to say this but I happen to have insider info. They don't want you hooking up with the archaeologist—at all. Mom did, but now she's changed her mind."

That had Brent's temper spiking for real. He cocked a brow. "So my mother gets to tell me who to date? I don't think so. I'm afraid to ask but, what's wrong with the archaeologist?"

"For one thing, she isn't local. She isn't staying put here for any length of time." When he saw Brent's scowl,

Ethan held up a hand. "Don't shoot the messenger. The way they figure it River's just passing through for a few months or however long it takes to excavate our ancestors. And keep in mind Dad isn't happy about that."

"We don't even know for certain it's a Chumash settlement."

"Dad says it is."

"And he's never been wrong before?"

"The giveaway seems to be the canoe sticking up out of the ground. The markings are definitely Chumash."

Brent moaned. "I'll have to take your word for it. With a bum knee I never made it to the hole to see for myself. This seems to be what my life is reduced to now. The county's put me on medical disability indefinitely. And my mother is running my love life."

"How can the county do that? It's been three weeks. How do they know you won't be able to return to your job in record time?"

"They don't. It has politics stamped all over it."

"Ah," Ethan said, beginning to catch on. "Jim Richardson. He was never shy about making it known he wanted the sheriff's job, been angling for it since before I ever left the department."

"Exactly. And now with the explosion, I'm out on my ass. It all works in his favor."

"You aren't suggesting Richardson could've done this to you, are you? Or hired someone?"

"I don't know what to think. All I know is I'm doing my best to get back to my job as quickly as I can before it's gone. Why do you think I've been religious about keeping my PT appointments?"

"Makes sense now. Okay, what do you want me to tell Mom about Saturday night?"

Brent took a long pull on his Anchor Steam. "See, this is why I'm pissed. Not only do I have a guy breathing down my neck for my job—may even already have it locked up inside the department—but now every time I turn around Mom and Dad are sticking their noses where they don't belong. How the hell am I supposed to convince River Amandez to come to a family cookout? At my age I'm too old for these stupid games."

"Do you want Mom off your back or not?"

"Look, just because I show up with the scientist, doesn't mean a thing. Chances are Mom will likely dig her heels in and try to fix me up with someone else like her hairstylist. Again. She did that, you know."

"Geez, I had no idea things were that bad. I mean, I was on the receiving end a couple of times but she let up on me…eventually."

"The whole thing's a bit of a joke at work—behind my back of course—how Lindeen Cody tries to fix her son the sheriff up at every turn. Why the hell do you think I worked so much? I also turned down invitations to the house at least once a week out of fear—fear that I'll walk in the door and some woman will be sitting there looking at me like husband material and want to go pick out places to register China patterns. You're lucky. You were at least two towns away."

"Plus, I'm off the market now."

"Do you miss it? Being out there? Dating?"

"Hell no."

"Does being a father ever scare you?"

"Honestly? For a while it did but not anymore. Nate's starting to crawl. Now you tell me something. Level with me. Are you done in law enforcement? Do you honestly believe this Richardson is out to thwart your return from within?"

"Is that what Mom and Dad think, too?"

"I know they're worried about you. Are you burned out because of what happened?"

"A little, I guess. But who wouldn't be with the hours I keep. Is it obvious?"

"Not to anyone outside the family it isn't. But remember, you were the first one to recognize burnout in me."

Brent nodded. "I worried about you. A cop can't sustain burnout for long before he endangers himself and others."

"I know you did. But my heart was never in law enforcement the way yours is, And as sheriff you don't have to be out every day in a squad car."

"That's true. Okay, here's the deal. I want my job back. But the reality is I might be done. If I can't win my appeal to get my job back and off disability status, they'll wash me out of the department for good. Not only do I have to get a clean bill of health from the doctors, I also have to pass all the hurdles with the shrink. Trouble is, if it should happen, I have nothing as backup, nothing planned when I reach this point. I damned sure don't want to work security detail no matter how pushy Dad gets."

"You're in no shape to do it either, at least not yet."

"Exactly, so you know about his covert plan to get me to secure the dig site for the tribe? It's another reason I'm ticked off."

"Yep. I know he's angling for you to get more involved in the excavation on a professional level to keep an eye on things."

"Sounds like he's expecting trouble."

"Let's face it, dig sites are notorious for attracting looters and protestors. You know that. And there'll invariably be a few of the tribe who show up to demonstrate against the archaeological site."

"Before I set foot on-site in an official capacity I still have weeks of PT left." Brent took another pull on his beer, stared out the window. "I can't imagine River Amandez agreeing to dinner at the Cody house."

"But it sure would needle Mom if she did."

"There is that. I'll have to think about it though."

"Don't wait too long. Women rarely like last-minute invites anywhere."

After mulling on it overnight, in the end, Brent took his brother's advice. He hadn't asked a woman out using such a ruse since high school. Since it was already Thursday, if he wanted to shore up a date for Saturday night he had to get his butt in gear. On that one thing he agreed with Ethan. Women usually didn't go for last-minute invitations.

Brent knew where to find her. At this time of day, she hung around the cliffs either making notations on maps she'd charted, or taking a slew of photos from the top of the cavern.

He also knew his father had gotten off the phone with her two hours ago. Marcus Cody had given her permission to crawl closer to that hole in the ground as long as she promised not to remove any objects.

Brent moved out the front door like a zombie dragging one foot. With all the enthusiasm of a man counting the steps to the hangman's noose, he crossed Ocean Street. He looked out at the sun-kissed bay and the glistening water. He'd forgotten how pretty the little inlet could be this time of year.

She was standing in the same spot as yesterday as if she'd spent the night there guarding what was hers. Today she had on jean shorts and a white top that already had smudges of dirt at the tail end. River Amandez didn't seem to care about anything at the moment but plotting the stretch of beach.

Veering off the concrete pathway, he stepped gingerly onto soft sand.

She glanced up just like before but this time she sent him a hundred-watt smile. His heart did a flip-flop in his chest. A part of him felt like that kid back in eighth grade again. He waited for her to make the trek down the hill to where he stood.

"Hi there. I'd give you the grand tour but I doubt you could make it up the incline. Thanks to your father I got to slide down into the crevice today. It'll have to be shored up some more before we get serious but I got some great shots to send to my team so they'll know what to expect."

Her enthusiasm reminded him of a kid with a new birthday toy. When she finally paused to take a breath long enough for him to comment, he asked, "Where are they? Your team?"

"It took them a couple of days longer to shift gears. They had to pack up the RV in the middle of Alabama marshland. That's where we were working, a Coushatta site. We thought we'd hit the big time there until we heard about this one. Now we're jazzed and ready to go."

"And Pelican Pointe is the big time? It's a shame we don't still have a newspaper. I'm sure the town would like knowing they're now in the big leagues when it comes to the spotlight."

She cracked a grin. "At the moment Pelican Pointe is it. And to answer your question, I'd say about now my team is somewhere in Texas, in the process of crossing that stretch of I-10 and fighting boredom behind the wheel. They have close to eight hundred miles of highway to travel from border to border in Texas alone. I expect them here this weekend though. And if I know Julian he'll try to stay on schedule as much as he can."

"How long were you in Alabama?"

"Hmm, let's see, almost five months. The place was a humidity nightmare that made for a brutal summer. Outside of the heat, among other things, we fought mosquitoes the size of bumblebees. I still itch at night just thinking about them."

"But it sounds like you were right at home. You certainly get excited about dirt. I've never seen a woman who had that gleam in her eye over mud and sand."

"True. Are you just out stretching your legs or what?"

"According to my physical therapist it's a requirement. How do you feel about barbeques?"

She gave him an odd look. "I believe they're as American as apple pie. If you're taking a survey, you can put me down in the 'for' column."

He grinned. "Then how would you like to spend Saturday night at one?"

Her grin vanished. "Are you asking me out on a date?"

"I'm asking the newcomer to my parents' house for a steak dinner grilled next to the beach under starry skies."

"Ah, so Marcus and Lindeen want me to come to a cookout? Sure. What can I bring?"

"Not a thing. I'll pick you up out at Promise Cove around five-thirty."

"That isn't necessary. I can drive into town, we can leave from here." Sensing an awkward moment and to prevent that from taking root, River suggested, "Why don't we walk over to the Diner? Maybe get a cup of coffee. I need to take five anyway," she said, mopping her brow with her forearm as she hopped down from the slope. Tilting her head to one side, she noted the look on his face. "You don't seem too thrilled about the invitation. Is something else the matter?"

Yes, he thought, something was definitely the matter. For one, he was too damned old for these kinds of silly games. At that moment, he could've easily given Lindeen Cody a piece of his mind. Probably wouldn't do any good anyway, he grumbled as they headed toward Main Street.

The Hilltop Diner did its best to look like a malt shop straight out of a *Happy Days* rerun. The black-and-white checkered floor hadn't been new since the place had opened its doors in 1965. Eight padded red stools were tucked under the black marble counter and bolted to the floor. All had been patched several times over with red duct tape.

The Wurlitzer jukebox at the end of the counter provided music from six in the morning to nine at night. In all that time it had only been out of order once. That was when Myrtle Pettibone had walked in, aimed a .22

rifle at her husband, Clete, and fired. It had been the same morning she'd caught the lying, cheating son of a bitch in bed with Nola Davenport. After considering all her options, Myrtle had dug out Clete's gun from its hiding place in the hall closet and followed him to the Diner. Even though Myrtle might've missed Clete's ear by a scant two inches that day, she'd caught the Wurlitzer dead center in its electronic heart.

It was the only time in almost fifty years the jukebox had been out of commission.

Even with all that, the dining area hadn't changed much since its opening. There were eight mismatched square tables and four red-vinyl booths that lined the front wall, each offering a window view to Main Street.

River and Brent slid into a booth across from one another.

Over pumpkin pie topped with pistachio ice cream, which he learned was River's favorite fall concoction, they deliberated the ins and outs of paleontology. For another fifteen minutes she went on and on about uncovering interesting tidbits in the books she'd read about his thousand-year-old ancestors.

When he could take it no longer, he finally stopped her in mid-sentence and said, "How can you eat that? I'm pretty sure you've ruined pumpkin pie for me for good."

"Oh please. This is delicious. Want a bite?" she asked, holding out her spoon.

"No thanks," he said as he dug into his own apple pie with vanilla ice cream.

She stared at the typical pairing on his plate and said, "No imagination with desserts, huh? Why am I not surprised? I might point out that anyone can order vanilla but it takes someone willing to experiment to come up with blending two flavors together to make them rock."

"Are you willing to experiment, River?" Brent asked, cocking his head in a devilish dare.

She grinned. "I'm a scientist. What do you think? Maybe if you told me what you have in mind, we could cut to the chase."

Brent waved his hand to get Mona Bingham's attention. The waitress sauntered over to their table with her order pad. "Need something, Sheriff? More coffee?"

"That'd be great, Mona. But what I really want is for you to bring us two thick chocolate milkshakes made with chocolate fudge ice cream and double chocolate syrup." He looked over at River, raised a brow. "Can you handle the triple-triple? Better tell me now."

She sighed. "I've never ever said no to chocolate before in my life. I swear between the Diner and Jordan's cooking, I'm gonna gain ten pounds while I'm here."

"You're what five-nine? Your work must keep you physically fit. Where'd you get a name like River anyway?"

"I come from a long line of Zuni people who were mostly farmers. Water is essential for survival. My parents wanted to give me a strong name hence; I'm River."

"I thought you were Pueblo."

River threw him an incredulous look. "Zunis are one of the Pueblo peoples. I guess I thought since you were Native you'd know that." Eyeing the expression on his face, she realized something else. "I'm surprised you don't. In spite of the fact your father's a walking information databank about the Chumash, you on the other hand, know relatively nothing about your tribe other than surface stuff. Why is that?"

Brent let out a long breath. "I'm afraid that's true. After growing up listening to his stories, I guess there was a point where I started tuning him out. Ethan did it as well."

"That's a shame because he truly knows his stuff. Would you like to tell me what's really behind this invitation to supper? Your father's great and all but he really didn't strike me as the friendly sort who would ask me over for a meal. He doesn't completely trust that I'll treat the artifacts with respect and the reverence they deserve. Of course, he's wrong…but that doesn't play into your angle."

"You're perceptive."

"That's what they tell me. So what gives?"

Brent decided to level with her and began to relay the plan. He knew almost immediately he'd made a huge misstep. Watching her eyes narrow, watching the temper flare in those dark brown orbs, he began to realize something else. He was attracted.

"So let me get this straight. You want me to show up, *uninvited*, like a surprise for both your parents?"

Brent knew he was in double trouble when she pushed her plate to the side so she could lean across the table to make her point.

"How dare you? Not only would that ridiculous idea embarrass your mother by inviting me without her knowledge— but you'd put me in a very awkward position with the man acting as liaison on *my* dig—therefore putting my entire project in jeopardy. I won't even address the fact that you would no doubt humiliate this Julianne woman." She wadded up her paper napkin, threw it on the table.

He was surprised it didn't end up in his face.

"Sometimes I don't even know what goes through men's brains or what passes as brain matter. Reasoning seems to fly out the window."

River stood up, dug in her jeans pocket for a twenty dollar bill which she tossed on the table. "I believe I'll pass on being part of your childish plan." She shook her head. "How old are you?" She held up her hand. "On second thought, I don't care. You're old enough to know better."

With that, Brent watched as River Amandez turned on her heels and stomped to the door while the other patrons suddenly got busy finishing their lunch.

About that time Mona brought over the two chocolate shakes, glancing at River's back as she disappeared out the door. "I take it you're gonna want these to go now, right?"

Before Brent could answer, he spotted Troy Dayton making his way inside. Troy passed River on the way out. The young man crossed to where Mona stood at the table.

Tall and lean with curly white-blond hair, Troy slid into the booth River had just vacated. The young carpenter nodded in Mona's direction, then Brent's. "How's it going?" But Troy caught the definite lingering tension in the air and added, "Did I miss something? It's a little early in the day to get stood up."

But it was Mona who answered for Brent. "He didn't. Get stood up that is. That archaeologist got mad about something. She just up and took off. She yelled at the sheriff here. How rude is that?"

Troy cracked a smile in Brent's direction. "Women troubles, huh? We've all been there. Not that long ago Mona dumped me over that whole Gina Purvis mix-up. It's been kind of a sore spot with us since, hasn't it, Mona?"

Mona eyed Troy. "I've never known anyone who got arrested for murder before. It sort of gave me the creeps to think you could've done something like that. Just thinking about it...gives me cold chills now."

Brent stared at Mona then back at the kid. Troy had been wrongly arrested for Gina's death. The guy had spent weeks locked up in county before the real perpetrator, Carl Knudsen, had crossed onto their radar. "You thought Troy was guilty all that time he spent in jail?" Brent asked.

Mona shrugged and admitted, "The cops don't usually arrest innocent people. I've had a tough time getting past it."

Brent studied the young couple. Even now it didn't seem like the relationship had any kind of a chance. But that was none of his business. He used his cane to get to his feet.

"Good thing we got all that straightened out and Troy was completely exonerated," Brent said loud enough for Mona and all those within earshot who still wanted to give Troy a wide berth to take in the declaration.

Brent looked over at Troy. "Your carpentry skills are excellent. When Logan finishes his lighthouse project, how about coming around to my grandmother's house? The cabinets need upgrading. You can give me a quote and we'll take it from there."

"Really? I'd love to do the work on them," Troy said, beaming. "Thanks, Sheriff. Was River really rude to you?"

"No, she wasn't. In fact, she put me in my place." And he should have his head examined for ever listening to Ethan's half-baked scheme in the first place.

"Why don't you two enjoy the shakes? While you're at it, order a burger and fries to go with them." Brent threw some bills on the table, adding it to River's twenty on the table.

As he hobbled off, Mona pointed out, "But this is way more than enough. I'll get your change."

"Keep it," Brent muttered. "Having to eat crow turns you off food for a while."

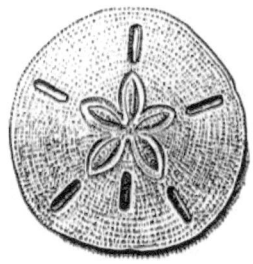

Chapter Seven

There was something about the thrill of a bomb going off and sitting back to watch it happen that stirred the senses.

To see the debris fly through the air, to witness the fire ignite and burst into flame, to watch the carnage firsthand had been pure joy.

It had all gone down exactly as planned. The meticulous timing had worked. The device had been brilliant, even clever in its design and simplicity.

The only problem was the sheriff had lived. He wasn't supposed to live. He'd had all these years to thrive and flourish. He should have been dead by now. Instead of planning a funeral, his family was in the process of pushing to get his job back.

The Codys obviously didn't know their son very well. They didn't know what he'd done, what he was capable of doing still. That's why he had to be stopped, for the greater good.

Because no one deserved to die more than Brent Cody.

Thursday night football found Brent settled in front of the flat-screen nursing a cold brew. It had been hours since the scene at the Hilltop with River and yet it still nagged at him. He'd already gone three rounds with Ethan over it for suggesting the harebrained idea in the first place.

Even now he rested his head on the back of the sofa and considered just how dumb he could be at this stage of his life.

"You shouldn't beat yourself up over it. Everyone makes mistakes, especially in relationships, especially in the early stages."

Brent's head popped up at the sound of the voice. He stared at the man standing in his living room wearing khaki shorts, a T-shirt that read *Nerds Do I.T. Better*, along with an opened Oxford shirt, the sleeves rolled up. Scott wore sandals on his feet and looked like a man comfortable in his own skin. Trouble was the guy he saw now had never made it back from Iraq.

"I've barely had half an Anchor Steam. I know damn well I'm not drunk. And I'm not taking any drugs stronger than ibuprofen."

Scott smiled. "It's not the alcohol. Remember when we were teenagers stealing a glance every chance we could get at Farrah Gosse in a bikini?"

Brent's right hand automatically flew to his heart about the same time he let go a loud sigh that filled the room. "Farrah Gosse, the foreign exchange student from France visiting the Crawford sisters for the summer. God, I couldn't have been more than sixteen then, and you fourteen. I might point out though what Farrah had on could barely be considered a bikini around here—two skinny pieces of fabric, one held together by string that barely covered all the interesting stuff."

"Farrah wasn't skinny, that's for sure. She was the most well developed sixteen-year-old in town that summer, had to be what, a thirty-six bust?"

"At least. That July and August I made up as many excuses as I could to head over to Pelican Pointe just to get a look at Farrah."

Scott nodded. "As I recall you used Autumn as the reason. You certainly were a remarkable good Samaritan that summer about helping out your grandmother whenever you could spare a minute."

That brought a laugh out of Brent as he uncurled his frame off the couch. "I was. It took some creativity on my part. Of course, it wasn't the same as Farrah with her swimwear. She wore red one day, black the next, although my favorite might've been that pale turquoise one with the little white polka dots."

"I remember the day like it was yesterday when Farrah took her top off right there on the beach like it was the Mediterranean or something."

"That day thank God I'd agreed to mow Autumn's grass and decided to go surfing in the bay afterward. I'm in the water, sitting on my board waiting for a wave. Next thing I know, off comes her top. Best day of summer vacation up to that point. I worked up the nerve to ask her out that afternoon. If only we'd had camera phones back then we could've captured the moment for posterity to use for…ah…later."

"I didn't know you ever asked Farrah out."

"After her topless day, are you kidding? I had to stand in line. Turns out, Farrah wasn't as…sociable…as her outgoing personality led her randy fans to believe."

"Ah. You tried to get past first base?"

"I tried but I didn't get very far. Good kisser though. I'd offer you a cold beer but…" His voice trailed off as he made his way into the kitchen and the fridge.

It was Scott's turn to put his hand over his heart. "Beer, one of man's true pleasures. I do miss it. Jordan's cooking, too. She's gotten better at it over the years. Whatever happened to that Ford Mustang you used to drive?"

This time Brent swore. "Drove it until I joined the army and met Cindy. She never liked that car and made me sell the damn thing to get a new foreign job. That should've been the first red flag right there."

"You never talked about Iraq when you came back. I guess there's a reason for that."

Brent looked away. "There's always a reason you never revisit war."

"Or a lousy marriage."

"Or a lousy marriage," Brent repeated before taking a swig of his beer, studied the man with the military-style haircut. "How about you? You want to talk about war, Scott?"

"No."

"I didn't think so. What's with hanging out with Megan Donnelly?"

"You never forget your first love. Megan was mine. And Jordan has Nick now. Hutton even thinks of him as her daddy, calls him that. Why shouldn't she? I never even got to touch my daughter in life, run my hand down her cheek, or hold her. If life seems unfair, try death. So what's the harm in revisiting how I once felt about Megan at seventeen?"

"Not a thing. It's the afterlife, *your* afterlife to boot. You spend it doing whatever you want."

"It may seem that way to you but…it doesn't work quite like that, not exactly. What's bothering you the most? The fact that you're alone at this phase of life or that someone wants you dead?"

"You get right to it, don't you? Do you plan to be the one to straighten me out with these late-night visits, Scott? I caught your vanishing act the other day at the pier. Plus, I saw you my first night here in this house. You were standing in the backyard like some vampire who needed an invitation to come inside."

"I don't need an invite."

"That's what I thought. What do you want from me?"

"How about you work on keeping yourself alive? How's that for starters?"

"Any ideas on that score? Because I could use some starting points."

"Sure. I'll help out where I can. After all, I have plans for you. You're needed around here more than you think."

"Who said I wasn't? What plans?"

But Scott had already vanished into thin air.

"Damn. I hate it when you do that." Brent raised his voice so that it echoed against the walls. "You're just like a woman, stir things up and then take off in the middle of an argument."

But the insult didn't get Scott to stick around to finish the discussion. He'd left Brent alone to think. And to talk to himself like an idiot.

Chapter Eight

At four o'clock Saturday afternoon River found herself sitting at the side of the Pacific Coast Highway, south of Pelican Pointe's city limits waiting for the first sign of the RV to round the bend. Because Julian was doing the driving and was known to have a lead foot, River figured her crew would get here in record time. She'd been texting Laura back and forth for two hours since they'd left Santa Barbara right after lunch. As they grew closer, Laura had kept her posted on their progress.

As soon as the motor home came into view towing a faded blue Jeep Wrangler, River laid down on the horn. She waved and watched as the RV pulled to the shoulder.

Getting out of her boxy SUV, River jogged over to the huge home-on-wheels with the foundation's logo on the side. She studied the driver, Julian Gustave, the bespectacled, studious man she'd known for more than fourteen years. A crop of curly chestnut hair fell across his forehead and it made him look more disheveled than usual.

As soon as Julian lowered the driver's window, River chided her friends, "Hey you guys, took you long enough to get here. Where are the interns?" she asked, peering beyond the front seat.

"What? No hello? No, how the heck are you? You ever try driving a gas-guzzling motor home from Alabama to California twenty-four-hundred miles and make good time?" Julian retorted in a teasing tone, adjusting his wire-rims. "And the interns are about a day behind us pulling all the equipment, making even worse time than we did. They should pull in here sometime tomorrow."

"We'd've been here sooner but this thing won't go over sixty miles an hour," Laura tossed in.

River smiled over at Laura. If she had to pick a perfect mate for Julian she couldn't have come up with a better one than the petite dishwater blonde who knew pre-Columbian facts and figures about indigenous people almost as well as River did. Not only that, Laura had a great sense of humor and was a kick to be around on a site.

"Laura's been itching to get out of this rig and spend one night in a real bed before the dig starts."

River grinned. "Good thing I snagged you guys an available room at Promise Cove for the weekend."

Laura grabbed Julian's arm. "Think about it, an actual bed and breakfast. I'm so there."

"Trust me, you'll love it. Beds so comfortable you won't want to crawl out of them in the morning and food to die for. Beats the greasy spoon we had at our disposal in Brasher Hills all to pieces."

"I might miss southern-fried everything," Julian noted.

"We'll get enough junk food over the next few weeks anyway. I'm looking forward to a real meal with real eating utensils," Laura said.

"Prepare yourself for eighteen-hundred-thread-count Egyptian cotton sheets so soft they feel like silk."

Laura sighed.

"You won't be disappointed in the food either. It's the best I've had in a long time," River assured them both. "Why don't you follow me to where you can park this monster and unhook the Jeep."

"Got us a spot all picked out?" Julian wanted to know.

"You bet, thanks to the county sheriff. It's within walking distance of the site. It's actually perfect."

"A sheriff? Please tell us you aren't already in trouble with the law in these parts," Julian teased.

"I'll tell you about him over supper," River promised as she headed back to her Wagoneer.

From the passenger seat of the RV, Laura watched River go and turned to Julian. "Hmm, interesting."

"What is?"

"Our fearless leader looks like she's intrigued by this cop."

"How the hell can you tell that by one comment, one look? For all you know this guy could be in his sixties with four kids and seven grandchildren."

"I don't think so. After five years, I know River. That look on her face suggests she's more than a little captivated by this sheriff."

"I didn't see anything but a jazzed woman who's ready to get crackin' on the dig. That's the woman I saw just now."

"Well, yeah, that, too. But how long has it been since River's had anyone in her life? Too long to even count. Since her divorce from that no-good bastard Wes, she dates less and less each year."

"She works practically all the time out in the boonies. Her job isn't conducive to meeting men. Besides, you know she's obsessed with her search, so much that she's closed herself off to men in general."

"True and the ones she does meet are interns, students, or have some type of connection to the foundation. And you know how she feels about dating any member of her team. She won't do it. I can't remember the last time she had a day off unless it was to go see her mother."

"Last Christmas. She went back to Santa Fe and refused to talk about it afterward. She did tell me she spoke to the private investigator. How much money do you think she spends on that detective each month?"

"Quite a lot I'd imagine. But she won't give up, Julian. She'll never give up. I wish we could do something to help."

"What would we do that we haven't already done? I've offered her money to help pay for the PI. She won't take it."

"I think that gets to her more than she's willing to admit. She's also lonely."

Julian sent her a desperate look. "I'm begging you, please, stay out of it, Laura. Your meddling will only spell trouble."

"You and I both know a dig site is like a movie set filled with gossip."

"Women," Julian muttered under his breath as he pulled the RV back out onto the road to follow the boss into town.

Once the two interns, Sandra McFarland and Walker Pruitt, showed up and got settled into the B & B, River held a strategy session that ended up turning into a wine-tasting event.

The heart of Promise Cove seemed to be the dining room. So that's where the team gathered around the table so that River could answer questions and go over the plan.

"Why don't we have more help?" Walker asked almost at once. "I expected the same size staff as we had in Alabama. Five people won't even be close to that. We're obviously short-handed here."

River smiled. "Wait until you see the narrow strip of beach we have to work with and you'll appreciate the skeleton crew. If we had any more people here we'd be tripping over ourselves. As it is, the Pelican Pointe Project will be very different from the one we just left, for that matter any other dig you've worked on before. I guarantee that."

"How so?"

"I'll go over that tomorrow at the site. It's easier for show and tell there than here. Besides, tonight is for making sure everyone knows their role and what I expect over the next few months."

"As long as we get to drink this divine chardonnay while we're in town I don't care what my role is," Laura admitted, emptying her second glass. "I've always heard great things about the California wine country. This," she said, holding up her glass, "does not disappoint. How far are we from Napa Valley anyway? I'd love to take a run through it while I'm this close."

River snickered and shook her head. "I knew it was a mistake to give Laura vino during a meeting. Try to concentrate on dirt instead of the white grape," River cracked.

"Come on, River. You have to admit this is an exciting time for us. A celebration of sorts is in order. And staying at this bed and breakfast, even for one night, is sheer heaven and a luxury we don't often get." Laura turned to Julian. "Maybe we could stay another night? What would be the harm in that? I'm even thinking of paying for it myself."

Julian smiled. "I'm not averse to spending another night here in a nice room with my woman," he said as he put his arm around Laura's shoulders.

River couldn't very well throw water on such enthusiasm. "Why don't we get through tonight and reevaluate the lodging situation tomorrow? Not one of us is itching to live out of that tin can for the next couple of months."

"Try bedding down in the travel trailer. It's in worse shape than the RV," Walker groused.

"Maybe they could cut us a deal here," Sandra suggested. "You know, share rooms, the guys stay in one, the girls in another. That's only two. I'd certainly be willing to bunk with one of you."

"I'm not sharing a room with Walker," Julian stated emphatically. "Laura and I have been together now for over three years. I'm not going back to bunking with a guy during a dig. I'll crack open my own wallet before that happens."

River suspected they'd be reluctant to leave the inn but she needed to nip this in the bud before it became an issue. "I told you guys, we'll reassess the RV and camper situation. I don't want us getting on each other's last nerve though like happened in Alabama."

"Digs are notorious for becoming little three-act dramas," Laura pointed out. "That's how Julian and I hooked up to begin with, a blowup between two stubborn anthropologists led to one of them walking off the dig, I replaced the boneheaded rival."

River grinned. "I remember that. Look, the owners have already offered a generous discount to anyone who wants to take them up on it. I'll leave it up to each individual. If you can work it into your budget, go for it. If not, it's the camper. So unless you're willing to toss in some cash to add to your per diem, you're still looking at an outlay to stay here."

"I can't afford to do that. I'm barely getting by as it is," Walker said as he turned to Sandra. "How about you?"

"'Fraid not. It's gotta be out of my price range. I'm a lowly student who still mooches off friends whenever I can. Looks like it's a comfy bed for tonight and back in the dingy travel trailer tomorrow," Sandra groaned.

An hour later River left her crew like that in grumble-state and closed herself off in her room. She opened her laptop to email Gil Conroy for an update. She hadn't bugged the private detective for two whole days. Even if it was Sunday night, Gil was used to her badgering him at all hours either by phone or email. In her message, she kept it short and to the point.

Anything come from the lead I gave you on Tuesday? If not, what about increasing the surveillance on Wes's mother's place? I know Hilda. She has to be keeping in contact with her son. Follow her, Gil. Please. I know Hilda has to be the key to finding Luke.

After hitting send, she tried to shift gears and get some work done on a progress report that the foundation expected by midweek. But after two hours of staring at the screen, she couldn't think of anything except Luke and the years she'd missed.

Whether it was the torment she felt catching up with her, as it so often did during any downtime she had or the excitement of starting the dig the next day, she didn't feel the least bit sleepy.

She also had a bad case of the munchies despite eating her fill of Jordan's roasted chicken at dinner. With a habit of craving chocolate late at night, she'd had the forethought to squirrel away a bag of fun-size Snickers. But she needed milk to go with one or maybe two.

Because of that, she got out of bed to pull on a T-shirt, stretch on a pair of yoga pants. She grabbed a couple of candy bars in her hand and made her way down the back staircase to the kitchen.

The old house creaked as old houses do, but as soon as she reached the last step something made her turn to her right. She caught movement over her shoulder and went into defensive mode, drawing back a fist, prepared to go for the nose.

"What the hell? Damn it! You scared the crap outta me. What are you doing down here this time of night anyway?" River grumbled.

"Technically, it's my damn house. And the way you're going on, you could wake the dead out at Eternal Gardens," Scott pointed out. "That chocolate addiction of yours is a bad habit. You know you'll have to brush your teeth again before going to bed, right?"

With one hand still resting on her stuttering heart, she fast-tracked her recovery enough to mumble, "Okay, *Dad*, thanks for the reminder even though you don't have to worry about such things. I'll have you know my dental appointments have been stellar," she added as she made her feet move to the cabinet, got down a glass. She went over to the fridge, poured the milk.

"By the way, you're right to think Hilda Patton is the key to finding your son."

At those words, the glass almost slipped out of her hand. "I knew it! Hilda's protected him all this time. Gil has to be there when she slips up. And she will. Slip up that is. She's got to. I have to hope for that," River said, peeling the wrapper off the candy. She took a huge bite before sipping the milk and did her best to maintain a calm demeanor. "I appreciate knowing that. It's a shame you can't tell me where to look for him."

"I wish I could. Your secret's safe with me, River," Scott assured her. "No one here ever has to know until you decide to unload."

"Thanks for that. Julian and Laura know, of course, but I don't share everything with them. It's too painful, especially because it's always the status quo."

"I know you keep things to yourself. You also keep your gift hidden from them, too. Is it because kids made fun of you at school?"

"Something like that," she uttered, letting the sugar and caramel combo kick in. "I wish you wouldn't harsh my chocolate high right this minute with painful memories, especially when I haven't set eyes on my baby since he was six months old."

"You have a special gift, River."

"Really? If that's true, if it's so special, then why doesn't it help me find my little boy?"

"I know exactly how you feel." When he saw the face she made, he added, "I do. Even though I can't wrap my arms around my child, I at least get to see her, make sure every day that she's okay. I can't imagine what it's like for you not being able to do that."

River softened knowing how difficult it must be for him around his child without being able to touch her. But then, she grew angry. "I'll tell you what it's like. It's pure hell. I want my baby back. I'd give up my job, I'd do anything to have my child back, to be able to see him, hold him, tuck him into bed at night, sing him a song. If I got the call right now that Gil had found him, I'd be there in a heartbeat anywhere in the world."

"I know that, too."

"Luke won't know me. It's been two long years. I missed everything, Scott. I missed Luke's first steps, his teething, his first words. He was only six months old when Wes took off with him." Tears streamed down her face. She suddenly lost the taste for the chocolate. Instead she felt like throwing up. At the loud sigh from Scott, she looked up into his face. "I want my baby back. Please, if you see anything, if you could tell me anything, anything at all. Please."

Scott rubbed his chin, cleared his throat to stall for time. "You tug at my heartstrings, River, you really do. You know it doesn't work like that. Why do I always have to remind people about that one thing?"

She let out the breath that had backed up in her lungs. "I don't know. Why doesn't it work differently? Why does it have to be like this? I didn't deserve this. And Luke damn sure didn't. Couldn't you make an exception, just this one time?"

Scott began to pace back and forth in front of the island. "Listen to me. You know Wes's mother is hiding something, has been since Wes went on the run. Your private investigator needs to stay on her. She sends him money, River. His parents are in on this and they both help him move around, stay hidden."

River eyed Scott and said, "You know that for a fact? Because I tried to get the cop in charge of Luke's case to see that and he never acted like it mattered."

Scott was tempted to tell her. But it wasn't his place. "Use your intuition, River, or whatever it is you call what you do."

"You think I haven't tried that? I've tried everything. I see the past. That doesn't help me find my baby. I've consulted psychics. I've spent time with shamans from every tribe across North America willing to give me an audience."

"It's because you're too close. Go with your gut. Where do you think your ex would've taken him? Didn't he have some favorite spot he'd always talked about seeing?"

"I hate these subtle hints of yours. I already told Gil to check out what you told me on Tuesday—the ski areas from Northern California to Idaho because Wes loves the sport. I'm still waiting to hear back. If I don't hear from Gil by tomorrow, I'll bug him over the phone."

After considering Scott's question for several seconds, she said, "Wes always wanted to live in the mountains, a region similar to his beloved New Mexico. He especially loved the Aspen area though, used to go skiing there every spring break he got from school."

"Then have Gil look there. You're going to find Luke, River. You will find your son."

"God, I hope you're right. Maybe I should take another leave of absence, check out the Denver area on my own?"

"Is that what you want to do? I'm telling you, confide in Brent Cody. He can help with this."

Since she wasn't so sure about that, she changed the subject. "How do you know so much about my gift anyway?"

Scott sent her a withering stare without bothering to reply.

"Okay. So you must know that I felt different growing up. The kids let me know it on a daily basis."

"You hated school. It's a wonder you did as well as you did. Look at you now, smart as a whip. Just goes to show that a person can overcome adversity, overcome feeling different."

"Smart as a whip doesn't help me locate my son."

"In the long run it will, trust me."

"I wish I could. It's a stubborn streak a mile-wide and the fact that I refused to buckle under the pressure to give up. I think Wes exploited my childhood when we met. In fact, I'm sure of it. He knew about the gaping hole in my self-confidence and knew that was my weakness."

"I'm sure that's true."

"I studied hard and got the tag as a nerd early on, maybe because I spent most of my time alone. When I met Wes…"

"I know something about being different. All the kids at school had their moms and dads. I had grandparents. Not that they weren't great but…"

"It wasn't the same thing. I get it. The fact your parents were dead made you different. But you still loved it here. I can see why. It's a beautiful place. You made a connection to the land, the cove, the town, long before you ever did with your grandparents."

"See, right there, that insightful nature of yours has to pay off in the long run. I'm curious about something. How long do you intend to make Brent Cody suffer?"

"What? Hmm, let's see, how about till hell freezes over?"

"That's pretty steep for a simple invitation to dinner that went awry."

Her shields went up. "What's it to you anyway?"

"He's a cop, River, and a damn good one. Think about it. He has connections that might help you find Luke. Did he ever mention that his father located a little missing girl up in Oregon? Miracles like that don't happen often. Take advantage of every inroad that might lead to success."

River stared at Scott, opened her mouth to speak but nothing came out. Her mind raced with hope. Then she came back down to earth. "I don't think Marcus likes me very much. I'm not exactly sure why."

Scott lifted one shoulder. "Doesn't matter. He'll help if you ask him. I hate to see you and Brent get off on the wrong foot because the guy listened to bad advice. I hate to see you miss out on a chance to find your son."

River's brow furrowed at that. "But I'd have to level with him about everything. Besides, there's no wrong foot here because there was never any foothold to begin with. Brent did mention that it was his brother's lame idea. But that hardly matters…and I emphasize the word *but* here.

Brent did not have to act on it. I'm curious about something though. Does Brent have the same kind of ability as his father?"

"If Brent does, he's never used it before, not outwardly anyway. It's widely known in these parts that Ethan has the greater gift."

"Hmm, what about asking the brother?"

"Go for it. Either one will help if you let it be known you need it."

"I take it you've known them for quite a while?"

"Ethan and Brent's grandmother used to live there in the same house where Brent lives now. Whenever they'd come over to Pelican Pointe to visit, we'd see each other around town. Ethan was the pesky little brother who tagged after us."

"No doubt fond memories."

"You bet. I'd be getting a haircut at the barber shop, the one old man Sanderson owned before it became the Snip N Curl. Or my grandpa might take me into the Diner to treat me to an ice cream cone. Brent and Ethan might be there doing the same. Brent was the very first guy in town who befriended me."

"Really. When was this?"

He scratched his head. "After I lost my parents in the car accident, I'd been living here about a year. It was summertime, I remember that. I couldn't have been more than six at the time. That would make Brent about eight. Like typical boys do, we played with our matchbox cars outside Ferguson's Hardware, went for a swim in the bay, and ran around town like heathens. It was then I guess Brent started coming out here to the cove. Here we got to play pirates without Ethan hanging around. With the age difference I guess I looked up to Brent, like a big brother. Now some bastard is out to do him in. Some days I think the world is unraveling on so many levels. There's so much meanness out there."

"That must be why you're looking out for Brent now and trying to fix the two of us up. It isn't a good idea,

Scott. I'm not a good bet when it comes to relationships. I'm too obsessed on finding Luke."

"No one could blame you for that, River."

"I'm not in the market for anything long-term, not ever again. I do kinda feel sorry for Brent though. I mean someone wants him dead. But that's never a good way to start a friendship much less a relationship. Besides, he seems a little lost right now. And I've got way too much on my plate."

Scott shook his head at that. "And you've never known what it felt like to be lost, River? Come on."

"Of course, I have but—"

"Then get to know him. He's at a crossroads right now and could use a friend. That's all I'm saying. Maybe the two of you could help each other."

"He has his family. They care about him."

"It isn't the same and you know it. He needs an ear. Lend an ear, River. What can it hurt? Be a friend. Ask for help. You want me to help you? I'm trying the only way I can."

She bit into the last part of her Snickers, drained the glass of milk. "Okay, but I'm no fixer of lost souls. I need major help in that regard myself."

Scott was tempted to argue with that. But then he knew River would never believe how things were about to change—in a huge way—and there was nothing she could do about it.

Chapter Nine

The next day along the dunes, Marcus Cody made it official. He gave River the all-clear to start work on the dig.

The first order of business was to erect a barrier to keep the tides from coming in. River assigned the interns to that job. Heavy-duty plastic tarps went down first and then enough sandbags were stacked two-feet high to create a dam-like wall to keep the work area as dry as possible.

"Make sure the seal is as tight as you can get it," River emphasized as she surveyed the barrier. "Otherwise this close to the ocean, we'll plot the grid only to have to bail water again and again."

When it came to defining and measuring out the range of beach, everyone pitched in to do the grunt work. They did north to south units first horizontally and then east to west, vertically. But even with that, it took them all morning to section off the measly strip of earth allotted them. Because of the narrow slit of landscape, they dug the hole in a rectangular contour, the same shape as the stretch of shore.

"Walker, this is the reason the Pelican Pointe Project is no ordinary dig. For one, the mudslide hollowed out a space that's no more than twelve feet long."

Though the cliff above them stood sturdy and rugged, the area around the base looked like a mini crater. "This slender strip of sand is all we have to mine so get used to bumping elbows with each other."

"But that's crazy," Walker said. "We're practically on top of one another."

River rolled her eyes. "I just said that. It is what it is and no amount of grumbling will change the measurements. You might as well make the best of it. We'll have to be extra cautious in excavating down to even the initial four inches around the circumference. Because of that it won't be easy. Now it's time to brush away the topsoil and get to work, see what's underneath besides that canoe."

"It'd be a lot easier to bore holes in the soil," Walker groused.

"You want to bore holes, you'll need to find another dig," River said matter-of-factly. It wouldn't take much more of Walker's bitchy attitude before she booted him off. "We utilize GPS coordinates, ground sonar and magnetometers. No boring holes, no invasive procedures. Not on my site."

Hands on hips, River decided it was time to remind the newbies of the rules, namely Walker. "Here's the order of things. All dirt goes through the sifter, no exceptions. Just because you don't eyeball anything, that doesn't mean something significant isn't hiding in there. We then log *everything* that surfaces into a database for accuracy. Everything gets bagged and tagged. Anything that looks like bone or fragments, anything that requires testing, we put in a separate container. Again, bag it and tag it. Take pictures with your phones if that will make it easier. We keep track of even the smallest piece of bone. You got that, Walker?" she snapped. "Because if you don't, tell me now. It isn't too late in the semester to switch sites. I'll gladly see that you're reassigned."

"No, I didn't mean anything by it," Walker backtracked. "I just thought drilling the holes would get us where we want to go a lot sooner."

"This isn't a race. You want fast results, you're in the wrong line of work," River continued testily. "Look around you. This is a delicate operation, probably unlike any I've encountered before. There are a lot of ecological things to consider here."

She ticked each one off by the fingers of her hand. "First, we had to conquer the tidal flow which we've done. Second, we have unstable ground here. Those two things won't change. Third, we're working with an incline, which doesn't help matters at all. That's why the plan is to utilize the natural stratigraphy. Fourth, we've established that we're dealing with a limited amount of space, fourteen feet is paltry. We have less than forty feet of shoreline to set up the workspace. Usually we get a much larger plot of ground. A farmer's field would be ideal. But we don't get to choose where the goods are, now do we? Fifth, we get any more rain it could weaken the side of the bluff even more. That happens, we're underwater again and starting from scratch."

She raised her other hand in the air for emphasis, stuck out her thumb. "And finally, you start boring holes in the ground around here even with decent sonar data and we could have damaged artifacts or worse, human remains in smaller pieces than what we bargained for. You destroy human remains, next thing you know I've got a pissed off Marcus Cody AKA tribe elder just looking for a reason to kick us outta here for good. That isn't happening on my site. Are we clear, people?"

"Yes, ma'am," Sandra wasted no time piping up.

That was fine by River, but Sandra wasn't the problem and neither were Julian and Laura. She waited for Walker to nod in agreement. When the man finally did, she added, "Good. Now quit standing around all of you and get your butts to work. And don't forget to charge your laptops at night. You do not want a dead battery forcing you to make manual entries out here that you later will have to re-enter into the database anyway. That's double the work."

An hour later inside the hole they'd allotted, River stood ankle-deep in muddy sand studying the remains of the canoe lodged at a forty-five degree angle.

"This is redwood," River muttered to Julian who stood up on the lip taking pictures with the zoom lens. "It's definitely Chumash, amazingly well-preserved. See the markings, here, here and here. Note the planks used on the sides, exactly the way the Chumash were known to carve out their boats and shore them up to make them seaworthy."

"What do you estimate the length to be?"

"Ten feet, maybe more. They were known to build tomols, some as long as thirty feet. It's a shame this one isn't that large."

Before reaching out to touch, River took off her latex gloves. She braced for the sensations she knew would bombard her. Running a bare hand over the brittle wood, her body went rigid as she stared straight ahead.

As if her eyes pierced the veil of time, she saw an active settlement, its people going about their daily lives. Several canoes were pulled up on the beach where fishermen unloaded their catch for the day. Other members of the tribe were still hard at work at their task out on the bay, their canoes bobbing in the swell of the harbor.

All at once the villagers began pointing to the horizon and shouting a warning of sorts. A storm loomed, River decided and watched as the skies darkened.

She shook off the vision, looked up at Julian to see his intent stare. Not for the first time River picked up the conversation where they'd ended it.

"What are the chances of getting this sucker out intact, Julian? How can we keep it from breaking apart in chunks? I can already feel how dried-out and delicate the wood is. I know it's asking a lot…"

"More like a miracle, River. Of course, intact would be preferable. But you have to realize we probably still have another four feet of layers to go through before we can even think about removing it. Not only that, but it looks like it goes back into the cliff. We'll have to extend the grid. There's no other way. And anything during that process could cause the planks to snap," Julian pointed out. "That's why we'll need to document what it looks like now in case it splits and we have to reassemble it later. Hell, it could already be in pieces underneath all this mud and we're not able to see it."

"I don't think so. We should start applying the preservation sealant today though, get it covered with plastic since the wood's been exposed to the air. We don't want it drying out more than it already has."

"Sure, I'll start the process now with what's sticking out of the ground. Is it okay to come on down there?"

"You bet. While you're at it bring the bucket of tools with you." With that, Julian dropped down into the hole, a space barely large enough for two people to work.

As they began to brush away the first precious layers of grit, River grinned, elbow to elbow with him. "We really are crazy for playing in the mud like this, aren't we?"

"We started out like this in Selenge, only not as coastal, but right next to a river as I recall. Do you ever wonder what would've happened between us if the site in Turkey hadn't come up?"

River studied her friend's face for any signs of lingering hostility about their brief time together, a matter of months really. Deciding he was just making conversation, she finally said, "We were just kids then on our very first dig. You and I both know we were all wrong for each other."

"That we were," he agreed with a grin. "At the time I really resented the fact you left me high and dry in Mongolia and headed to Turkey though." He lifted one shoulder. "I was so immature. Can you believe it's been fifteen years since then? A lot has happened. I wish you'd never taken that anthropology class and met Wes Patton."

She sighed. "That makes two of us. As far as leaving you high and dry in Mongolia, just remember, when I got to Ankara I did major grunt work just like Walker and Sandra are doing now," River reminded him. "And it wasn't pretty."

"It never is. Glad you put Walker in his place this morning. The guy's a major pain in the ass. He drove us nuts during the summer."

"I know. Keep a tight rein on him, will ya? If he slacks off, I want to know about it."

"Sure thing."

Cocking a brow, River proceeded to wiggle her eyebrows up and down. "Want me to have Laura come down here in the hole? That way you two could roll around in the mud together. Just don't damage my canoe in the process."

Julian laughed. "Nah, we did a lot of rolling around last night in that queen-sized bed we had at the inn. Laura really is lobbying to stay there instead of the RV."

"I've decided I don't want to spend the next two months feeling like a third-wheel most nights in the camper with you two. I don't want a repeat of Alabama when I was forced to bunk with you guys. It's time you two had your privacy and I had mine."

"That's appreciated but what about your budget? Can you do that *and* keep your detective looking for Luke? I know our grant doesn't cover lodging and the foundation's per diem is meager."

"I'll sleep in a tent right here on the beach before I give up the private eye." As she turned to climb the ladder up, she stopped and glanced back at her longtime friend. "Julian, you don't resent the fact that I'm heading this dig, do you?"

"Nope. You call the shots. I discovered years ago on that site in the Midwest that I don't like being in charge. I'll leave bossing people around up to you. You're good at it. Who's doing security around here anyway? You want us to take shifts for the time being?"

"If that falls to us and the crew is forced to do both, it will extend the dig well into next year. I'm sure the tribal council won't want us here any longer than we have to be. Besides, Marcus says he's handing the job off to his son, the recuperating sheriff."

"Really? So you intend to make nice then?"

"Sure. Why not? It beats the hell out of the alternative."

Chapter Ten

For three days straight since his last PT session, Brent could get around without his cane. He'd managed to walk down to Main Street and back without hunching over in pain or falling down. Thanks to a physical therapist who was as tough as any army drill sergeant he'd ever had there was light at the end of the tunnel.

He couldn't run yet, or even jog, but it was a step in the right direction.

His appointments with the department shrink were progressing. After they'd addressed the confidentiality issue, he'd found a level of trust. A couple of sessions had gotten him to open up about the daily pressures of his job, something he'd suppressed for years. And since his time in law enforcement might be coming to an end, he thought it best to unload his anger about it to the psychiatrist.

He had to wonder if he'd miss his job. If he was honest with himself, he'd struggled the past year to maintain any kind of momentum at all. Why had he been able to recognize Ethan's burned-out state of mind two years earlier but not his own now?

When the doorbell rang, he went to answer it and was shocked to find River Amandez standing on his stoop. She held up a bag he recognized as coming from the Hilltop Diner.

"Peace offering," she explained as she made her way past him while Springsteen belted out *Born in the USA.*

"Lunch break. Nothing like bonding over a meal, and artery-clogging burgers and greasy French fries are the best."

"We're going to bond?"

"Yep. At least we'll give it a shot. So where do we do this?"

"Kitchen."

"Got any ketchup?" she asked, following as he led the way. "French fries demand a condiment. Mustard works, too."

He sent her a dubious look. "No one should disgrace fries by smearing mustard on them."

"I do. I forget how sheltered your culinary life is." She dropped the bag on the counter and turned. "Hey, where's your cane? You're walking minus the cane. I can tell it still bothers you some but that's amazing. Look at you, you're caneless."

His mouth curved up. "I'm making progress. I hate that damn cane. Who wouldn't? And it's been almost a month. The physical therapist says I'm healing right on schedule for an injury like mine."

"Not being able to get around would drive me nuts. Got a Coke?"

The music changed to the Stones' *Time Is On My Side*. A confident Mick assured the listener that his baby would eventually come running back.

"Uh, yeah. I thought you were furious with me."

"I was. But your father tells me you're in charge of keeping an eye on my dig. It's better if we make peace."

"I agree."

"Good. Then let's eat these before they get cold." River dug into the sack, divvied up the food while Brent got down glasses and filled them with ice.

They sat down at the kitchen table like they were old friends on a picnic.

"I didn't know how you liked your burger so I had it cooked medium well with lettuce and tomato. You can always drag them off to the side if they disgust you. I had 'em cut the onions though. Hate those things but I realize not everyone feels that way. So I got mustard on mine, mayo on yours. But we can switch if you prefer. I'm not opposed to mayo just not on my burger."

"No, I'll eat it. In fact, it's perfect."

River's lips curled up and with it admitted, "I cheated. I told the waitress who took my order, I believe her name was Mona, the burger was for you and the cook fixed it the way they knew you usually ordered yours."

He grinned as he picked up the salt, shook a generous supply onto the fries. "Max Bingham, that's the name of the cook. His food's become a staple since I came back here."

River held the bottle of ketchup in the air, waited for Brent to nod in approval before squirting a mound of the red stuff onto the paper container for sharing and dipping. "So you don't cook?"

"I nuke stuff."

"I'm an expert at nuking stuff myself."

"I bet you eat out a lot going from dig to dig like you do. It gets old for me. But every time I try to prepare a meal it's a disaster of some sort. I'm pretty sure I didn't get the cooking gene."

"I can cook. I just don't usually have access to a stove."

"Do you miss having a base? Doesn't it get old always being on a dig?"

"At times. But the dig is usually my home. While I'm here in Pelican Pointe I'll make myself comfortable for the duration whether it's in the RV or staying out at that cute little B & B."

"How could you possibly make an RV home?"

"It's not that easy… especially lately…when you're forced to share it with a couple in love. Yuck."

"That would be…awkward."

"Exactly." The song changed to U2's *Native Son* which prompted her to ask, "How long have you been the top cop around here anyway?"

"Not that long. I intended to make the army a career. It never occurred to me I'd end up in civilian law enforcement. But when I decided to hang it up after three tours in Iraq, I joined the sheriff's department."

"How did you get to be sheriff in such a short amount of time? You aren't that old."

Brent grinned. "Gee, thanks. I started out as a lowly deputy. Turns out, the department was rife with cronyism and corruption when I joined up. I decided to do something about it. I ran for sheriff on a platform I'd clean things up, start from scratch, get rid of all the dead weight. During the election, I must've gone to more than a hundred barbeques, kissed hundreds of babies and had photo ops at each stop. By the end, it felt like I'd pressed palms with a million hands. At the time my opponent said I was simply cashing in on my time in Iraq and didn't know anything about being the sheriff. Turns out, he did me a favor with that line."

"Because you won."

Brent nodded. "Got sixty-two percent of the vote. But I made a lot of enemies along the way. That thirty-eight percent was rather vocal about my lack of experience at the helm. And when I shook up the department, that made a lot of enemies within. There were a lot of hard feelings at first but they eventually learned to see things my way. At least I thought they had. I hate to even consider that one of them took it to the next level and tried to end me. "

"Politics is an ugly business."

"It is. And that's one of the reasons I'm on disability even after I can clearly get around enough to sit behind a desk to do my job."

"Someone there wants you out for good? That doesn't seem fair. And I hope you don't mind me saying this, but a little scary as well."

"I don't know that for certain. But it's looking that way. Now, I'm reduced to doing your security detail."

"Your father roped you into this, didn't he?"

"Oh yeah. But he truly wants to make sure our people are represented when you start digging for bones. You shouldn't take it personally."

"I don't, not really. We don't even know there are remains at this site yet. There's a village there, yes, where people lived and worked and had families. But human remains could be forty miles up the coast." She did her best to sound convincing.

It didn't fool Brent. "You don't believe that for a minute."

She smiled. "No. I don't. It was a large, thriving village, a busy one at that. Not just a campsite either but their permanent environment. Remains are there. We may have to dig down deep and then go back in under the cliff to get to them. But the remains are there somewhere."

Brent stayed silent for a few minutes, studying her face, her confidence. "You have some special gift that tells you that. You do, don't you?"

Without answering, she blinked in amazement before it dawned on her. Scott's words echoed in her head. *If Brent does, he's never used them before, not outwardly anyway.* "You have it, too. You just don't bother using it very much. Why is that?"

"I guess you could say I took the path of least resistance as a kid. I was Native. First strike. My father was a bit of an oddity. Second strike. He embraced his psychic ability and ran with it. But at the time the whole thing embarrassed me. I didn't want people to know and my father was out there every day making sure they did." His shoulder came up in an easy shrug. "What can I say? I was young. It became a habit, something to hide, to back away from."

"But you do have psychic abilities." She sensed the struggle in him.

"I prefer to call it my gut feeling. It isn't as strong in me as it is in Ethan anyway, never has been."

"It wouldn't be because you have to exercise it the same way you do your brain. How do you know how strong it is, if you never utilize it?"

"I know. Okay? I've seen Ethan find a little three-year-old girl in Wilder Ranch State Park when I didn't know where to look. I've seen him use it to get women. Believe me, The Force runs strong in Ethan, not me."

She smiled at that. "Just because you don't use it to get women into bed doesn't mean it isn't there."

About that same time, they both heard a succession of loud pops coming from outside in the distance.

"Was that gunfire?" Brent asked, dropping his burger back down into the wrapper. He got up from the table to snatch up his cell phone on the counter. Instinct had him punching in nine-one-one. More pops alerted him to more shots and a potential serious situation. "That *was* rifle fire."

"The dig!" River shouted as she got to her feet. "It isn't the first time we've been shot at during an excavation," River explained as she tried to dart past Brent to the front door.

But Brent grabbed her arm to stop her progress. "Wait a damn minute! You aren't running out there until I get some backup here and check this out for myself."

When dispatch picked up, Brent identified himself. In clipped words, he apprised the person on the other end of the phone of his location and that he might have a possible ten-thirty-two in progress. He reached for the weapon he kept under the seat cushion. The entire time he watched River squirm beside him, itching to dash out the door to check on her crew.

"You don't understand. My team's out there. I left them to come here. I have to go see if they're okay." River took out her iPhone and thumbed in a text message to Julian.

But Brent had a job to do, too, and held firm. "I know that. And we will. But not until I know what's going on." While he kept her arm gripped, they moved together out

the front door and down the porch steps. Rifle fire
continued to echo from a distance. They made their way
across the street about the same time a smattering of
curious people began to stream outside from the little
touristy shops along the beachfront.

"Get back inside, all of you and stay there until I tell
you different," Brent demanded in the direction of the
onlookers. He shoved River toward the closed door of the
watering hole known as McCready's. He was surprised
when the lock turned.

When the bar owner, Flynn McCready appeared, Brent
told River, "Go in there and wait for me until I tell you
that it's okay to come out. Got it?"

"But what about my crew? They might be in the line of
fire while I sit here doing nothing."

"I'll see to it they're evacuated."

With that, Brent finally let go of her and was surprised
when River added, "Be careful."

Flynn filled his own doorway. A big man, originally
from Dublin, who'd once spent plenty of time in the ring
as a boxer, stepped aside to make room for River as she
scooted into the dimly lit pub.

Flynn pointed toward the lighthouse. "Gunman's on the
cliffs, Brent. I'd say it's a high-powered rifle probably one
with a scope."

It was then Brent saw the shotgun Flynn held. "You
take care of River and let me handle this." He might be on
disability but he'd be damned if he'd let Richardson
handle this situation when it was in his own backyard.

At the first sign of sirens closing in fast, he added,
"There, it seems my backup is already on the way. Now
get back inside both of you. And Flynn, do me a favor, try
to keep the gawkers to a minimum. Coax them into the bar
if you can and keep them there. I don't care if you have to
give out free, watered-down drinks to do it."

"Count on it. I haven't heard any shots in five minutes
or so," Flynn reported. But just as the bar owner spoke the
words, another round of gunfire went off.

"It's coming from the cliffs all right." Brent took out his cell phone, dialed dispatch a second time. "I need SWAT. I need choppers in the air with a marksman onboard. Get me Nightsun to illuminate the area. I want it so bright I can pick out a fly. I have at least one confirmed shooter, maybe more, with a vantage point. He's in a high-risk area, too. I have civilians on-site at the lighthouse and on the beach below in danger of getting hit. That's why you need to come in from the south. If our sniper should get a kill shot, I'm giving the go-ahead to take him out."

Listening to Brent's part of the conversation, River couldn't help it. Drawn to his intense eyes, she felt that familiar tug in the belly she hadn't experienced in years. How long had it been since she'd acted on that kind of urge anyway? But this wasn't the time for lustful thoughts. She didn't need to get tangled up with anyone. It was a bad idea. Too much on her plate to consider a quick roll in the hay. But those take-charge eyes of his made her heart flutter in a way it hadn't.

Make sure my crew is okay," she told him when she stepped back outside where he stood. Looking into his dark soulful face, she tiptoed to reach his ear and acted on instinct. Whispering, she said, "When this is all over, I want a dance, sheriff. Make sure I get it. Understand?"

Despite the situation, Brent almost smiled. "I can arrange that. While I'm waiting for my ride, hand me your cell phone for a second."

River reached in her jeans pocket, pulled out her iPhone, handed it off. She watched as Brent punched the keypad in rapid succession before giving it back.

She reached out her hand for his to do the same. When he complied, she entered her number, handing it back with a grin. "I'll say one thing for this town, you do an interesting lunch."

At that moment the first patrol car screeched to a stop driven by sheriff's deputy Dan Garver. Brent took a step toward the cruiser and said, "Go on back inside, River. Stay there."

"Stay safe, Brent." She watched as he climbed into the passenger seat and took off down Ocean Street—and toward the shooter. A panicked feeling took over until she glanced down at her phone. It dinged with a text message. And it wasn't from Julian. It read:

When you get mad I love the fire in your eyes.

"Dispatch lit up like Christmas with several different calls, not only yours, reporting gunfire," Garver relayed with an excitement only adrenalin produced. "The radio's been on overload. You sure you're up to this?"

"Just drive the car, Garver," Brent snapped. "Our first order of business is to evacuate those people below on the beach." He picked up the mic to radio central, gave instructions to get it done. With the directive out of the way, Brent turned to Garver. "What about injuries?"

"None so far. Just those scared people trapped on the beach near that dig site. Then there are the workers up at the keeper's cottage on the hill. Shooter opened up on them, too. Luckily he missed."

Even sitting in the cruiser, both men heard more popping sounds coming from the direction of the cliffs.

"You ever shot anyone, Garver?" Brent asked, eyeing the twenty-five-year-old cop. When the man swallowed hard, Brent had his answer. "Will you be able to do it? I need to know now if the situation calls for it."

Garver nodded. "Sure, I can do it if I have to."

"Good to know," Brent muttered as the cruiser continued along the road up to the bluff.

"I've only shot at paper targets before though," Garver added, feeling the need to confess his inexperience.

"That's fine. Were you any good?"

"Good enough to get a badge. I'm a decent shot."

By this time they were passing through the main entrance to the lighthouse where chaos reigned.

The Smuggler's Bay Lighthouse and its keeper's cottage were on the left hand side of the car. To their right, some fifty yards away, a thick forest of cypress, scrub oak, and California pine dotted the coast line to the north. Brent noted the trees made for an excellent place to hide if you wanted to avoid detection for any length of time, a shooter's paradise. Locating the precise location of the gunman would be best done by air.

Logan Donnelly, the owner and sculptor renovating the place, met them at the entrance. He ducked behind the car to lean one arm on the driver's side door. In the other hand, he gripped a Ruger bolt-action rifle. Logan peered into the vehicle and used the barrel of the weapon to point to the thicket of trees. "The shots came from the woods. You don't want to charge in there though, Brent. Troy and I tried that. We had to back off when whatever nut is in there turned his cannon on us. We were pinned down for a few minutes until I made it to Paul Bonner's truck to get his deer rifle."

Brent stared at the artist with the waist-length hair. "With a baby on the way, I'd rather you got yourself and your crew, all of them, out of here and evacuate. I don't want them in the line of fire any longer than they have to be. By any chance did you get a look at this guy?"

Logan shook his head but added, "This may sound crazy but I think it might be Sam Turley. I had to let him go two days ago because he showed up drunk at seven in the morning. He was pretty pissed about losing his job. That isn't all. Ever since his brother Sal got locked up, he's been spiraling down into deeper depression, getting more angry and hostile by the day. Before his drinking binge, he'd show up and spend eight hours in rant-mode. When I fired him it might've pushed him over the edge."

About that time a bullet pinged off the hood of the car. "Damn it!" Brent shouted. "Logan, get in the backseat. Get us out of the line of fire, Garver. Back that way." He pointed behind them.

The minute Logan climbed in, the deputy put the car in reverse and skidded all the way back to the main gate.

"If it is Turley and he wanted to hit you, he could and would," Logan pointed out.

"You're right about that," Brent agreed. "Sam's hunted his entire life. He and Sal are both sharpshooters. Not only that, Sam knows those woods like the back of his hand."

"Whoever's out there shot out every damn window in the keeper's cottage. He tried to take out the new beacon we installed last week. He did all that without putting a bullet in anyone. That's why my guess is, it's Sam Turley trying to make a point."

"So his frame of mind's been even worse than it usually is? Great," Brent mumbled. "In your opinion could we open up a dialogue with him, get Sam talking before he kills someone?" Brent suggested.

"I don't know. He's a stubborn cuss. Maybe talk to him about his little girl. Sam just recently discovered he has a daughter over in San Sebastian. That also contributed to his anger. Talking about the little girl might get his attention enough to surrender."

Just as vans with the SWAT team inside began to pull up alongside the cruiser, another shot rang out. This time it hit the dirt six inches away from the front tire. "If he keeps shooting at us like this he's gonna end up dead," Brent said as he opened the passenger door to make a dash to set up the command post.

He wasn't fast but he made it there in one piece. Reaching the head of the tactical unit, Brent dropped down behind the truck and told the sergeant in charge, "From what I've been able to determine the shooter's location is at approximately eleven o'clock. That's where I want you to put the Nightsun. Light that place up. He's had this site pinned down now for nearly thirty minutes with no signs of letting up."

At that moment, Brent caught the unmistakable wap wap wap sound of four incoming Puma choppers. Two remained offshore while two circled the woods overhead.

From his position, Brent kept up a line of communication with the team in the lead chopper. But when he found out the marksman couldn't get a bead on the sniper, he turned to Garver who had eventually sprinted over to the command post. "Give me the bullhorn," Brent groused. And with that, he began his first attempt at getting the shooter to talk to him.

Six hours later and a little after nine that night, a tired and hungry Sam Turley finally walked out of the woods sans weapon to give himself up.

Dropping to the ground, Sam began spouting a list of reasons why he'd gone on his shooting spree. "Brent, I didn't hurt nobody. I just wanted to show that damned hippie freak Logan a lesson after he fired me."

"Yeah, you taught him a lesson all right. Never hire a drunken idiot and expect anything more out of him. And to think at one time I believed you were the lesser of two evils. I thought Sal was mean. But this…"

"But…but…I didn't hurt a single person, Brent. I could have but I didn't."

"No, just scared the crap out of everyone in the process. Look around you, Sam. This stunt of yours set the taxpayers back a pretty penny with your stupidity." Brent turned to Garver. "Read him his rights and get him the hell outta my sight," Brent demanded.

Brent was about to text River to tell her the situation was over, when he looked up and saw her standing outside the entrance among the throng of news vans.

"What are you doing here?"

"You never got to finish your burger. You have to be hungry. According to locals, the only places still open to eat are The Pointe or McCready's."

"Those two choices are about as extreme as you can get it. One's pricey with atmosphere, piano music. The other serves basic bar food and noisy. But then you know about the pub. There's a third choice and I'm starving."

"What did you have in mind?" River asked.

About that time several reporters rushed up to Brent and shoved microphones in his face to get his take on the situation. He instinctively drew River to his side in protective mode. While cameras flashed, as video rolled, and everyone threw questions at him all at once, he stood with his arm wrapped around River's waist.

Fifty miles away down the Pacific Coast Highway behind the orange door of a seedy motel room, the live feed and image flashed on the television screen. While the news anchor rehashed the story, while a reporter gave a play-by-play of the last several hours, the headline ran across the bottom of the screen as breaking news. The shooter had been apprehended, some redneck hick who obviously couldn't hit the broad side of a red barn.

Why couldn't the gunman have been more accurate? Why couldn't he have taken out Brent Cody when he had the chance?

Rage built.

Brent Cody needed to die.

It was a heavy burden. But if success did come, bringing it about would be the challenge.

Looking around the four drab walls there were indicators of a determined mind. Various supplies scattered around the room told a story. Gun powder, batteries, a cell phone, an alarm clock, an egg timer, nails, ball bearings and other ordinary items littered the bed, the dresser, the floor. There was so much stuff, there was barely enough room to make the walk to the bathroom.

The clutter meant victory would surely come at a price, a price that would have to be paid no matter what.

Chapter Eleven

Brent dragged River back to his place for frozen pizza.

As they cleaned up their mess from lunch, which they'd left out on the table, River studied her host. "You look exhausted. Are you sure you're up for this? I sorta invited myself along."

After sliding the frozen pie into the oven, he turned to look at her. "We both know you didn't. Besides we have to eat. I saw the RV and the camper utilizing the lot across the street from the rescue center. Are you and your team settling in okay?"

She sent him a sheepish grin. "They are. Julian and Laura are in the RV. Walker and Sandra share the camper. I'm a little embarrassed to admit it but I'm still staying out at the B & B."

"There are perks to being the boss."

"Sure there are, but that's not why I decided to bunk somewhere else. In case you haven't noticed Julian and Laura are a couple, have been now for quite some time. On the last dig it got...awkward, to say the least, with me in the Winnebago."

"I imagine so."

"Exactly. That's when I started sleeping in the travel trailer most nights. But taking on brand-new interns here, I have to turn that over to them."

"So Walker and Sandra aren't a couple?"

"God no. I'll be lucky if they don't kill each other in their sleep. Anyway, I've decided I'm not pitching a tent on the beach to make things work this time." Her lips bowed. "I'm treating myself to the B & B on my own dime. Well, I get a per diem so I'm paying the difference out of my own pocket."

"Makes sense. Want a beer?"

"I'd love one." She dropped into one of the chairs at the table. "I should probably mention you were the main topic of conversation this afternoon."

"Gossip is a prerequisite in a small town, especially when one of its residents goes off the deep end like Turley. Pelican Pointe ranks pretty high on the buzz-o-meter in the gossip department."

River found that amusing enough to needle him. "I learned quite a lot about you." Noting the wrinkle on his brow at that, she smiled and added, "It was a long afternoon spent waiting for word you nabbed the sniper. Anyway, once my crew made it off the beach we settled in at McCready's. Half the town wandered over before it was done. Flynn served sodas and snacks until four o'clock then started cutting the price of suds on tap. Like everyone else there, I'm afraid my crew and I went a little wild with the brewskis. And during our time together with everything half-price we had to talk about something."

"Or someone," Brent prompted.

"You were voted most popular."

"Lucky me. What did you learn?"

"That you're a good guy, a little aloof at times, but a rock solid citizen otherwise. Of course, this guy with a mane of white hair, chimed in. I think his name was Hawkins. He got everyone talking about your wild side when you were younger. Something about the time you disappeared with Donna Sullivan, the veterinarian's daughter. When no one could find either one of you, Donna's father, Bran, along with your grandmother, had to send out a search party. There were two schools of thought. Either the two of you were abducted or you eloped."

Brent rolled his eyes. "Christ. We were fourteen. I remember that day though. We'd gone off looking for sea shells, went a little farther down the beach than we'd planned. We lost track of time is all. When Donna and I finally made our way back home—the way everyone acted—you'd have thought we had stripped naked and had sex right there in the church parking lot."

"You stick to that story, Romeo," River cracked as she took a sip of her beer. "Flynn said for two weeks afterward he expected Bran to get out his shotgun."

Brent rolled his eyes. "Donna and I shared a first kiss. That's it. And what is this aloof thing? I'm as down-to-earth as home canning."

A laugh snuck out of her throat. "That sounds like something my grandmother would've said."

"Mine always used that expression when she referred to people she considered were the salt of the earth. I take it your grandmother's gone."

"She is, died about six years back. I miss her quick wit."

"I have a feeling you inherited that." Brent leaned back on the counter, studied River's face. At the mention of family, it seemed as though she'd closed off right in front of him. His cop instincts kicked in, he prodded. "What about the rest of your folks?"

He saw her wince at the question then remembered how she'd acted on the dunes the first day he'd met her. She hadn't wanted to talk about anything personal then either, particularly, Santa Fe.

"What about them?" she shot back.

"Since you travel so much, don't you miss them?"

How in the world could she begin to answer such a simple question? Was Scott right? Was this someone she could confide in? He did have such trusting eyes. Instead of giving in to divulging secrets though, she countered, "You seem close to your family."

"Family can be a pain. But yeah, I'd say we're close. Sometimes too close."

"Your mother tries to set you up because she loves you. She wants to see you happy. It's kinda sweet."

"Then Lindeen Cody must be rolling in sugar."

The timer dinged about that time signaling the pizza was ready. No one was more relieved than River. She stood up to help. "You slice and dice. I'll get the plates if you'll point me to the right cabinet."

"Second from the right."

"Got it."

They twisted open two more beers, piled plates high with slices of the pie before taking their bounty into the living room.

As they dug in, she asked, "Did you ever have to shoot anyone, Sheriff? I know today ended peacefully but...it doesn't always end like that, does it?"

"You don't really want me to answer that, do you?"

"I guess not. That's an answer in itself. Flynn mentioned you were in Iraq. Three tours. That's quite a lot experiencing confrontation firsthand." She noticed him bristle and close off his emotions. When he remained silent, she added, "Sorry. Didn't mean to bring up bad memories."

"I might point out you aren't exactly an open book either. You and my dad made peace yet?"

"Headed there. I don't trust easy so I understand the way he feels and that I have to show him I won't screw the tribe over with the relics we find. Your father wants to make sure the Southwest Tribal Foundation is solid in that regard. I'm here to show him we are."

"Why do you have trust issues?"

She'd opened her big mouth on that one. "The truth? I was married to the lowest of the low. It ended badly."

"Is that all? Who doesn't have an ex like that?"

"Not you, too? I'm sorry. I guess there are way too many assholes in the world, both male and female."

"I'm not. Sorry, that is. I'm well rid of her." Brent wasn't sure why but he felt he needed to pry further. "What was his name?"

"Wes Patton. Turns out the lying bastard couldn't keep his pants zipped up around a female, any female for longer than five minutes. He wasn't picky about them being legal or twenty years older either. If they could somehow further his ego, he was all over them."

"You're lucky to get out of that kind of marriage. I hope he served time."

"Ah. Well. He got locked up all right. Trouble is it wasn't long enough. That's how I ended up with—" Her voice trailed off realizing she'd almost tipped the scale.

Brent understood she didn't intend to elaborate so he decided to commiserate instead. "I hear ya. I was married to a lying piranha. I knew even before I left to head overseas she was unfaithful."

"Wes was a serial cheater. I'm not sure how he found the time for all his girlfriends but somehow he did."

"You aren't still hung up on him, are you?"

"Hell no. He was a sleazebag of the worst variety," River said, guzzling her beer. She eyed Brent. "You still pining for the faithless two-timer who got away?"

"God no. I came home from deployment, found Cindy, that was her name, seven-months pregnant. I knew the baby damned sure didn't belong to me. I hadn't been back in California for almost a year."

"Ouch." Maybe Scott was right. Maybe this man would understand her situation and be able to do something about it. For a few seconds she hesitated, but then, Scott's words came back to her. *Confide in Brent Cody. He can help.* What good did it do to believe in spiritwalkers if she didn't intend to listen to one? She decided to do a little end around first though. "The final straw for me was when I walked in on Wes in bed with one of his students. Did I mention Wes had been my post-grad anthropology professor at one time? That's how we met."

She shook her head at the memory. "I can't believe I was ever so gullible. Anyway, what I didn't know at the time was that Wes had a habit of going through his female students faster than a shark swims through water. It's a fact Wes had plenty of pickings he could sink his teeth into right there in the classroom." She decided the alcohol she'd consumed was loosening her tongue.

"The administration usually frowns on that sort of thing."

"I don't think they knew about it until…the thing is the eighteen-year-old student he was shagging at the time I caught him in the act, had a younger sister. Fifteen. Turns out, Wes had talked her into bed, too. For almost a year, every time I went out of town on a dig, the son of a bitch used our home as some sort of groupie hangout. By the time I finally figured out Wes was out to score with any skirt he could lift up, I'd wasted two years with the bastard. I have no idea why he even bothered getting married in the first place." She took another sip of beer.

Brent wasn't sure why, but she made him want to talk, to tell her what he'd shared with no one else. "*He* was there that day, the day I got home and walked into the apartment. The other guy was right there. I'd left my gear in the car so I could carry in all these ridiculous flowers I'd stopped to buy. As I came through the front door with my arms full of roses, I heard two people going at it hot and heavy in the bedroom. I went to check it out. I got as far as the bedroom door. There the two of them were bouncing around on the mattress. And then Cindy spotted me, froze like a deer caught in the headlights. She crawled out of bed and that's when I saw the belly. I dropped the bouquet and couldn't get out of there fast enough. Talk about feeling like an idiot."

River tapped her beer bottle to his in the way of camaraderie. "Then here's to two idiots who finally saw the light of day and got rid of the cheating assholes disguising themselves as loyal spouses."

Brent followed suit, clinking his bottle to hers. "I've never admitted this to anyone before but Cindy never knew the definition of loyal. I caught her cheating before I left for Iraq. I should've filed for divorce then and there. But she begged me for a second chance and I wanted to save my marriage."

"Why do you suppose we do that? Why do we think people will change if given enough chances when they likely will continue down the same path? Wes showed me his selfish side plenty of times and each time I chose to ignore it."

"I can tell you why I did it. First of all, I wanted the same thing my parents had. Second, it's embarrassing to know the person you gave your heart to is basically—"

"Scum," she said, finishing his thought. She sucked in a long breath and hoped Scott knew what he was talking about. Blurting out her revelation, she stated flatly, "I have a son. He'll be three next February. The twentieth of February to be exact."

Brent blinked. "You're a mother? And yet you travel so much of the time? How do you do that? Does he stay with his father? Your mother maybe?"

So many questions. She had to be crazy for opening up the floodgates like this. "No."

She tipped the beer up, finished it off in one big gulp. She pushed away the pizza that had smelled so good earlier, saw him still staring at her. Why did those piercing eyes have to hurt so much? "My mother has Stage-6 Alzheimer's. She's in no condition to babysit."

"Okay. I'm sorry. So she's back in Santa Fe with your son?" He saw the pain flicker in her eyes.

"Not exactly. My mother's back in Santa Fe in a nursing home."

"But you don't have custody of your son?"

The disdain in his voice was noticeable. Irritation bubbled up in her throat like bile. She knew she should have kept her mouth shut. "No," she muttered.

When she started to get to her feet, Brent grabbed her arm. While he somehow knew there was a lot more to the story, he braced himself for the rest of it. For a mother to lose custody, it had to be bad. "You might as well tell me now."

River blew out a huge sigh and stayed where she was. "You think I don't see how you just judged me without even knowing the circumstances?"

"Then tell me so I won't."

"Screw you. I don't have to tell you anything."

He tried for patience. "How did you lose custody if you were married to cheating scum?"

Her shoulders slumped. "Oh, all right. Once I discovered what a philanderer Wes was and to what extent, I filed for divorce. Within weeks I discovered I was pregnant. The adultery was excellent grounds for the divorce. About the time I had the baby though, a boy I named Luke, Wes didn't give a crap about anything but getting out of the mess he'd made. He wasn't even at the birth. And once I left the hospital he didn't even come by to see his son."

A bad feeling was beginning to inch up his spine as he listened.

"When Luke was a week old, the cops arrested Wes."

"Ah. Let me guess. So now the professor's facing statutory rape charges because of the fifteen-year-old."

"Oh yeah. The age of consent in New Mexico is sixteen, so when the parents found out their fifteen-year-old had slept with a revered professor, they filed a complaint. It didn't take the authorities long after that for them to pick up Wes. Because of his arrest, the judge gave me sole custody. I was thrilled. I had Luke and Wes was locked up. After two miserable years my life was finally starting to look up."

She reached for her bag and took out a wallet, slid a photo out of the leather sleeve. She handed the picture off to Brent.

He studied the baby in the photograph, the big brown eyes, the mop of sleek black hair. For some reason, hearing the details and looking at the snapshot caused relief to swell inside his chest. "So what happened?" But even as he asked he somehow got the gist of what she was about to say.

"Wes spent about four months in jail. But then because his family had a stellar reputation in Santa Fe and came from old money, they fought to get him out. With Wes's standing in the world of academia, I guess that tipped the court in his favor, and the judge let him out on bail. Things might have been okay if the district attorney hadn't approached me to testify against Wes. After I gave my deposition, Wes's family didn't take it too well. Their son was looking at ten years in prison. I had no idea giving that deposition would be such a huge mistake for my baby and for me."

Brent sucked in a breath, his appetite for pepperoni gone. "Facing a long jail term, Wes abducted his son." It wasn't a question.

"He did. One day before his trial began, Wes talked his way into Luke's day care facility while I was at school and…and I haven't seen my son since." A sob caught in her throat, tears ran down her cheeks. "Luke was only six months old at the time. I missed his walking, his first words. I've missed out on everything. I've been searching for him all this time, spending every dollar I could get my hands on to put toward finding him. Eventually though, the police went on to other cases and just…stopped looking. That's when I hired a private investigator. But the entire thing has gone nowhere. I have to face facts. My baby might be gone forever. He'll never know me."

Tears came for real this time like a dam bursting and water spilling over the wall. He reached over, took her hand in his and wasn't surprised when the strong woman he'd come to know, fell into his arms. "My God, River. I am so very sorry. I'll help you find him."

She shook her head. "No one can. I know his parents are helping him financially. With all their money, Wes could be anywhere, Canada, Mexico, maybe even in Europe somewhere. He obviously planned this out in detail before he went on the run."

Brent pushed her hair off her face, cupped her chin. "I'll say it again. I can help find him. What's the name of the detective originally assigned to the case, not the private investigator you're paying, but the one in law enforcement."

"Ortega. Tony. I check in with him regularly at least twice a month. But he never has anything new. It's like he's given up, Brent, or maybe it's a low priority. Either way, if the cops give up, what else is there? It's like I'm supposed to give up along with them. And I can't do that. I can never do that."

"Of course, you can't. No decent human being would expect a mother to ever do that." It was then he noticed the puffy eyes, how tired they looked, how glazed over they were. "River, how many beers did you have at McCready's while you were waiting for me? Did you eat anything during that time?"

"Three. I think. Okay, maybe four. And I'm pretty sure Wade Hawkins might've bought a few rounds of tequila shots somewhere in there, too."

"With all that alcohol what did you eat?"

"Some peanuts and a few chips."

He moved her head from side to side, gazed into her brown eyes. "You can't drive in your condition, River. You're sauced. Not only that, you look exhausted. I don't know why I didn't see it sooner."

"Probably because you've had your own drama to deal with. You think I'm too drunk to drive?"

"I know you are."

Her shoulders slumped. "'K. I might not be able to get behind the wheel but I can do this." Her words slurred but to prove her point, she leaned in, touched her lips to his.

Brent dragged her up against him to ravage her mouth. She tasted like spicy pizza with a hint of Anchor Steam in a blend that had him ready to move to the bedroom.

The burst was instant, all heat and sensation. Tongues danced in that time-worn prelude to mating. Lust hung at the fringes as they sunk into the kiss together.

River felt as if she came to life in his arms. She wanted to devour. Her hands roamed to his hair. Her back arched as he met her taste for taste, bite for bite.

But just as she streaked her nails over his skin, Brent broke off the kiss.

Instead of ripping off each other's clothes, he rested his head on her forehead. "River, for what I have in mind, you've had way too much to drink."

"I do feel kinda sleepy," she admitted, letting her head fall onto his shoulder.

When she grew silent, Brent looked down, fingered a few strands of her hair before tucking the loose ends behind her ear. He tilted her chin up, prepared to take her mouth again before realizing she was sound asleep. The little snort she made had him chuckling. He reached down to take off her shoes. At the movement, her body sunk back into the cushions even further. He readjusted their positions on the sofa, covered her with a throw.

Instead of cleaning up or moving to the bedroom, Brent decided to remain right where he was. He settled back, let his head fall on the headrest. His eyes fluttered closed. The long, tension-filled day caught up with him. In two minutes he was sound asleep, River's bare feet still draped in his lap.

Chapter Twelve

River opened her eyes with a mouth as dry as Santa Fe dust. She tried to swallow and found it difficult. Her legs tingled like heavy logs had fallen across them. She couldn't seem to wiggle her feet and discovered she couldn't feel her toes.

She opened one eye and was blinded by bright sunlight sliding through the slats in the blinds.

Before raising her aching head, she felt a lump on her belly. When she reached down to determine what the source was, she heard, "Ow! That's my eye."

"Sorry." She lifted her head an inch, took in the tuft of black hair curving into her stomach. Her fingers strummed through the mass until Brent's head snapped up.

Their eyes met. "Hi. I guess we both must've sacked out. Good to see you're still alive."

"That's a matter of opinion. I think my tongue is swollen," she said, putting her hand over her mouth. Through her fingers she announced, "I've got the morning breath from hell, too. Stay away. Got any mouthwash?"

"Not on me. Bathroom," Brent uttered still trying to focus.

"What time is it?"

Before he could answer she gave a leg kick and bounced up and down. "Move. I have to pee. Bad."

Brent sat up, freeing her limbs and watched as River made a mad dash for the bathroom.

One glance at his watch had him shouting down the hall after her. "It's almost nine-thirty." He heard an expletive come out of her mouth along with something about how she needed to get to the site.

At that moment the doorbell rang.

"Christ. What now?" Brent grumbled as he used the palm of his hands to rub his eyes awake before finally getting to his feet to answer the door. He was still trying to get the fuzz out of his brain when he peered through the peephole only to see his father standing on the porch.

"Great, just what I need right now." He turned the knob but he wasn't happy about it. In the native tongue of his people, Brent greeted his father. "Haku, kʰoko."

Marcus eyed his oldest offspring with a certain amount of curiosity. "Haku, kwop, you were still sleeping? The day is late for such things."

"Yes, well, it's a late day after a yesterday filled with a ton of stress."

"Which brings me to ask, why didn't you let your second-in-command do the honors and handle Turley? You know that Richardson fellow is gunning for your job. What if the situation had turned out badly?"

"Because I was here and Richardson wasn't. Plus, my knowing Turley's history worked out for the best."

"That and got you a lot of press coverage this morning. Rumor has it Richardson was pissed about that."

"Then Turley's stupidity worked out to be a bonus for me, didn't it? Don't you just love politics? I'm just glad the idiot didn't kill anyone in the process," Brent grumbled before he added, "You drove all this way from Santa Cruz to let me know Richardson was steaming because I got the spotlight last night on the news?"

"That and to see my oldest son, maybe walk him over to the dig. You're getting around better these days. Now that they've started the excavation, it's time I turned this over to you. Your mother doesn't like me making that long drive to Pelican Pointe every day."

"Save it, Dad. I'm not buying it for a minute."

But about that time both men heard the toilet flush down the hall indicating Brent wasn't alone. A few seconds later River emerged from the bathroom. "Good news, I found the mouthwash. You have my favorite. Cinnamon flavored. Yum. I used it to get that bad taste out of my mouth from—" River's stream of words came to an abrupt halt when she reached the living room and spotted Marcus.

Both men stood staring at her until Brent said, "I believe you two know each other. I need coffee." As he ambled past her doing his best not to hobble, he paused long enough to brush his lips to hers in the lightest of kisses. "Sweet taste. Always did like cinnamon," he said as he moved into the kitchen.

She watched him go and said to his back, "I need to get to the site."

From the other room Brent told her, "Then go. As soon as the coffee's ready I'll bring you over a cup across the street. How do you take it?"

"Thanks, that'd be great. Black, no cream or sugar." She turned to deal with the father. "Mr. Cody, were you looking for me?"

"In a manner of speaking, of course I didn't realize you'd spent the night here with my son."

River ignored the obvious scorn in his tone. After all, she was a grown woman who didn't intend to give Marcus Cody the satisfaction of seeing her squirm—about anything—least of all her personal life. They still had yet to find understanding and trust concerning the dig anyway. Because of that River straightened her spine. "As you know, our work was interrupted by the sniper Brent arrested last night. We haven't yet finished the tunneling around the canoe and may not until the end of the week. It's a slow process because I want to try to keep it intact as much as possible. When we extract it, I'll send word to you through Brent."

Without another syllable to anyone, River strolled to the front door, threw it open, knowing full well that with every step Marcus Cody glared at her back.

Brent poured freshly brewed coffee into a thermos for River while his father bored holes in him from the side.

"That didn't take long," Marcus snarled at his son.

Brent knew he wasn't talking about the coffee. "Don't take this the wrong way but I wish you and Mom would butt out of my love life."

"How could we possibly take that the wrong way? Your mother was rooting for Julianne."

"There's not a single spark between Julianne and me. She knows it and doesn't want hard feelings over it between neighbors."

"Maybe it's because you've only been around Julianne at the…"

"We went out once," Brent interrupted. "Didn't tell anyone because we knew there would be this kind of outside pressure. I don't know any other way to say this. I've tried to be nice. But I'm not dating Julianne Dickinson, not now, not ever."

"That's plain enough."

"Good. Now try to convey that to my mother because she'll have to accept it sooner or later. Let her know she can stop asking Julianne over to the house for dinner."

Marcus sighed. "Easy to say, harder to do. This woman won't stay here in the area. You know that, don't you? She's been all over the world. Why would she settle here?"

Brent knew they were no longer talking about the first-grade teacher. Since he'd voiced much the same opinion about River himself to Ethan, he'd be damned if he'd admit it. "*The woman* is smart *and* funny, a helluva combination these days. And she has a name. It's River."

"Does Pelican Pointe look like a place where *River* would settle down for good though? The foundation website keeps track of all the digs she's been involved in. It reads like a travelogue."

Brent already knew that because he'd been curious enough to Google her, too. "Which is one reason we haven't set a date for the wedding yet."

"Smartass. I've sensed a very troubled past within that woman. From the time your mother and I drove down to Santa Barbara with her—"

Brent waved him off. As much as he loved his father, his temper flared just thinking about what River had told him last night about what her ex had done, how he'd cheated her out of precious years with her son. "If I'm not mistaken I come by smartass naturally. And before you say anything else, I'd like to caution you that my business, my love life is just that…mine. If River and I decide to…do whatever, it's not a damn bit of anyone else's business."

"You never did respect my ability."

"That's one leap to another. You know damned well that isn't true. I've brought you in to consult on many cases, off the record. And you know why that is. If it ever got out that the sheriff used your talents on a regular basis, I'd've been drummed out of the department long before now. You've been amazingly accurate over the years. But need I remind you that there were times when you've also been well off the mark."

"Are you saying I'm wrong about this woman?"

Brent flinched at the use of *this woman* one time too many. "I'm saying you don't have all the facts. Not having all the facts, you invariably draw the wrong conclusions. You could cut her some slack, you know. Sometimes I don't understand that certain talent you have and where exactly is goes when you fail to pick up on things."

"When it concerns my sons, I'm too close, although I was right about Hayden. What are you saying?"

"I'm trying not to. Ever heard of keeping a confidence?"

Marcus let out a loud harrumph. "Who would I tell?"

"Dad, you just admitted you were too close to pick up on a decent vibe. Let it go."

"Okay, okay. I'm not sure I'll mention the fact she spent the night here to your mother."

"Suit yourself." Brent took out the carton of eggs, cracked four into a bowl, started whipping them up before turning on the burner to the stove. He got out the tub of butter, scooped up some to drop into the pan.

"What are you doing?" Marcus asked. "I've already eaten."

"That's good because I'm making River scrambled eggs and toast to go with her coffee. Then I'm taking it across the street. She deserves a hot breakfast and I plan to see she gets it."

"So, what happened after you disappeared to go find the hunky sheriff?" Laura pondered as soon as River reached the site. "We closed the place down last night and you didn't come back."

"His father showed up."

"Last night?"

"No, silly. This morning."

Laura made a face. "Ugh. But the sheriff's gotta be forty, right? He's a grown man. What did you do?"

"Doesn't matter how old he is. A dad is a dad no matter what."

"Wait. This morning? You spent the night? River, you just met the guy. That has to be some kind of record for you."

"Just hear me out. To make matters worse his father mistrusts all outsiders. And what I did was get out of there as fast as I could."

"And you're an outsider?"

River nodded. "We all are. But I'm the one interested in his son."

"So you admit it? Wait. You spent the night? Wow. That isn't like you either. It usually takes you weeks to even warm up to a guy."

"No point denying I'm attracted." When she saw Laura's eyes go wide, she added, "Nothing happened between us other than a really hot kiss."

"So if the father hadn't interrupted, something might have happened between you two this morning? Ah, I get it. I can see by that look in your eyes you're already expecting a repeat performance."

"Probably. I also did something really, really stupid."

"A kiss isn't stupid. It's a nice buildup to foreplay and a precursor to see if the guy in question knows his stuff. And from what you say, the sheriff does."

"Oh yeah. Not complaining here. But I told him about Luke."

Laura's mouth gaped open. "You did what? Oh, River. That's so unlike you. What made you do that?"

"I don't know. I've been kicking myself since I got out of that house because of it. The only thing I can think of is that while we sat at the bar waiting for word, I had four beers and several shots of tequila over a span of hours before I ever walked up to the cliffs. I guess the combination of all the alcohol and seeing him handle the crisis situation somehow loosened up my tongue. At least that's my story and I'm sticking to it." With that, River decided to change the subject to something a little more fascinating. She told Laura about the local legend known as Scott and the fact that Pelican Pointe had a resident ghost.

Just as Laura began to pepper her with questions, River looked up to see Brent making his way along the strand. Walking with a slight limp, he carried a thermal cup in one hand and a paper sack in the other. River wasn't sure which was more appealing, the man or the prospect of coffee and whatever food he'd brought.

She trudged down the incline to meet him on the pathway. Inside her chest her stupid heart set up its own little dance. Remembering the kiss they'd shared she went hot from head to toe all over again.

"You look like you could use caffeine," Brent said as he handed off the stainless steel mug.

"You're a saint. My head's pounding from the alcohol last night and the lack of coffee this morning."

He held out the bag. "Think you could keep down scrambled eggs?"

She grinned. "I'll give it my best shot."

From up the hill and behind her there was shouting. "River! River! You have to see this," Julian yelled. "Get back up here."

"Sounds like they've found something," Brent concluded.

"I guess they have. Julian doesn't usually get jazzed unless it's big. I'll go see what it is. Be right back."

But once she got to the hole and peered down to where Julian was practically dancing a jig in the confined space, she knew whatever it was would be huge. She used the ladder to climb down, stood toe to toe with her anthropologist.

The way Julian had brushed the dirt aside it didn't take long for River to make out the framework of skeletal remains. She scanned the grid, realized the bones stretched the length of L-7 to M-10.

"By the size, I'd say it's obviously an adult," River determined. Squatting on her haunches, she examined the outline more closely, running fingers over the bones. As soon as she made contact, the vision hit her almost at once. She saw a bronzed hunter, peering out from behind a thicket of Ponderosa pine, waiting patiently to send his arrow into a passing deer. Dressed in nothing but what amounted to a loincloth around his waist, his damp skin glistened in the sunlight. His body was painted. He wore beads around his neck. In the background waves rushed to shore as the water sparkled on a hot summer day. River watched as the man brought back his bow and let the arrow fly through the still air. The warrior hit his target, bringing the doe to its knees.

From above, Brent watched her go off into some kind of trance. He didn't think it was from focus on her work or due to solid concentration. But then her head had popped up and she had been back to herself. It had lasted no longer than forty-five seconds or so.

As she stood up, she said, "Okay, people, we take soil samples around the frame. Then we back off until I can get the rep out here." When she glanced up though, Brent was staring down at her.

"Are you sure what you've found are human?" Brent wanted to know. "It could be nothing more than a few animal bones."

"I'm one-hundred percent certain. If you'll come down here a minute, I'll show you the outline of a jawbone sticking out of the mud. And with it, you can see the teeth are almost worn down to the gum line. Considering this often happened in tribes by a very early age, I'd say this is probably a male no older than twenty-five."

"Since you're the expert, I'll have to take your word for it. As of this morning I've been given rep status by the man himself and the tribal council."

"Really? Okay. Then we'll need your expertise and approval before we begin the process to disinter."

Brent nodded. "The tribe will no doubt want a ceremony before that happens. So you should probably expose as much as you can of the area around the bones to determine exactly what you've got. If there are more remains, the tribe will perform only one ritual even though it will likely shut you down for more than a day, maybe two. One ritual, one shutdown."

River nodded. "Good thinking. My crew and I gladly accept those terms. It will probably take us another four days, maybe longer, to excavate completely around this particular skeleton and at the depth it's embedded."

"In the meantime, I'll get on the horn and let them know what you found. You should know though, there are a lot of people who won't be happy about this."

"I know. It won't be the first time we've encountered resistance."

Just as Brent expected, by two that afternoon word had spread around town. A crowd gathered along the pier and boardwalk to talk about what the find meant for the town. That included a few members of the tribal community who grumbled and protested, waving their signs in the air. They made it known they preferred their ancestors be left in the ground where they belonged, undisturbed. Then there was the curious along with those trying to figure out how to make a buck in the process.

Either way, Brent had been directed to hire a few local men to keep the onlookers at bay.

Knowing employment was hard to come by in the area, he'd hired Harold Boedecker and Zach Dennison as the security detail for guard duty. The three of them would split time at the site in shifts. At fifty-two, Harold was the oldest. That's why Brent assigned him daylight hours and the easiest shift. Since Zach was the youngest at twenty-six, he drew graveyard. That left Brent's shift sandwiched in between both of them from afternoon to midnight.

Brent wasn't happy about it. But how else did he plan to pass the time stuck on county disability? He supposed that just because he still hobbled wherever he went didn't mean he couldn't sit on his ass for eight hours and keep sightseers away from the cliffs.

From sheriff to second-shift rent-a-cop was a helluva demotion though.

The forced leave of absence hurt his pride. That's why he intended to do what he could to get his job back. And another reason he continued to put in all the time required at his PT with the goal of eventually leaving it behind him entirely.

Hopefully he'd be able to zigzag mentally past the shrink by giving clever answers to a bunch of silly questions. Ultimately though, even he had to admit, the decision to give him his job back was entirely out of his hands.

There were days he was tempted to give in and hang up his badge himself. But then his stubbornness would kick in and he'd find some reason to keep fighting.

As he stood in his kitchen admiring the patch of purple cornflower Hayden had planted the previous spring, his mind wandered to his growing attraction to River.

Since that first day, there was something about her eyes that drew him in. He couldn't help but wonder if his father hadn't arrived that morning what might have happened between them. If River had stuck around, he was certain they'd have ended up between the sheets. He liked considering that possibility.

Even now, thinking about that sleepy-eyed, mussed-up look he'd seen, made him want to get her naked—the sooner, the better.

"River's a looker all right. No doubt about that," Scott said from the other side of the counter.

"What the hell's wrong with you? Just because you're a ghost doesn't mean you have the right to intrude on people's thoughts. Every time you do that you're like a voyeur."

"That's a little over the top, don't you think?"

"Over the top? I was thinking about…"

"River," Scott finished, grinning and wiggling his eyebrows up and down. "Got it. In the way that brings a smile to a man's face. You don't know it but if you'd look in the mirror right now, you're almost glowing."

"Glowing? Now who's over the top? I have to help her find her son. I placed a call to Ortega. He has yet to call me back."

A smile crossed Scott's face. "I was hoping you'd say that. It's a start anyway."

"Is that what this was all about? You could've just asked. I'm a cop."

"Part of it. Not all of it. Don't rely on anything Ortega tells you though. River and the boy need you to do your own investigation."

Brent's heart sank. "All this time and Ortega's been stonewalling her? Why?" But even as he got the words out, realization dawned. "The family's paying him off?"

"They are. Just as River digs to excavate bones, you may have to dig several layers down to uncover answers."

"Count on it."

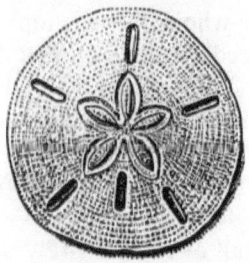

Chapter Thirteen

Saturday nights were meant for unwinding. For the second time that week, River and her crew found themselves rubbing elbows with the locals inside McCready's.

With two visits under her belt, River had already discovered the ins and outs of the dive. Rain or shine, Flynn McCready manned the bar seven days a week from the opening salvo at four in the afternoon until closing time at one a.m.

Regulars knew that two days a year McCready's closed for a solid twenty-four— Christmas and Easter Sunday. Customers expected to find bowls sitting out on the old mahogany bar brimming to the top with traditional pretzels or peanuts in the shell.

Waitresses Noreen Halpin and Bree Dennison split time working the sparse nine-hundred- square-foot seating area. In addition to that, they covered the area where the two pool tables stood. Even though the bar didn't serve actual meals, both women saw to it their customers got good service. Noreen and Bree stayed busy taking orders for simple appetizers like chips and salsa, nachos drenched in cheese and jalapenos—or for the truly adventurous—mini pizzas fresh out of the microwave in the back room that passed for a kitchen.

River scanned the standing-room-only crowd. She watched as Walker and Sandra went another round with a young married couple, Paul and Abby Bonner, in a game of darts while Julian and Laura rocked together on the smidgen of a dance floor.

Once Ricky Oden, the founder and lead singer of Blue Skies, had taken the stage, River had never seen a place come alive so fast. The man's silky, smooth voice had the throng on its feet swaying and stomping with *Roll In My Sweet Baby's Arms*.

Watching the couples on the dance floor, River thought of Brent Cody. It was hard not to. Since falling asleep on his sofa, when she wasn't bugging the private detective, she'd done nothing but think of the guy for the past two days. She knew right at that moment where he was— guarding her dig site.

On a chilly fall night like tonight, she should probably take him something hot to drink. After all it was nearing the witching hour. With any luck, he might want company this time of night. That warm thought was interrupted by her brusque intern.

"The consecration ceremony isn't until Monday," Walker complained. "We're stymied until then. I don't like it when we're in a holding pattern."

"No one cares what you like, Walker," River returned. "Be grateful we're at a standstill and not butting our heads up against the tribal elders."

"River's right," Julian agreed a little winded from the jump and jive on the dance floor. "No big discovery like this goes down without getting the blessing of the shaman when we hit human remains—whatever tribe it is, whatever continent we're on—that's fairly routine, Walker. Better get used to it."

"Lucky for us the tribal rep suggested we uncover as much as we could, otherwise we might not have found the other set of remains this morning. That's the silver lining," River noted.

"Hey, with most of the two skeletons revealed it would be surprising if we don't find more," Laura indicated. Like any good excavator her voice held a certain amount of hope that other bones buried for centuries at that spot could be unearthed.

Noticing River's antsy demeanor though, Laura leaned in to River's ear. "I bet if you asked Flynn nicely, he'd fix you a tall coffee to-go."

"What for? I drink coffee now it'll keep me awake."

Laura tilted her head, met River's eyes. "You know what for. Go take the hunky sheriff some wake-up juice. Or offer to tuck him in for the night."

River rolled her eyes. "I was just thinking the same thing. But really, I need to back off."

"What on earth for?"

"Because I'm pretty sure since learning about Luke, the sheriff's gone out of his way to avoid me."

"Hmm, he didn't strike me as a jerk, but then you never know."

"I never said that."

"Leaping to his defense? An even better sign."

Disheartened but too stubborn to admit it to her friend, River tossed back, "Don't be silly. I'm not in the market to take a bunch of BS from any man, not anymore."

By the time Brent got Zach to cover the last two hours of his shift with a promise that the younger man could come in two hours later on Monday—it was almost ten-thirty.

It wasn't too late to take River up on her invitation. After all this was his turf. Sort of. The ins and outs of McCready's, especially on a Saturday night, were as familiar to him as if he'd gone back in time as a teenager. His grandmother's house had been practically across the street, her gift shop farther down the block. Even then, McCready's had held a certain amount of mystique to a male teen just coming into his own. He remembered it had been a loud place to blow off steam in a town where there were no other places like that to hang out. The fact that it was off-limits to him only made the pub more enticing. Back then, he couldn't wait until he was old enough to go in, buy his first drink. He'd taken care of that before his first tour of duty in Iraq on a visit to Pelican Pointe to see his grandmother.

Now, even with wall-to-wall people and in a dimly lit room, Brent had no trouble zeroing in on River. Her hair hung loose down to her waist. The white lacy-looking summer dress she wore brought out her cinnamon skin. The little violet flowers in the pattern showed she had a definite feminine flair. The thin purple sweater she had layered over it didn't look like it would keep a flea warm. But the outfit was sexy as hell because it showed off her tall, lanky body.

Something inside him moved. It made him want to scoop her up and whisk her out of the room to some dark place where he could nip and nibble. But since she was sitting with her friends, he doubted that would happen anytime soon. That's why he was surprised when she glanced across the throng of people and locked eyes with him. Those chocolate orbs didn't look away as he crossed to her.

Damn it, River thought. He didn't look like a jerk now. Dressed in a light-colored pair of jeans and a button-down white shirt, with his bronze skin, he looked too good to ignore.

"I see you're getting around a lot better," River said, holding out her hand. "You up for that dance, Sheriff? If I promise to be gentle and keep you from falling down, will you dance with me?"

About that time the music changed to *Blue Eyes Cryin' in the Rain*. Brent decided he could handle slow and soulful. He took her hand and led her to the paltry strip of dance floor. They bumped their way along into the crowd until his arms slid around her waist.

She, in turn, laced her arms around his neck. They swayed to the beat with barely enough room to move.

While Ricky worked his magic with the lyrics, they linked together in harmony, body to body, heat to heat.

When Ricky went into his rendition of *Carolina in my Mind*, his lilting voice kept them wrapped up. She felt his hands move over her back, her butt, and arched into him. She caught her own fingers raking through his hair.

Caught up in each other, his mouth found hers. Fire met fire.

An ache, a yearning she hadn't known moved over her, into her, through her. She wanted to meld her body to his.

Even though the song ended and Ricky started his version of the lively *Lay Down Sally*, Brent couldn't, for some reason, let go. But when other bodies began grinding and bumping into theirs, they reluctantly moved off the dance floor and went back to the table.

"Want a beer?" she asked.

Their eyes remained on each other. "Not really. Want to get out of here?"

"I thought you'd never ask."

She followed Brent out the back door of McCready's and onto the little stretch of beach near the dunes. River breathed in the cool fresh air as they walked along under a fat moon and a clear, starlit sky.

"Have you heard from your private detective?"

"No."

"You should know that I've contacted the FBI about Luke."

"Did they tell you to buzz off?"

"Hardly. I hate to be the one to have to tell you this but Ortega's been stonewalling you all this time. I suspect the Patton family's been paying him off."

River stopped, her feet seemed stuck in cement. Some inner instinct had made her distrust Ortega from the start. But hearing it confirmed by someone else, another cop no less, didn't keep the anger from boiling up and spilling out of her mouth. "That son of a bitch! How dare a detective do that to an innocent baby?"

"How dare he do that to the *mother* of the innocent baby?"

"My feelings exactly. Ortega had to know Wes's history with women. How do you explain a cop taking up for a guy who took a fifteen-year-old to his bed? Does Ortega know we're on to him?"

"Ortega doesn't have a clue. But the FBI was curious to know why he never called them in on the case in the first place."

Her jaw dropped open. "At all? What recourse do I have? You know, forget about Ortega for the moment. Does the FBI think they can find Luke?"

"They notified every agency in an official capacity by sending Wes's mug shot out internationally via fax. They also made up an age-progression photo of Luke." He drew a piece of paper from his back pocket. "Thought you'd like to take a look at it."

River swallowed hard, her hands trembling a little as she took the paper to stare at the image. Luke's face had gotten leaner, no longer baby fat rounding out his puffy little cheeks. It broke her heart.

Brent watched at tears welled up in her eyes. Before she started crying, he added, "Using credit card and bank alerts, they'll let me know if they get a hit on any accounts belonging to his parents. Any large amounts of money that go out will be a red flag."

River's heart sank. "So it's basically the status quo, the same old same old I've been hearing for years. Blah, blah, blah."

"You aren't listening, River. After all this time, the FBI is ramping up their efforts by getting the word out using all the tools they have available to them. That wasn't done before."

"You know, Brent, I was told at the time the police were doing everything they could to find Wes and Luke. Obviously that was not the case."

"Ortega was holding back. Now I'm running a check on Gil Conroy to make sure he's legit."

"If Gil's being paid off, too, I've been screwed over by the system as well as everyone I reached out to in Santa Fe."

"Who recommended this private detective to you? I hope it wasn't anyone connected to the university or the Patton family."

"It was actually Julian."

"Ah. Do you trust Julian?"

"I do. These past few days, I thought you were avoiding me."

"Why would I do that? Avoiding a beautiful woman isn't my style unless she's a whack job or high maintenance. I do my best to steer clear of those."

"I bet. How do you know I don't fit into either of those two categories?"

His lips curved. He took her chin, tilted it up. "Just my gut feeling. Here's what I know. You have a fiery temper when it's something you feel passionate about, you've been unbelievably wronged by an ex. You won't give up looking for your son, and you have the most incredible eyes I've ever seen."

"You like my eyes?"

He grinned. "I love your eyes. Your smile isn't bad either." To prove it, his hand went to the back of her neck. He yanked her into him, angled his head and crushed his mouth to hers. His hands moved down to her ass and he lifted her up off the sand.

Her cheeks went hot. She felt like a raging fever suddenly spiked. Her breath backed up in her lungs.

But just as things were hitting a rhythm, the kiss ended and he set her feet back down on the ground. "I want you, River. Even though I know you aren't nearly ready to take it to that level yet."

"Since we almost made out on the dance floor back there, I hope you know I'm not playing head games here."

"That's what makes it so difficult. But I get it. And it's probably a good idea for both of us."

Hearing that, she pulled him to her. Her hands circled the back of his neck. "And that, Mr. Cody, is what makes me want you even more. Seeing as how I caught a ride with Laura tonight, why don't you take me back to the B & B before I jump you right here on the beach?"

Filled with lustful thoughts, he grinned as he threw an arm around her shoulder. "Great idea, let's get out of this chilly wind and go make out in my truck."

Once they reached Promise Cove, he parked his pickup at the edge of the driveway near the road for fear of waking the kids sleeping inside.

They sat in the dark in the Silverado and stared at each other. Both unsnapped the button to unfasten their seat belts at the same time.

"What do you have on your agenda for tomorrow?" Brent asked.

"I scheduled a meeting with the team for around ten o'clock."

"On Sunday? What a taskmaster."

"Not really. Julian and Laura know the work keeps my mind off things. The meeting isn't mandatory. But what else does my crew have going on in a town this size? They've settled in for the long haul. How else are they going to spend their time? What can I say, we love to dig. Why do you ask?"

"How about ditching your own meeting? There's a place I'd like to take you."

Her eyes sparkled with amusement. "I just bet there is. I'm pretty sure you could get me there, too, without too much effort."

He grinned back. "I like the sound of that. But there's a physical place I'd like to show you. It isn't far from town. We could have a picnic. I'll supply the food."

"You've definitely piqued my interest. Where is this place?"

"North of here, up the Coast Highway a bit. You'll love it."

"Hmm, I can't wait."

"That's good because I've been waiting all night to do this." He dragged her over his lap and lowered his lips to touch hers.

Almost straddling him, she curled into his chest, matching his moves, searing heat to scorching burn. They set an urgent pace. Tongues thrilled, tasted and teased.

"I could sneak you into my room," River said in a breathless sigh as soon as they came up for air.

"I haven't done that since…never mind."

"Since your wayward misspent youth with Donna Sullivan?"

"You make me feel young again, River."

She laughed. "Brent, you talk as though you were as ancient as Methuselah. Forty is the new twenty-five. Don't you know that? There's only a seven year difference in our ages. If you're old then so am I."

"Funny, but right this second I don't feel so old."

"Did anyone ever tell you that you're cute when you're being silly?"

"Here, let me show you cute." And with that, he took her mouth again. His wandering hands began to work on the buttons of her sweater. Soon River was arching her back while his fingers worked their magic on her breasts.

A little after two a.m., River crept back into the inn like a fifteen-year-old who had missed curfew.

She couldn't say why but she found the need to tiptoe into the house using the back door that went into the laundry room. On her way to the back staircase, a lone figure appeared just inside the kitchen. Startled, River jumped.

"It's just me," Jordan said, jumping a little herself.

"What are you doing up this time of night?" River asked.

"Scott woke up with a cough and sniffles. I think he's coming down with a cold."

"Fever?"

"Just a tad." Jordan eyed her guest who looked as though she'd gotten caught slipping in through the window instead of the door. Her long hair was mussed. The buttons on her sweater weren't hooked in the proper holes.

"Your cheeks look hot. Do I need to feel your forehead or was that Brent Cody's truck I heard pulling out of the driveway?"

"Uh, we were just...talking." The minute she met Jordan's eyes, she knew the innkeeper wasn't buying it. "Okay, we made out a little. Okay, a lot. He wants to take me on a picnic tomorrow."

Jordan snickered. "That's why your clothes are buttoned wrong and your cheeks are rosy red."

"It's a chilly night."

Jordan grinned. "Sure it is. You need food for a picnic I'll put a basket together for you."

River's jaw dropped. "That is so sweet. But you don't have to do that. Brent said he'd take care of the food."

"Hmm, I can't see Brent Cody in the kitchen unless he's making a sandwich."

"He fixed me scrambled eggs the other day."

"Really? Now see, I've always gotten the sense Brent was a diehard bachelor who relied on takeout, especially with his job and the hours he keeps."

"I'm right there with you. I would never have considered him much of a cook but he surprised me. The eggs were delish." River studied the innkeeper and added, "You look like you have something you want to say."

"Brent's a good guy. He's the best sheriff the county's ever had. He came here personally in the middle of the night to arrest Kent Springer after Kent tried to set fire to the house."

For the second time, River's mouth dropped open. "Your house? But Pelican Pointe seems so quaint and perfect."

"Like any place, I guess we have our share of rotten apples."

"Like the serial killer Brent arrested. He mentioned it."

"A definite low for the town. Before we finally figured out who was responsible for killing Gina Purvis, we were all starting to look at each other and wonder. And poor Troy Dayton had to sit in jail an innocent man before the DA would let him out."

"You don't think whoever is trying to hurt Brent lives in Pelican Pointe do you?"

Jordan shook her head. "Brent hasn't spent all that much time here, other than to visit his grandmother and his brother. I'd say whoever is after Brent is someone from his past, maybe someone from his own department."

"That's horrible."

"Are you nervous about spending time around him because of it?"

"Nope, I figure he's the top cop. I ought to have a little faith in his talents."

"You're smitten."

"I am not. Well, okay. Maybe a little."

"It's tough sometimes to admit it. That was the way it was with Nick and me."

"Really? Because of Scott?"

"That and the fact we were both in a bad place at the time. Neither one of us wanted to give in and just let things be as a couple. Loss is difficult enough to deal with but when you complicate matters by being attracted to each other at what feels like the wrong time…"

River thought of her baby. Would she even recognize him? What kind of mother thought that way? "I know loss," she blurted out.

Jordan eyed her guest with new insight. "I thought as much. Look, it's late. Go to bed. We'll sort this all out when you're less distracted."

"Okay. Sure. It's just that Brent Cody is a major distraction I hadn't counted on."

"I know just how you feel. It seems to always hit you hardest when you never see it coming."

The whispered voices grew louder and louder. They were keeping the path clear, directing the effort where it should be—how best to end Brent Cody. Sometimes though, the headaches made it hard to think—to see exactly how it would all work out in the end. But then the pain had been here before. For such a long time it was part of the equation and dealt with as such.

Sleep refused to come. The mind wouldn't shut down long enough. The voices kept echoing against the four walls of the motel room. Shadows inched along the doorway to the window all the way to the bathroom, until they stilled in the illusion and the darkness.

And in the blackness, madness prevailed.

Chapter Fourteen

The next morning started off with a dreary, gray marine layer that shrouded the tops of the tall cypress in mist. Even though the clouds wanted to spit and drizzle, River already knew that by noon they'd see the sun.

At nine on the dot she spotted Brent's pickup rumbling up the lane. After throwing her backpack inside, she slid in next to him in the front seat while the Red Hot Chili Peppers blasted their way through the truck's speakers.

"You're prompt."

"One thing about cops they appreciate a schedule. Not that we're on one today." He picked up her hand, kissed a few fingers all the while he made the turn to head north.

After several miles, she noticed that he kept a watchful eye on the rearview mirror.

"You think someone might follow us."

"No harm in caution."

"You don't talk much about someone trying to kill you. Why is that? People are worried about you."

"Why do you say that?"

"Because Jordan cares for you. It seems she doesn't forget how you were there to arrest that dunderhead who tried to set her house on fire."

"Nick's the one who called it in. But I made it a point to slap the cuffs on the bastard myself. Hutton was in that house tucked in her crib. I don't even want to think what might've happened if Nick hadn't caught Springer red-handed."

Another five miles they drove in amiable conversation, him pointing out fields of wild strawberries, wildflowers, and her taking it all in, landscape so different than what she'd grown up with in Santa Fe. The ocean on the horizon to their left provided a misty fog over the gray water. In contrast, the pretty rolling countryside to the right gave her a continuous change of scenery.

There were undercurrents of attraction, a little flirty dialogue, along with a subtle effort to avoid bringing down the mood by talking about sad subjects, like Luke.

She appreciated the fact that the cop in him hadn't bombarded her with ten thousand questions about it. And he could have. It was as if he knew dissecting it wouldn't give her the answers she so desperately needed.

When Brent turned the truck onto a bumpy road that ended in front of an iron gate, she looked around at the pretty canyon in the distance and the closer rolling hills. A dusting of red and gold poppies on a grassy backdrop completed the picture postcard.

While Brent grabbed the backpack that held their sandwiches and drinks and picked up a blanket he'd thought to bring—she reached for her own pack—the one Jordan had stuffed with her homemade trail mix and a bottle of wine and cheese. She shrugged it on over her shoulders.

Gathering up the additional blanket Jordan had supplied, River eyed the weight of the food they intended to lug around. "By the looks of things, if we get lost, we certainly won't starve," River determined as she hefted the load. "There are enough provisions here to feed a family of four for a week."

"No chance of getting lost. I've been making this hike since I was two. It's this way." Brent frowned as they started off side by side through a hilly meadow thick with knee-high grass and a smattering of butterfly weed. "That does look too heavy for you. Give me the gear you're carrying. It's still a bit of a walk from here."

"No, I've got it. But will you be okay to make it that far on your bum leg?"

"I'll make it. Promise me you won't tell a soul about what you're about to see."

"If that's a euphemism, it's a damn good one. Of course, I won't."

"No pictures either."

"Brent, stop worrying. I left my Nikon back at the B & B because you said to. And my camera phone's back in the pickup because there's no service way out here."

When the trail narrowed, he went first through the brush to lead the way. She followed in single file, trudging up another incline and down a ravine.

"Do you want me to girl-scout swear or something that I won't blab about your double-secret undisclosed place?" she asked to his back.

"Nah, your Pueblo word is good enough for me. You know Native traditions as well as I do."

She decided to delve into something she'd been curious about since her conversation with Scott. "Which Native traditions are we talking about specifically? How do you stand on spiritwalkers? And have you seen any recently?"

"Have you been talking to Ethan?"

"Nope. But it's a known fact Pelican Pointe has itself a resident ghost, a spiritwalker, a very strong one, I might add."

Brent stopped walking which caused her to bump into his backpack. "Have you seen him? Scott?"

"Of course. Talked to him, too. Surely you knew he was doing his best to get us together. I think."

That sounded just this side of crazy. But since Scott had indicated as much, it did have merit. "What's it to him anyway?"

"That's what I said. Have you talked to him?"

"Now and then."

"I knew it. Be more exact."

"It means that since coming to Pelican Pointe I've seen the infamous Scott a couple of times myself. Why is it you don't sound like you want to hightail it out of town because you've encountered a ghost?"

"Because I've seen a few before Pelican Pointe."

"Okay. Now would be a good time to elaborate."

She told him about all the other encounters she'd had over the years at other dig sites, from overseas to stateside.

"So this is no big deal to you?"

"Scott's different."

"How so?"

"He knows things. He knew about Luke. How I don't know. He just does. It must come with the afterlife."

Lumbering along behind him they finally came to a trail wide enough for both of them to walk side by side. "Could this trip get any more top secret or what? I feel as though I'm on a covert mission or something." Her sense of direction kicked in. "Wait. Are we headed west again toward the ocean? We are."

He grinned. "You either have good instincts or you smell the water."

Her lips curved up as they came to a little clearing. "A little of both. You don't need a compass?"

"I could find my way here in the dark."

The sun chose that moment to peek through the clouds. They stopped long enough to watch the marine layer lift and break apart over the bluffs to the north. As the slight breeze carried the remaining fog out to sea, she looked around at the countryside.

Rock formations came into view on either side of them. She noticed etchings in some of the stones, engravings and symbols representing earth and sea and knew that wherever he was taking her, it had to be special.

She studied him as they plodded over scenic knolls, through wooded patches of fir and birch, and came to a clearing of sage and rosemary growing wild. To River, the man looked like a warrior on the hunt minus the bow and arrow.

She'd already noted he hadn't gone on the hike without bringing along his trusty .45 in case there was trouble—or they happen to spot a snake. The gun was strapped to his waist. The thought of slithering reptiles had her glancing at the ground and her feet. But she couldn't blame him for toting the cannon. With someone out to get him, he couldn't leave the house without coming prepared.

About that time though, the rugged trail abruptly dead-ended into a slight drop off.

Jutting rocks met up with dunes and fragrant sea grass. Below them the ocean glistened like a collection of sapphires. Hilly mounds of sand created a little valley where two adjoining rocks naturally came together to form an A-frame shape.

She looked closer. Oak and pine guarded the jagged opening with an added overgrowth of tough manzanita to discourage people from getting inside.

"Ohmygod. Is this what I think it is?"

"Sacred ground."

She slid her pack off her shoulders, turned in a circle to really get the lay of the land. The surrounding banks offered an array of berries and wild vines curling up and over the rock. Sand dunes butted up against stone and pillar. But the narrow opening to the cave was the draw.

"That and much more. No photos, you said. That means…" She made her way past the ground-hugging red bark, ducking under low-hanging branches to enter the cave. Waiting for her eyes to adjust to the difference in light, she took in the brightly colored pictographs on the walls and ceiling, distinctly Chumash.

Her breath caught. They were like those she'd seen in Santa Barbara. Some were whimsical like the one where people gathered in obvious celebration of some sort. There were a few different versions of the sun. All told a story.

Those paintings in Santa Barbara had been off limits, no way to venture up close and personal—but these, these glinted back at her—almost magical. The boulders themselves seemed to come alive, layer by layer, despite the rough texture. It was like stepping back in time. She could imagine the artists taking turns coming to this exact spot hundreds of years in the past to create from the rudimentary paints they'd made themselves.

She itched to touch the depictions of turtles, fish, all manner of animals, some with serpentine shapes amid tribesmen on the hunt. Figures had been outlined in bold reds and blues and greens for emphasis. Those that hadn't were simply carved in the stone with no use of color but rather etched with precision enough to make out the dance or a deer or a rabbit.

"What do you call this place?" she wanted to know as the blanket she carried dropped to the floor of the cave where she stood.

"In Chumash it loosely translates to the dunes and cave under the stars." When he saw her brow crease, he added, "Look up. Notice the natural skylight. It's sunny now but at night, it's a great place for stargazing. It probably saw a lot of action at night. If you get my drift."

She grinned, glancing upward at the craggy dome above her head. Sunlight drifted down in streams of gold from several splits in the rock formation in the ceiling. "This place must be amazing at night, like having your own personal observatory. Starlight dunes and a cave. What more could you want?" she emphasized. "Imagine this in its natural state centuries earlier. What a magnificent place for the elements to come together! Can we stay until dark?"

"You read my mind. I was hoping you'd want to."

"Are you kidding? I may never want to leave." She twirled around, took in the walls again. "My God, Brent, your ancestors had such a flair for color and art and innovation. I mean, I've read the books, know they were magnificent boat builders so they could navigate the sea and make the most use of it. I dragged your parents through the Santa Barbara Museum of Natural History until they looked like they wanted to collapse. So I know... But somehow this makes it all more real. Up close, it makes an impact. Why isn't this place included in the history of the area? I found no mention of a cave on any of the charts or maps I researched. How has your family managed to keep it off the radar all this time and not crawling with tourists?"

"It's private land, owned by my grandfather's people for centuries. I've been coming here all my life."

"Wow! I don't even want to risk touching it for fear I'll spoil it in some way. I should've known Marcus Cody was holding back. He drove me all the way down to Santa Barbara, in the opposite direction I might add, to make certain I didn't go near his own personal part of history right here. It worked." She rocked back on her heels and tossed in, "I guess I can't blame him."

"If he knew I brought you here—"

"He'd be furious. Got it. He won't find it out from me but he's bound to—I don't know—pick up on some kind of vibe. I don't want you in trouble with your own father because of this."

"I'm sure he will know, maybe even sense it now, but I'll deal with it when he does because I intend to tell him myself at the right time."

"Brave man. Have you ever brought—?"

"No, it's a sign of trust. You trusted me enough to tell me about Luke. This is my way of returning the favor."

Her hand flew to her breast. "I'm blown away by that." She stepped to him then, ran her hand down his cheek. "You have an incredible heart, not to mention an incredible mouth."

He hauled her up and against his chest. They were eye to eye, dark chocolate to dark chocolate. He bent his head to meet her lips. Tugging, nipping in need and want, they let themselves enjoy the buildup, the edge, right up to fireworks. "I've half a mind to take you right here."

"Oh that can be arranged." She sought out where she'd dropped the blanket.

His eyes tracked hers and twinkled at the implication. He went over to pick it up, spread it out over the hard ground.

All the while his movements let her know what was about to happen. That's why she was surprised when he said, "So you see things in the past just by touching them? That's quite a gift. How long have you known you could do it?"

"Who told you that?"

"I do have my own sense about things. Besides, you mentioned as much. And I saw you at the site when you went somewhere else, like in a trance but not."

She sighed. "The past comes alive for me. It always has. If only I could use it to somehow help me locate Luke."

Knowing Luke was a sensitive subject, he suggested, "Let's try something." He dropped to the blanket, patted the space beside him. "Sit down and tell me what you feel in here, what you see." When he saw the questions form on her face, he added, "It's okay to reach out and touch." To prod her a bit, he tugged her toward him, keeping her hand in his.

Prompted, she sat down next to him, settled into the lotus position.

When she was ready, they reached out together and glided their fingers along the stone wall. Flashes, bits of images, shot through both. They saw a bustling village where its people went about their daily lives of living and getting things done in organized fashion.

Teams of boat builders gathered onshore. At one end of the beach, the men carved out the trunk of a sturdy redwood as they used its length to shape and form what would eventually become a twenty-foot-long tomol.

Farther down the stretch of sand, another group of men worked to smooth out logs using their meager tools of sharkskin, shells or bone. Yet another team busied themselves with planking and sealing the sides of an already carved out canoe with glue they'd made from pine pitch so that it would hold together in the water.

Some distance inland, large thatched dome structures made from willow reeds and cattails were scattered throughout the encampment. Smoke curled up through the tops.

Nursing babies nestled against mothers in their time-old tradition. Women sat in groups cracking and peeling acorns out of their shells then sifting the kernels into flour. They would in turn, leach out the bitter tannin of the nut by dousing the mixture with water. For hours they worked at prepping the grainy texture into mush and then into dough that would set overnight to be cooked in the oven pits they'd built into the hillside.

As some labored over meal preparation, others strung together beads from the olivella shell that would adorn their dresses and capes.

Using stone bowls and pots, they tended to the communal fires set around the campsite while their supper of oyster stew or black abalone, simmered over the hearth.

Once night fell though, the work came to a grinding halt as the villagers came in from their chores and gathered to eat. As the stars began to wink to life, the place took on a festive atmosphere. Shamans began to sing. Children joined in, keeping time to the song with the clam shell rattles their mother's had made them.

Children.

At the sight of little ones, Brent sensed River had seen enough. He squeezed her hand to bring her back to the present and noticed her shivering. "Are you cold? Here put on my jacket."

She shook her head. "No, it's okay. I'm not really, at least not when I'm with you." With that, she burrowed her body into his.

Brent removed his jacket anyway and draped it around her shoulders. In the waning afternoon light, he angled his head to find her mouth. Tender and gentle, he drew the kiss out until finally he said, "I'll go out, gather wood for a fire. It'll make it nice and toasty in here for when—"

The idea had her purring out a sigh. "Oh. A fire would be lovely. And we have all manner of food to hold us for the rest of the day."

As he got to his feet, she offered, "Mind if I help?"

"Nope. Let's go," he said tugging her up and out into the bright light.

Together they hunted down every available branch and twig and stick they could find. She gathered dry leaves to use for kindling. After twenty minutes or so, arms loaded down, they made their way back inside with an air of sexual tension hanging between them brimming on the surface.

Brent kneeled in the center of the room at a shallow, circular pit in the floor. It looked as though it had been used many times before. He took out matches from his pocket, lit the leaves.

At the first snap and pop of fire, impatience nagged at him. River sensed it, too. "Just so you know I'm not that hungry for food."

His toothy grin in response warmed her to the bone. She saw the want in his eyes, as they flickered with the same longing she felt. Because of that, she went to him, took his face between both hands, brought his mouth down to fit hers.

All the while her blood heated and shot straight to the core. A fine white spear of need kindled and caught.

They toed off their shoes where they stood.

He peeled off her top, slid off her jeans. She helped him out of his.

Wrapped in each other, a hot white blaze had him grabbing her ass, hefting her up and off the floor.

Her arms laced around his neck, her legs went around his waist.

They sunk like that to the blanket and shifted to deal with the rough floor underneath. His fingers explored curves and folds. He leaned her back. Hovering over her, his muscles bunching, he skimmed downward with his tongue. Grazing, he placed gentle kisses on her belly, that portion that protruded a little where she'd once carried her son. His lips drifted to her center, found her wet and ready.

Firelight shimmered off the walls. The bold colors turned to shadows as she closed her eyes. Pleasure built and soared. She felt like she'd taken flight. She climbed to that gilded level where giddiness vied for dizzy. It took hold until she fractured into glorious bits of soft golden beams all around her, through her.

But then an urgent demand rose in her. "Now, Brent! Now!" she begged.

He reversed their positions, leaving him to the stony surface beneath. Guiding her over him, he murmured softly to her in the dialect of his ancestors. Using the language of the ancient Chumash, he spoke of endearments he'd never felt before.

They began to sail as one, ever higher, through wild seas, through billowing whitecaps to water as smooth and sultry as silk. When the surf broke and evened out, they floated and drifted on the glossy waves. Afterward, they lay tangled, bundled as one.

Out of breath, he asked, "Are you cold?"

A little winded herself she whooshed out, "I'm as warm as I've ever been. Couldn't you tell?"

"I could. I'm not even certain we needed the fire since we made our own."

"Can you imagine it? Making love in this place, so special, so remote and knowing we aren't the first to do it here."

He cocked a brow. "How do you know that?"

"I can see it, feel the history. Can't you feel the vibe? It's a good one for sex. And because of it, I feel as though we're the only two people in the world right now."

He ran his fingers through her hair. "Right now, we are. Take a look at those stars above us."

It was the first time she realized dusk had fallen. She breathed in the cool evening air and glanced into the glimmering night sky overhead. "Those stars look like we've been sprinkled with glitter of our very own. Look there, see the W shape? That's the constellation, Cassiopeia."

"And see the double star, the brightest in the southern sky over there," Brent pointed out.

"I feel as though I'm back in another time period, maybe getting another chance at not making the same mistakes I have before tonight."

"Shh. Mistakes in life are inevitable no matter what century you find yourself in. Besides, I like it just fine right here where we are."

She kissed his cheek. "Thanks for that."

He bumped his hip to hers. "Hungry?"

"Starving."

"Then let's dig in. Clothing is optional."

They didn't bother with their clothes. Instead they wrapped up in the blankets and then opened the wine she'd lugged from the truck—a more than decent chardonnay. They unpacked roast chicken thanks to the cook, Max Bingham, at the Hilltop Diner and potato wedges, seasoned with rosemary and olive oil.

"I had no idea the Diner prepared food that tasted so delicious," River admitted as she patted her stomach. "Or maybe I just worked up an appetite," she tossed out with a gleam in her eye.

"Not many people know this but Max used to work as a chef back in Texas for a chain restaurant. At some point he lost his job and he and Margie hooked up, drifted to California and somehow ended up in Pelican Pointe. Even though Max can throw a terrific meal together, I'd say it's more like we both worked up an insatiable hunger." He ran a hand down to her bare breast, toyed with a hard nipple before taking it into his mouth.

"Mmm, looks like you're working up another."

With that, she shoved him to his back and straddled his naked torso. At the need she saw swimming in his eyes she started riding hard to prove it.

Chapter Fifteen

Finding human remains always brought out the press. It had been a minor miracle they'd been able to stave off the blitz of reporters until now.

The Southwest Tribal Foundation, or more like River's boss, Emilio Matias, believed it best to deal with the event head on. Because of that, he'd called a press conference for bright and early Monday morning and left it to River to handle the local television reporters.

They advanced on the site out of Santa Cruz, and as far away as San Francisco and Los Angeles. They fired questions at the project leader, intending to put River on the hot seat.

There was always one in the crowd, some persistent journalist like a dog with a bone, who wouldn't let go of an issue, determined to hog the Q & A session. Today, a perky blonde out of Santa Cruz who identified herself as Tamara Davis just wouldn't shut up.

"How do you respond to those people who say you and your crew are nothing more than tomb raiders?"

"I'd remind them that this site was not officially a tomb, none that we knew of anyway. No one had an inkling this type of settlement existed here until a mudslide revealed what was underneath. And learning about the past always helps us with the future."

"What about the rumors that the site will be cursed after the removal of the bodies?"

"That's a popular belief in Native American legends. But I should remind you that the Egyptians and Peruvians felt much the same way. There's even one myth about the Ice Man found in the Alps that says disturbing the dead results in death for all those who participate in the removal."

"Aren't you scared of that?"

River smiled. "Not really."

"What exactly are the kinds of things you've found so far other than the human bones?"

"Along with the canoe, which we have yet to fully extract, we've found various shell beads, bows, arrows, steatite used for carving the jewelry they wore, mostly serpentine pieces, and a good number of stone bowls. The list goes on and is really too numerous to mention in detail. The complete list appears in the media packet you were given."

"Do you plan any trips down to Simi Valley to get a better feel for the painted caves there? Those belonged to the Chumash as well?"

The blonde had done her homework River decided as she pointed out, "You can't go see Burro Flats without obtaining special permission. The land's owned by Boeing. Even though I've put in a request to see the pictographs there, it isn't likely me or any member of my team will be heading down there anytime soon." Because of the way she'd spent her Sunday thanks to Brent, she'd already experienced the ultimate in cave dwellings anyway. So why leave the area? It wasn't like Burro Flats could top "Starlight Dunes."

"In your opinion do you think this site was used for human sacrifices?"

Ah, thought River, the opportunity to set the public straight on that score. She'd wondered when someone would get around to that leap of logic. She shook her head. "No. There is absolutely no indication that the Chumash lived any other way than to value their families and their traditions. They were among the first boat builders. They fought for what was theirs by defending their territory against the invading Shoshone on occasion but they were not known to war with anyone unless provoked."

"How did they live?"

"They thrived off what the land and the water provided. They held dances and ceremonies to honor nature, the summer and winter solstices, told stories around campfires, and fed entire villages with their keen expertise in hunting and fishing."

She looked good on camera, Brent decided as he watched River answer questions with some definite skill at PR and a fiery passion for her work. But then she usually looked damn good doing just about anything wherever she went.

He still remembered last night and how they'd moved together in the light and the dark. Since they'd moved like that several times over, he noted she hadn't minded making love in a cave. In fact, she'd seemed stoked at the setting and right at home in the wild.

About that time the dogged newscaster turned her head, shot Brent a lethal stare. It was then he remembered Tamara. They'd been quite the item—for about six weeks—two years earlier. The breakup hadn't been without resentment on her part.

Brent shifted his feet as River put an end to the news conference. As soon as she was sure the camera stopped rolling, Tamara wasted no time storming over to where he stood on the sand. He braced himself for a confrontation with a very pissed off female still holding a grudge after all this time.

While the sunny blonde read the sheriff the riot act, River stood back and took in the show. It wasn't every day a tall, lanky hunk faced down the wrath of a woman who obviously wanted to get in his face.

Even though she couldn't read lips from this distance, River could make out the gist of the encounter. Someone had unceremoniously dumped someone via text message and they were still miffed about it. As soon as Tamara finished her profanity-laced bluster and headed for her news van, River strolled over to Brent. Calm as glass, she deadpanned, "Women. What're you gonna do, huh?"

"You heard all that?"

"Didn't have to. That was one ticked off female. Lesson one. You should never break up via text or email."

"That isn't true. I read on the Internet texting is the best way to avoid a scene."

"You mean like that one?"

Brent roared with laughter. "You have a point, even if she did wait two years to do it." For some reason, he felt the need to touch her. So he went on instinct, plucked her off the ground and took her mouth right there on the beach. They went at each other until he plopped her back on her feet.

"Seems to me you do that a little too well for someone who takes dating tips seriously from the Internet." River shook her head in sympathy. "I had no idea anyone actually read those blogs. By the way, thanks for handling the council this morning. We'll be able to remove the first skeletal remains by mid-week. I'd say the second will take a couple of days longer because of how far down the bones are embedded."

"I'm glad I could be the go-between. The council has a tendency to dial up their lawyers if they aren't happy depending on the degree of dissatisfaction."

"Don't I know it? Come on," she said, putting her arm through his. "I'll buy you a lousy cup of coffee Julian made and give you the dime tour inside the RV." It had been a good long while since she'd flirted. But after the day they'd spent together yesterday, she drew him closer, leaned in to nibble on his ear and whispered, "And if you're very good, I'll get rid of my crew so we can make out before I have to go back to work."

They hadn't made out but they had laughed and talked over the worst cup of coffee Brent had ever tasted and he'd drank some pretty awful stuff at the sheriff's department.

At noon, Brent wandered over to meet his brother for lunch at the Diner, whistling the entire way. There was a distinctive spring in his step. He couldn't remember when he'd felt so lighthearted about anything. Today he walked in through the door relaxed and upbeat.

He spotted Ethan sitting in the largest booth in the corner with a group of men he recognized as Nick Harris, Logan Donnelly, and Wally Pierce, owner of the gas station. The men huddled with Ethan over coffee. They looked as though they'd already been there a while and were deep in discussion.

Ethan waved him over and Brent slid into the booth next to his brother. "What's up with you guys? You look like you could use something stronger than caffeine."

Logan scratched the back of his neck. The recently married Logan, whose wife Kinsey was expecting their first child in March, was clearly uncomfortable.

Brent glanced around the table until his eyes landed on the sculptor. "Did I interrupt something?"

Logan cleared his throat. "I know that team of archaeologists found a second set of bones at the dig site. Are you certain these are centuries-old bones? Is there the slightest chance they could belong to one of Knudsen's victims and we're just now finding that out?"

Brent shook his head. "River assures me that the carbon dating came back to late fifteenth century, somewhere between 1450 and 1490. It's as close as they can get and pretty damn accurate."

Logan blew out a breath. "That's something, I guess."

"You were worried there were more victims out there? Can't say I blame you any."

"I'll always worry about that. Rumors are rumbling around town that other young girls went missing and we just didn't find them. Yet. People fear Knudsen kept back certain info regarding his kills and that maybe whatever they find at the dig site might have something to do with him."

"I'll do what I can to squash those rumors mainly because River's team has dug down more than five feet now. I doubt Knudsen or his partners in crime would've bothered with that kind of depth. I don't mean to be insensitive but—"

"When your sister dies at the hands of a brutal serial killer, there's not much else to get sensitive about," Logan said. "Just tell me straight."

"Okay. Then consider this. The other victims, including Megan, were found in much more shallow graves, no more than three feet. Keep in mind the bones in question at the dig site never would've come to light at all without Mother Nature's interference. That's how far down they were in the ground. They still haven't excavated the second set of remains. They haven't even extracted the canoe yet. The entire site is definitely pre-Columbian. According to River, the whole thing is a major find. So rest assured any bones found near that area will be scrutinized by experts."

"That's good to know then," Logan concluded. "Although I'm convinced Knudsen may have more victims."

"You're probably right about that," Ethan said in agreement. "Most serial killers never give up all their victims."

"That's what bothers me," Logan confessed.

"Knudsen's trial is a ways off still. In fact, it could take another couple of years for him to get to trial. There's still a chance he'll try to negotiate a plea deal before that. Look Logan, I know what happened here with your sister,

Megan, weighs on you. I'm actually surprised you decided to stay here and settle down, raise a family."

"I like the idea of my child growing up here. And I think Megan would like that as well."

"Just don't plan to send them to school here," Nick complained. "Hutton starts kindergarten next year. There's no school in this town. Jordan and I are committed to bringing the town back from economic disaster, but that's one huge drawback for us we never considered. We're already dreading the fact that Hutton will have to get on a bus to ride all the way over to San Sebastian for class. And we'll have to bring her into town in order to do that. Promise Cove isn't even on their bus route."

"That means she'll have to get up at the crack of dawn. I know because Kyra's in the same boat," Wally groaned in agreement. "She's been going to the preschool at the church. But once next fall gets here, she'll be right there with Hutton. Lilly and I believe that having to spend all that time on a bus is ridiculous for a five-year-old. And before we know it, Joey will be right there beside both of them."

"That's just plain silly," Ethan remarked. "I don't want Nate hopping on a bus to make a forty mile trip out of town every day."

"I don't like the idea of that either," Logan stated. "San Sebastian is too far away for that."

"Then why don't you guys do something about it?" Brent said in challenge.

"Like what?" Nick asked. "Other than build a school here, I don't know what else we could do."

"What about the old elementary at the corner of Landings Bay and Cape May?" Brent suggested.

"That place is falling apart," Wally pointed out. "They closed it down twenty years ago when enrollment dropped to under fifty. That's how long the kids have been riding the bus over to San Sebastian and how long it's been sitting vacant."

Nick raised a brow, intrigued by the idea. He exchanged glances with Logan. "But could it be renovated? What kind of shape is it in?"

"As long as it's structurally sound and doesn't have asbestos issues, or any type of mold problems, any building can be remodeled," Logan stated.

Ethan shook his head. "But that doesn't solve the enrollment issue. What if there aren't enough school-age kids here in town to fill it up? I mean Nate doesn't start school for another four years but if you could swing this, I'm in."

"Okay, then the next questions to get answered would be what exactly would it take to get a school opened in less than a year's time with limited registration?" Nick asked.

"A lot, I'm sure," Brent returned easily. "So the real question would be how motivated are you guys to see it gets done?"

"Not to mention a project like that would take major bucks," Wally noted. "Even though we'd probably need nothing short of Santa Claus to pull it off, I'm in, too."

"Is it possible to raise that kind of money in such a short amount of time?" Logan pondered. "Is it even doable?"

"What do you say after lunch we go take a look at the building, decide from there?" Nick proposed.

Logan drained his coffee cup. "As someone who just happens to be putting the finishing touches on my own personal project—not to mention I'm about to embark on fatherhood for the first time—I hope to one day send my kid to a local school. If it isn't here, then where?"

"So what are you saying?"

"I'm up for another crazy-ass, new project."

"Good," Nick said. "Because this one will take more than Santa Claus, it'll take a damned miracle if we could pull it off."

That sentiment turned out to be true after lunch when the men drove over in caravan style and spent two hours walking around the abandoned building.

Looking at it up close, it was hard to believe the old school had once seen hundreds of students from kindergarten to sixth grade come through its doors on a daily basis.

Now, two decades of disrepair had not been kind to the one-story structure. Most of the letters had fallen off the front of the building. Those that remained spelled out something indecipherable. "eli an Po te Ele t ry Sch" was all that was left.

Windows were busted out. The moist marine air had done its damage by rusting out the foyer around the entryway.

The interior had suffered the same fate as the outside. Vandals had trashed the administrative offices, the classrooms, sprayed graffiti in the restrooms, cafeteria and gym areas.

"And I thought the keeper's cottage was a mess," Logan admitted. "Wally's right. This will take some major bucks."

"But is the building sound? Is it worth it?" Nick wanted to know.

"If we could pull this off, I might change careers and decide to do this for a living," Logan muttered as he tested a load-bearing wall for its sturdiness.

"You mean renovating old places?" Wally asked. "I've seen what you did with the lighthouse. You could earn a nice living at it."

"Yep." Logan scratched his chin. "I haven't created anything new since I got here. And right back atcha because I've seen what you can do to a transmission and an engine," Logan said to Wally.

Nick shook his head. "You think you haven't created anything new, huh? Seems to me, the last time I checked, someone brought a lighthouse back from the dead, remodeled the keeper's cottage, and painted a mural that's practically a tourist attraction in the middle of town. I'd say that counts as creativity beyond the norm."

"He's got you there," Brent added. "Look, I hate to miss out on the rest of the fun, but since I'm the only guy here who isn't married and doesn't even have a stake in this, I've got to get to my rent-a-cop job."

"At least there's no silly uniform involved," Ethan joked as he walked Brent outside to his truck. "I gotta say your change of heart about heading this security detail surprises me. You don't seem to mind the gig all that much. Or could it be because of the perks, or rather one gorgeous perk thrown in, that's changed your mind?"

"River's amazing. I've never met a woman as strong. It's sexy as hell."

Ethan grinned, recognizing a change in his brother. "You any closer to getting back to work, officially?"

"No. It seems the county is going out of its way to throw out all kinds of stumbling blocks my way."

"Like what?"

"For starters, that I'm unfit mentally and physically to resume the office."

"You're kidding? After cleaning up the department like you did? That definitely stinks of political motivation."

"You're telling me."

When Brent turned to head to his pickup, Ethan called out, "Hey, bro."

"Yeah?"

"That nutjob who's after you is obsessed. I can't get a bead on him. He moves around a lot."

Brent nodded. "I appreciate your trying."

"And Brent?"

"What now?"

"Be careful out there."

"You got it."

While Brent spent his afternoon hanging out with the guys, River took the time to stroll down Ocean Street. After twenty minutes she ended up standing in front of Hidden Moon Bay Books. It wasn't, of course, by accident. She'd intended to stop in because for weeks she'd been curious about Ethan Cody. She was dying to find out how deep his psychic ability ran.

But since she couldn't just walk in the door and ask if the mystery writer would help her look for her son, she had to play it like a tourist.

She'd sought out psychics before. Some had been nothing more than cons. But she couldn't see the sheriff's brother posing as a scam artist.

There had been a few that had given her leads. Anything she felt viable, she always passed along to Gil Conroy. She wasn't sure Gil followed up on all of them. But at least it made her feel like she contributed to the search in some way other than standing on the sidelines.

River stepped into the shop with tables filled with fragrant candles, an assortment of fresh herbs, and rows of bookshelves filled to the brim with hardcovers, paperbacks, and audios, a reader's haven.

A portable crib set up at the end of the register area held a sleeping baby. River decided that must be the reason there was no bell above the door.

She glanced around to see a prominent table dedicated to Ethan Cody's two bestsellers. Generous stacks of each one dominated the tabletop.

River reached over to thumb through the pages.

The blonde behind the counter sent her a wide smile of approval at her taste in thrillers. "Come on in. I was hoping you'd finally stop by."

"You were?"

"Sure. I find it fascinating what you do. I once wanted to be a forest ranger so I appreciate anyone who works outside in the weather, enduring the elements like you guys do."

"Heat, sun, bitter cold, yep, that's us. Don't forget the bugs we encounter."

"Eww, I forgot about that. Are you looking for anything in particular? Except, of course, the one you have in your hand. That one is riveting. It's about a ship that vanished off the California Coast set in present day."

"Sold. I'll take it, along with his second book."

Hayden sent her a wide smile. "I like you already."

Chapter Sixteen

Skulking around in the dark wearing night vision goggles was a pain in the ass. But when the marine layer rolled in thick and heavy off the water it was a necessity, especially if the strike proved a success. The timing had to be perfect as did the aim. Having a steady hand on the trigger would surely get the desired results this time.

No one would expect a climb down the side of a cliff in pitch-black darkness. Only a fool would try that or someone who didn't give a shit about their safety. That's what made it a brilliant tactical foray into the camp of the enemy.

Death was the goal. Brent Cody's would be beautiful. It wasn't just the definitive payback. It was the only acceptable form of retribution.

The copse of trees on top of the cliffs made for a good hiding place and an excellent perch in which to keep an eye on the man's movements below. So far, all the sheriff had done on duty was to sit on his ass or stretch his legs. His ego had to have taken a hit at such a menial position.

But then the son of a bitch should be dead anyway so it hardly mattered. At the very least he should be back on the job by now. Why wasn't he? Probably milking the disability angle. Instead of top cop in the county he'd been relegated to what amounted to mall security—couldn't be a more fitting demotion for the asshole unless it was the ultimate—an ugly casket buried six feet in the ground.

A choir of chirping crickets broke the monotony. Scouting Brent Cody from this angle was so much easier than taking him out at ground level near the dunes.

A sitting duck is what he was—a gift of opportunity really. The dig site below made for a difficult climb down. But it wasn't impossible.

Good thing agility ran in the family.

The fog had rolled in leaving the quiet of night broken only by the gentle lap of the ocean as it washed up against the pebbled shoreline. Approaching the midnight hour, Brent had spent the last uneventful eight hours on the job listening to that slap and ebb.

He would admit to no one that tonight the continuous back and forth rhythm had almost lulled him to sleep a time or two. As the gentle rush of waves met beach, he expected any minute to see Zach Dennison rounding the dunes to take over for him on the sunrise shift.

Since Zach and his sister, Bree, shared a little bungalow on Cape May, left to them by their father who died last June, Brent figured Zach could use the work. It was rumored around town that the two siblings had considered leaving Pelican Pointe and heading to San Jose for better-paying jobs. They were having a tough time making ends meet. That was only one reason Brent had thought of Zach for work. The other, was that they were a couple of decent kids who badly needed to catch a break.

While Bree spent almost every waking hour either taking courses at the junior college in San Sebastian or working four to midnight at McCready's, her brother, Zach, picked up whatever odd jobs he could around town. He'd missed out on the lighthouse project last spring because he'd gone out of state to Colorado to work construction.

Their father's death might've been what brought Zach back to Pelican Pointe but it wasn't why he stayed. Zach's kid sister, Bree, had just recently turned twenty-one, old enough to cart drinks at the bar. Brent knew that worried the big brother. After all, he could relate. Over the years there had been times he'd felt much the same way about his little brother. For years Ethan had seemed to drift aimlessly without direction. Who would've ever thought the man who'd once tended bar and played in a band— would have found marital bliss—along with a solid career doing something he loved?

If that didn't show that sticking it out with family could turn out for the best, nothing did.

In Brent's mind family came first. He was sure that was the reason Zach had stuck around over the summer in Pelican Pointe. He recognized that about Zach. That's why he hoped like hell the Dennisons didn't leave. Too many people were packing up and heading someplace else these days.

Even if he didn't live here permanently, Brent didn't like to see the little town lose any of its residents. When that happened enough times, chunks began to fall away that you could never get back. Folks had to have a reason to stay.

Just that morning, the town council had made it official. They'd voted to move forward with a major renovation to re-open Pelican Pointe Elementary. The old building would have to undergo upgrades and changes. It would take dedication on the part of everyone in town to see that it happened. After all, families with children couldn't keep packing their kids off to school in another town. It was embarrassing.

Brent might not have to worry about things like that. But seeing the determination on the faces of fathers like Nick and Wally and his own brother, Ethan, did make a man wonder about all those what-ifs in life.

If River Amandez ever got her son back, would she head back to Santa Fe? Would the woman finally put down roots there in her own hometown? The fact that she was young meant she still had plenty of time to meet Mr. Right, to get her life sorted out. If everything ever fell into place for a woman like that, would she consider having more kids one day when she met said Mr. Right?

He admired her persistence, the way she hadn't given up on finding her child. Hell, who was he kidding? He couldn't wait to get her in the sack, a real bed this time, preferably his own.

Since he'd started his shift, they'd flirted with each other via text off and on all night. They'd bantered back and forth with suggestive byplay that had his juices revving up, even now.

Deep in those kinds of thoughts, the next thing Brent heard was someone yell, "Get down. Hit the dirt! Now!"

Brent ducked and dropped to the sand about the same time a gunshot crackled through the air. Several seconds went by as he lay there realizing someone had just taken a shot at him. It pissed him off. He heard leaves rustling. Then the sound evaporated into the wind and the waves. He got to his feet and took off in the only direction that made sense, the path leading to the dunes and down to the pier.

But he saw no one ahead of him. Turning, he scanned the cliffs for any movement. He saw nothing but the light wind stirring through the California scrub dotting the side of the bluff.

Just in case the shooter had outrun him, Brent took off as best he could around the bend. And ran smack into Zach Dennison. Wheezing a little, Brent shouted, "Did anyone run past you?"

"Not a soul. I was halfway to the pier when I heard gunfire. Are you okay?"

Instead of answering, Brent scratched his head and scanned the street to the east and southward. No movement anywhere. "They didn't vanish into thin air," Brent muttered. Surely they couldn't have scaled the side of the overhang. "They had to have come this way," he reasoned.

"I didn't see anyone but you."

"But you were right there on the dunes. You warned me to get down." Brent caught Zach expression and felt a defensive band tighten his chest. Was it possible Zach thought he had fallen asleep on the job? "I didn't imagine this."

"I didn't say you did. I was just making my way across the street when I heard cannon fire. But it wasn't me who warned you."

It was then Brent realized he was in no shape for a climb up the side of the cliff.

"You want me to take a look around? Check up the hill in case they scuttled back to the top through that heavy brush over there."

Wondering if maybe he might have fallen asleep after all and dreamed the entire incident, Brent wanted verification from Zach. "You can confirm you heard a gunshot, right?"

Zach nodded. "I heard that clear as day."

"That's something, I guess. After we get this on report we'll head up to the lighthouse, check to see if anyone parked there for any length of time," Brent suggested as he took out his cell phone to make the nine-one-one call.

By this time he looked up to see Ethan running up to him. Ethan clutched a service revolver in his fist. "I heard gunfire. You okay?"

Ah, a second person verifying he'd heard shots never hurt, Brent decided. For some reason that made him feel better. "I'm fine," he puffed out. "But I have to follow where I think the perp ran after he fired. Unfortunately, that's the side of the cliff."

"You'll never make it up there, Brent," Ethan pointed out.

"That's why we're taking your minivan and you're coming with me," Brent retorted. He turned to Zach. "I want you to stay here and make sure no one gets down to that beach. If there are any footprints, I want casts made. We'll have to wait for daylight for that though."

Brent glanced across the street just in time to catch Julian and Laura darting toward him and into the mix. He shook his head. The last thing he needed was a group of people gathering out in the open. "I'd be a helluva lot better if busybodies didn't decide to check out the situation for themselves," Brent grumbled, putting out a hand to stop the couple from coming any further. "Go back inside the RV. You don't want to be standing out here vulnerable to gunfire."

"I called River. She's on her way," Julian shouted from his position near the pier.

Brent's first reaction made him feel like he was back in middle-school, a starry-eyed teen, excited at the prospect of getting to see his best girl in study hall. Then, like any sane man, he remembered it was almost midnight and someone had just taken a pot shot at him from an unknown location. "I wish you hadn't done that. The last thing I need is to have River, or anyone else for that matter, caught in the middle of another round of shots. That includes the two of you."

"I thought maybe she needed to know there was trouble out here again," Julian said.

While relating what had happened to the dispatcher, Brent keyed in a text message to River that read:

Stay put at the inn. No need to head into town. Everything's fine here. I'm fine.

But while he'd been on the phone, McCready's regulars had streamed outside, curious to see what was happening near the wharf. They began to mill around the back door, a few even headed down to the beach.

What was it about people hearing gunfire and running outside to check it out? Weren't they supposed to fear getting out in the open?

Again, Brent reminded them all to move back inside and stay there out of the way. But just as he finished with one warning, River's ancient Wagoneer shrieked to a stop. He watched as the woman hopped out and scrambled over to where he stood. The yoga pants and little top she wore that didn't reach her midsection had his eyes on automatic perusing her body. The image of how detailed he'd explore every curve and fold inside the cave flitted through his brain. Under the circumstances, he did his best to rein in those lusty thoughts.

But from three feet away he saw the fury dancing in her eyes. Brent wasn't sure if she was angry with him or the situation. Either way, he felt the vibration she gave off—all the raw and heated energy between them bubbled to the surface. She had her hands on her hips, and looked like she was in no mood for an argument. Her chin jutted out and he saw her straighten her spine, ready for a good bout.

"Julian told me what happened. I don't think it's a good idea for you to continue to work the site anymore. This is ridiculous. Someone's out to see you dead and you're out here vulnerable to anyone lurking around. There's no reason to argue with me about it because I've already called Marcus and told him how I felt. And you know what? He agreed with me. And he's in charge. And if I have to, I'll ban you from the site by telling the council you're a security risk to my project."

As soon as she let him get a word in, he said, "I think you might be right."

"There's no point in being stubborn about this one point because…what did you say?"

"Even though there's no proof yet this was directed at me, I agree with you. But I don't see looters firing at the security detail just to get at the bones and the few antiquities you've found so far. My being here is a detriment to the project."

She huffed out a relieved breath. "I lined up all my reasons on the fifteen minute drive into town. I didn't think you'd be reasonable."

"I got that," Brent stated, more than a little amused by her concern.

"We've had to deal with looters before at other projects. They usually come at night, grab what they can in one fell swoop, and the stuff ends up for sale online. What makes this one so unique is that you can only get to this site from one source unless you count coming in by boat or dropping down from the cliffs."

"My thoughts exactly," Brent muttered.

"Plus, it's like you said before, the few relics we've managed to find, we've locked them away for safekeeping. They aren't out in the open to steal."

Brent nodded, pleased she understood his line of thinking. He took her by the arm, leading her to where she'd be safer if the gunman came back. But before he went, he turned to Zach. "Are you ready to start your shift? You can back out of this whole thing now if you want. I'll understand. You didn't sign on for this kind of trouble."

"I'm no quitter," Zach replied. "Besides, I don't think they were looking to steal relics just now. What they wanted they got. And that was you. Either to scare you or take you down."

River threw out her hand. "See. No one's buying that this had anything to do with thieves."

When Brent caught the worry on River's face, he began walking her toward the house. He reached into his pocket for his keys. "Do me a favor. Wait for me inside."

"Where are you going?" River wanted to know, alarm rising in her throat.

"I have to check out the cliffs, specifically the lighthouse area. And I'm about to look around inside my own house before I leave you here alone to make sure there's no one hiding under the bed."

"Now you're scaring me. You think the person crawled down the side of the cliffs to get to you? That reeks of desperation, Brent." The thought of just how serious the situation was frightened her. "Did you ever think that maybe you should hire someone to…?"

"Guard me?" Brent finished, as he led her into his living room. "I'm perfectly capable of taking care of myself. I don't need a bodyguard."

"That's a stubborn male response if I ever heard one."

"How about we argue about this when I get back?" He went into the pantry in the kitchen and brought out several plastic baggies.

"What are those for?" But she knew, even as she asked that it wasn't every day she saw a cop in action. Until coming to Pelican Pointe she hadn't even considered the dangers they faced on a regular basis.

"If we happen to find anything that is. After I eliminate where the shooter originated, we'll discuss my stubborn male response then. Whoever fired at me certainly didn't disappear into thin air. They had to go somewhere and it wasn't along the strand or into town."

"You can't go alone. Let me go with you."

For some reason that made him smile. "I like hearing that but Ethan's volunteered his time to the county tonight. I intend to take him up on it."

"Okay, but be careful." She rose on tiptoes to touch her lips to his.

Brent wrapped his arms around her. "Be here when I get back. Okay?"

"Trust me, that won't be a problem."

On the winding drive up the cliffs, Brent replayed the scene in his head right before the gunshot. Someone had yelled out a warning. If it wasn't Zach, then it had to have been Scott, his friendly shadow of late. Nothing else made sense. The thought of Scott had him casting an eye around the area for any sign of him—or for any stranger lurking about. He saw nothing but darkness and shadows.

Ethan broke the tension by cracking a joke. "Zach says your woman fired you just now."

"She did no such thing. I agreed that my being part of the detail might pose a hazard."

"Your woman fired your ass," Ethan chided as only a brother could. "The thing is she acts like she genuinely cares about you."

"I'm sure she cares about her project."

"Zach seemed to think her reaction was all about you."

"Zach's young and with that comes a certain amount of gullibility."

"Spoken like a jaded victim from the heart wars. Let me ask you something. Do you intend to go on forever letting Cindy ruin your outlook on matters of the heart?"

"I'm doing no such thing. I got over Cindy a long time ago."

Ethan brought the vehicle to a stop at the top of the bluff and turned to study his brother. "Are you sure about that? Or are you still carrying around a shitload of resentment that every woman is like that heartless viper?"

"Oh great, now in addition to Mom and Dad, you're trying to run my love life. You don't know a thing about it."

Ethan sighed, fully braced to hit that pocket of resistance. "I am not trying to run your life. And I don't know anything about it other than the one-line explanation you gave us at the time laced with expletives before demanding we never bring it up again."

The glances they exchanged indicated a clash of wills coming before Ethan added, "But I also don't want to see you getting to a stage in your life where you share it with no one because you're distrustful of the opposite sex."

A defensive shield went up. "River isn't like that."

"Now see, that right there is a good sign that you feel something about River you haven't felt for any woman in a very long while."

Another barrier shot out, cold and cautious. "Ethan, you need to back off."

Ethan nodded. "Sure. But you're scared shitless. What you're feeling has you petrified. When you take that plunge it hits you in the gut like a steel rod. I know, okay? You think you're the only one who was ever on shaky ground with a female?"

"Is that how you felt about Hayden?"

"Hayden and her situation scared the crap out of me. I was anything but confident we could make our relationship work, given our differences and her circumstances, let alone ever marry the woman."

"River has some issues."

"I know she does. But then everyone has something in their past that isn't pretty. Hayden was no different. Remember I was so mistrustful I finally ran a background check on her. We all don't get where we are without carrying around some baggage."

"I won't break a confidence."

"That's a good sign, too. Just don't be stubborn about asking for help in that regard."

They finally crawled out of the van to begin looking around. It didn't take them long to realize the area was deserted. Even with flashlights in hand though, it took some time to find anything in the blackness.

Brent and Ethan walked the area around the lighthouse and trekked to the woods and back again. Both brothers discovered tire tracks near the forest of trees about the same time. Studying the trail of footprints leading away from the soft impressions, they came to the same conclusion.

"Small car, like a Mazda maybe," Ethan said to Brent. "Different treads indicate the tires don't match."

"Shoe size isn't that large either, maybe a size seven or eight."

"That's small feet for a guy."

Brent nodded. "Someone no taller than five-eight for sure, maybe shorter."

"A woman maybe?" Ethan cocked his head, stared at his brother's face in the murky gloom. "Could be a pissed off girlfriend, maybe the wife of a felon you put away. You pissed off any girlfriends of your own lately?"

"Not that I know of. Whoever it is has good aim. If I hadn't dropped to the ground when I did that bullet would've hit its mark."

"Interesting. Why did you drop to the ground when you did?"

"I'd say I have Scott Phillips to thank for that. It was his voice I heard."

"Good thing he was looking out for you. Let's see, a woman who hates you enough to blow up your house *and* take a shot at you. That isn't just pissed off, bro, that's warped. Like I said before, obsessed. I hope you realize that whoever it is intends to keep trying until they get the results they want."

"I got the message when my house went boom. Look, fast-food wrapper there," Brent said, shining the beam very near the edge of the cliff. He took out one of the baggies, slipped the paper inside. "Just our luck it was left by one of Logan's crew and not the shooter."

"You never know. If they staked this area out for hours, it might mean they ate a meal here. Might get DNA from it."

Brent eyed the fast-food packaging sealed in the plastic. "DNA won't do much good unless we get a match. That restaurant is off the interstate, a good fifty miles from here. They're obviously staying away from town so as not to draw attention to themselves. But they have to be staying somewhere."

"That's why we need to check out all the motels within a hundred miles of Pelican Pointe."

Brent slapped Ethan on the back. "You think like a cop turned writer who now churns out mysteries for a living. And Ethan?"

"What?"

"Thanks for the pep talk."

"No problem. But Brent…"

"What?"

"Staking this place out at night, climbing down from a hundred-foot drop off point is nuts."

"Yeah. I know."

They stayed another hour, gathering evidence, taking pictures with their cell phones. It was too dark to do much else.

By the time Brent got back to the house, River had cranked up his stereo. While Clapton complained about pretending, the music blasted him as he walked through the front door.

"Find anything?" she bellowed out over the song.

His eyes landed on her bare midriff. "I found a beautiful woman waiting for me back home. It can't get any better than that."

Because his fingers itched to touch her, he streaked his thumb down her cheek, tugged the other hand through her massive hair. Heart racing with impatience, he brought her into him, crushed his mouth to hers. All the pent up emotions of the last two hours had him backing her down the hallway to the bedroom.

As they went, eager to get his hands on her, he yanked her top up and off. He got rid of her bra while he toed off his shoes. Together they stripped.

She tugged at the button on his jeans, ripped down the zipper. He stepped out of his pants, and yanked down hers. One pair flew to the right. The tee he wore, he dispatched to the left.

By the time they reached the bed, no barrier remained. He filled his hands with supple breasts, leaned his head down to feast on a pink nipple. They fell back onto the mattress. That energy he'd seen earlier was still there, throbbing, vibrating beneath him.

His tongue slid along her neck then lower, trailing slippery lines down her torso. But then he reared up, gripped her hips like a man starving and drove into her.

As she sunk back into the pillows, she considered him. His hair was slightly longer than when she'd first met him, so much that it curled up at the ends. The carefree style suited him. After what they'd just done to each other, he looked tousled and more than a little full of himself.

But since he was in the middle of nibbling her ear, she decided to give his smugness a pass. In the hopes of round two, a certain amount of encouragement couldn't hurt. When he moved to her neck, the little nudge she gave him seemed to work.

"Tell me I hit the right spot."

"Mmm, feel free to hit the right spot again." She brought his mouth up to meet hers.

"Oh I intend to," he boasted, right before he ran his fingers between soft folds.

She spiraled upward, fast and loose then shattered into his palm. Pleasure spread through her in bursts of pinks and soft lavenders. "Two for two," she breathed out, mellow as she'd ever been.

"Now go to sleep," he said, kissing her brow.

"What about your portion of the second round?" she murmured, fighting not to drift off.

"It's after three a.m. The second round for me will have to wait. I'm beat. Now go to sleep," he repeated. "Think of something nice to keep your dreams going till morning."

Burrowing into his chest, she purred, "Perfect. Then I'll dream of you and Luke."

Four hours later, at seven-thirty, she woke to a buzz in her brain before realizing it was her cell phone ringing from the living room where she'd left it. She rolled out of bed making a mad dash to reach it before the call went to voicemail.

Grabbing her panties off the bedroom floor, her pants in the hallway, she retrieved her shirt near the living room.

By the time she reached the ringing device, all of the usual questions had darted through her brain. But then she recognized the number on the display and the area code. It wasn't Julian or Laura about the dig. It wasn't the nursing home with news about her mother. She pushed the button to take the call as nervousness filled her heart with dismay. It was always like this whenever Gil Conroy called—hope first, before despair took over—because he would always deliver the same bad news in the same monotone voice.

In the other room Brent stirred. When he noticed he was alone in bed, and then heard River's voice coming from the living room, he threw back the covers.

From the hallway, he watched her close off to deal with the caller. Not just literally but figuratively, she blanked her face, steeled her spine as if bracing for a blow. With each clipped volley, while the conversation played out, Brent stared at her face. It wasn't good news. That much he could tell. He saw the tension carve out lines between her eyes and forehead, each one telling him she wasn't happy with what the person on the other end had to say.

"But if you just kept closer track of Hilda, I'm sure you'd get some info we don't—" Her voice trailed off as she continued to listen to what Brent assumed was an explanation of sorts from her private detective.

He saw her shoulders droop before she ended the call with desperation pooling in her eyes—and tears.

She glanced up, noticed Brent. "That was Gil. The last lead didn't pan out."

"I'm sorry, River. Look, don't be down. You've been strong now for a long time. Something will turn up."

She blew out a breath. Worry and fear could cause a woman to take desperate measures. "I want you to ask your father and brother to see if they can get a bead on my son."

Surprised by the suggestion, he did his best not to show it. "I don't know why I didn't think of it myself."

"Because you knew I wouldn't have agreed to it. I needed to come to this on my own. But I'm tired of waiting. I want…no, I *need* any input I can get at this point. I'll do whatever I have to do to find my son."

"Okay. Sure. I'll call them both and set it up. You'll need to be there, of course. You weren't planning on getting them to do this without you, right?

"No, I knew I'd have to be there."

"Good. How does your schedule look for tonight? Because before you answer, I have to close down the dig. You and your crew are stymied until I get the casts taken of those footprints from the beach area. I'll do my best to see to it you're back in business by noon though."

"That's fine. I'll let Julian know. I need to go back to the B & B anyway and take a shower."

"Shower here."

"I suppose I could but I still need a change of clothes."

"Ah. Wear one of my shirts then. You could put your yoga pants back on. They make you look sexy as hell." When she didn't laugh or smile, he reached for her hand, pulled her into him. "There's no need to be nervous about asking my family for help."

"Easy for you to say," she grumbled. But her mind unwittingly shifted gears. She stared back at the bronzed naked man in front of her. "You interested in cashing in your ticket for round two?"

He grinned. "You're standing here in my living room wearing nothing but panties and a bra. What do you think?" he pointed out. "Since you aren't completely dressed yet anyway—and it's still early—why don't we both save time and shower together?"

She ran her hand down his bare chest. "Now that's the best idea I've heard all morning."

An hour later, while Brent watched crime scene investigators take molds of the footprints and tire tracks on the beach and the cliffs, River's situation began to weigh on him.

If his father and brother couldn't help in locating Luke, what would they do then? Even though he knew both men possessed a talent, it didn't guarantee success. But he had to put his faith in them and he had to make sure River did that as well. That had to mean something, didn't it? That she was willing to reach out to his family.

Brent spotted Troy as the younger man worked around the lighthouse, putting the finishing touches on the foundation. Brent waited while Troy ambled over to where he stood.

In his easy way, Troy said, "Mona and I made it official. We called it quits last night."

"Sorry about that, Troy. But when a woman doesn't really believe in you, it's time to recognize that fact and move on. It might hurt for a while but you'll be better for it."

Logan overheard Brent's counsel and put in his two cents. "Good advice to follow, Troy. The less time you invest with a woman who doubts you, and has nothing good to say to you, the better off you'll be in the long run without her."

"I know. I know. But I'm gonna turn twenty-one at the end of the week and have no one to celebrate it with."

Brent exchanged looks with Logan. "Legal age to drink, huh? That's a rite of passage for any man. I say we throw you a party you'll not soon forget. Remember all those people who showed up in your corner out at Promise Cove when you were released from jail?"

Troy nodded and grinned. "I do. Warmed my heart to see all those people I never knew felt that way about me welcoming me home. Then they made those speeches and—"

Brent whacked Troy on the back. "Heartfelt sentiments all of them. We'll see you turn twenty-one in unforgettable fashion. That's a promise."

Chapter Seventeen

That night, River wasn't sure what to expect at the Santa Cruz home of Marcus and Lindeen Cody. But the more she thought about it, the more she wanted to give the whole idea a pass. By that time though, Brent had pulled to a stop in front of a cute 1920s Craftsman. Painted a sweet cream color, the beach bungalow had a well-manicured lawn, flower beds that popped with red and gold gerbera daisies and clusters of chrysanthemums.

River let out a loud sigh. "Do you think my coming here was a mistake?"

"Hey, if you believe in psychic abilities, Dad's no slouch in that department. He and Ethan both have a trail of successes."

"It isn't that. In fact, I've sought out psychics before. It's just that your parents were so warm to me when I first met them. Now, your father acts as though he doesn't even like being in the same room with me."

"My parents don't know you. But they will," Brent assured her.

"That's what I'm afraid of though. I'll have to give them certain details about my time with Wes. It isn't pretty."

"All I'm asking is for you to give them a chance. I guarantee they'll do the same for you." Crawling out of the pickup, Brent noticed Ethan's minivan parked in the driveway. "Looks like you get the full Cody treatment tonight. I was hoping Ethan would make it."

River got out and stood at the curb, clearly not happy about the full court press. But she would do this for Luke. "Great. Might as well get this out of the way and spill my guts to the entire Cody clan all at once."

"No need to be self-conscious."

"Easy for you to say. I'm curious. Before we go in there, I know you don't consider yourself as gifted as Ethan, but how do you come to terms with a supernatural guide like Scott? How do you explain a spiritwalker like him?"

"I don't. Nor do I explain my father or Ethan. I'm not without a mystic side to me though because I've seen all three do amazing, inexplicable things. The same powerful gene must've skipped me."

"You know that isn't true. You *sensed* my gift. I didn't even have to tell you about it."

"That's because I saw it in action."

"Not sure I buy that. I think you have some ability. You just don't practice it enough."

Before they could delve into the subject further, the front door burst open. Lindeen Cody stood in the doorway with hands on her slim hips, waiting.

"Are you coming in or do you plan to stay out there all night on the street?"

"Hi, Mom," Brent said, leaning over to kiss his mother's cheek. "Sorry we're late. The meeting with the adjuster took longer than we'd planned."

Lindeen patted the side of his face. "Fred Darby's been our agent for over thirty years. I hope he did right by you. River, don't just stand there planted to the concrete, come on inside. Nice to see you again. I'm sorry about your son. Brent told us about the entire situation."

River shot a look at Brent that clearly said she wasn't completely ready for this. "Thanks for agreeing to help me."

"The search for a child is such a serious matter, we thought of asking a contingent of others to join us, but Brent said it's best if we try it with Ethan and Marcus tonight first. We'll let you decide if at some point, you'll want the entire power of the tribe for this event—because that can be arranged."

"I appreciate that," River said as she followed Brent into the living room.

Marcus greeted his son with a slap on the back and extended a hand to River. "I know you didn't say anything about staying for supper but Lindeen insisted on thawing out some steaks. I don't remember if you're a vegetarian or not."

"Nope. Steak sounds good."

Ethan nodded in approval but it was his wife, Hayden, who said, "The Codys love a good outdoor party."

"How's the dig going?" Lindeen wanted to know. "Marcus may not tell you but he appreciated the way you arranged to have the ceremony go on all day."

"I was getting there," Marcus grumbled. "The elders were impressed. That's hard to do. Anyone want a beer?"

"Sure," River said. "The tribe hasn't protested my site in weeks and for that I'm very grateful. The least I can do to show that is to give them an all-day event before we remove any remains. You talked to them, didn't you, Marcus?"

"I might've mentioned it," Marcus said as he headed into the kitchen. "You've handled everything fairly. We're grateful for that."

"I don't know how much Brent told you guys but…"

Hayden didn't let her finish. "Your ex is the lowest bastard for doing this to you and your son. I can't even imagine what the last two years have been like for you." Hayden reached over and ran her fingers through her son's thick black hair. "Believe me, if someone snatched Nate I'd want them to suffer. But if that person was an ex, someone I once trusted, like his own father, it would devastate me."

River smiled. "I'm going to like you."

"I thought we'd established that already," Hayden said, giving her a sisterly grin.

It wasn't until after supper and they'd cleaned up the kitchen that everyone settled in the living room with their chairs in a circle.

Ethan put on music, flutes and drums that started out slow and built. Lindeen walked around the room lighting white and green candles to strengthen the power of sight while Marcus began to burn sage for cleansing and healing.

"So you've been trying to find the boy by any means possible, right?" Ethan asked, kicking off the discussion.

"I've done everything possible despite incredible odds," River replied, sending Brent a drawn-out look. "Brent recently confirmed one of the detectives on the case may have been taking money from Wes's parents early on to squash the investigation. That's when Brent got the FBI involved."

Marcus nodded his head. "A step in the right direction but the greedy cop is a difficult factor to overcome after all this time. It's a difficult situation."

When Brent noted the crestfallen look on River's face he felt they were getting off track. Hope was all she had, so he countered, "Difficult but not impossible, right?"

"I suggest you have the FBI focus on the ex's hobbies, like the sports activities he loves," Ethan suggested. "This Wes seems to be a creature of habit despite doing his best to keep a low profile. The thing I can't figure in the whole mess is if the parents are funneling him a shitload of money and he has unlimited funds at his disposal then why is he constantly on the move? That's what I see. Why hasn't Patton settled into suburbia somewhere using his obvious stash of phony IDs?"

"I think I have an answer for that," Brent offered. As all eyes focused on him, he explained, "Since bringing in the FBI, Ortega must have gotten in touch with Wes's parents who in turn made contact with their son directly.

That sent him into panic-mode at the idea the FBI was involved. As Hayden found out, getting on the radar of the feds is an entirely different kind of ballgame. Even the coolest, calmest felon will get a little shaken knowing a federal agency is breathing down their neck. They think twice about doing certain things. The notion that at any moment they could be found out alters the dynamics quite a bit."

Hayden agreed. "That's a fact. You think River's ex might be feeling the heat, so he gets edgy enough to move again? Makes sense. Let me tell you, being on the run is no fun. In fact, after a while it starts weighing on you. I can't imagine the stress of having a child in tow."

"Which means he's capable of screwing up, making mistakes," Brent finished.

"That's what I've been hoping for," River said, sucking in a breath at the stark reality of the last two years. "Just one mistake. I really never saw Wes as a father figure who would get involved with his son. He isn't the type because everything was all about him. For example, I can't imagine him giving up his pursuit of women. That leads me full circle. I try to imagine him paying that much attention to his son's well-being now." Her voice broke. "What I'm afraid of is…what if…what if he gets fed up with toting him around, gets desperate, and does something…unimaginable to Luke."

Brent's arms circled her shoulders. "There's no indication of that so far. Surely after all this time he's bonded with the little guy."

"I hate to be the one to mention this. But I'm sensing the kid isn't happy at all," Ethan chimed in.

Brent glared at his brother. That's not something he wanted Ethan to spill, especially right this minute when River was so vulnerable. She didn't need to have that detail shoved in her face. "There's something I need to show you in the kitchen, Ethan." His head bobbed in that direction.

But River would have none of that. "Don't you two dare get up and head off in the other room. I want to hear what Ethan has to say, all of it. Please do not hold back because you think I'm too fragile or delicate to handle what you see. I've been dealing with this for too long as it is. I'm tired of being put off and letting Wes win. I need to know."

Ethan eyed Brent, shrugged. "Sorry, but the little boy is forever living in temporary places. I see a string of hotels and motels, small out of the way apartments, recently. Your Luke is easily confused. His father constantly calls him by different names and he has trouble keeping up with the story he's supposed to remember."

No one in the room was more surprised than River when Brent added, "Luke has no structure, no regular time schedule. One night he's forced to go to bed at eight, the next he's kept up until the wee hours of the morning. He's been left alone several times only to wake up in a strange place, scared and disoriented."

Everyone gaped at Brent with open amazement.

"Since when do you *see* anything like that?" Marcus asked. "It's significant. Since when did you start using your natural ability?"

Brent ran a hand through his hair. "For a couple of days now." He turned to River, took her hand. "That day at the cave, you and I connected, soul to soul, spirit to spirit. I'd say you brought it to the surface for me in a big way."

"I did? You didn't say a thing."

"You took her to the cave?" Marcus demanded, clearly upset. "You know it's off limits to outsiders. The healing spirit is powerful there."

"That's right. I did take her. And I'd do it again. Because I don't consider River an outsider. And you shouldn't either. I'm not sure how this stuff works yet. My head's filled with so many images I'm having trouble keeping them all straight. And one of them is this. I'm curious about something I haven't been able to understand. Are you aware River has her own special gift? And if not, why not? Why weren't you able to pick up on her ability? You met her before any of us did, spent time with her, took her on a trip south in a closed up space for hours. You're usually more in tune with things like that."

"I'm curious about that, too," Ethan wondered.

Brent went on, "You seemed to focus on any negative around you instead of the positive. Why is that?"

To River's credit she felt she needed to defend Marcus before this got out of hand. She glanced over at the much older man. "Before you answer that you should know that my grandmother spent years teaching me how to block it, my gift, that is. Every time I touched a certain item and could see the past, she had it in her head that if people found out they might make fun of me or somehow exploit that part of me if they knew. So she showed me how to handle it, most times, anyway. As I said before, it doesn't do me any good in locating Luke."

"There's enough energy in this room, we'll locate him," Lindeen assured River as she patted the woman's hand. "You just wait and see." She sent her sons a stern look. "I expect a degree of respect where your father is concerned. But you might as well tell them Marcus."

"None of this doubt or drama is helping River locate her son's whereabouts," Marcus pointed out.

Chastised to a point, Brent stared at his father, but persisted. "If this is a test, I'll play along. I know you've always let us walk our own path, hoping we'd eventually arrive at that place in life to appreciate our roots as much as you do. While you were busy guiding others up to that point, you stepped back and let your own sons find their footing. Tough to do for a father."

Brent saw the respect shine in Marcus's eyes so he went on. "Despite zeroing in on the negative you saw in the people we chose to have around us, you let us make our mistakes, to learn, to hopefully grow. You didn't warn me off Cindy when you could have."

"At the time Cindy was a painful, sometimes destructive path you needed to take. In spite of wanting to keep our children from hurting, from suffering, it's oft times clear we cannot."

"So we needed to experience our own growth, find our own metaphysical well-being, is that it?" Ethan asked. He could see it now and all the blunders he'd made to get to this one happy point in his life. He met his father's eyes. "That time I spent bumming around in a band and tending bar, the aimless feeling I had about life, you never said a word to discourage me. You knew I'd eventually get it out of my system."

"I hoped."

River and Hayden exchanged glances. But it was Hayden who'd been privy to the Cody dynamics for much longer than River, who said, "I'd say that's a family breakthrough that doesn't come along too often. But that still doesn't help River find her son," Hayden added in frustration. She sent Ethan a pleading gaze. "You've assisted other people, surely now you can do something for a mother to find her baby."

Ethan glanced at Brent, who in turn, looked at Marcus. It was, as if father and sons were united, determined to get the job done tonight.

"I just don't want to give you false hope," Marcus cautioned River. "I want to make sure you understand that."

It was Brent who replied, "Appreciated, but at this point false hope might be a step up."

"All right." Marcus linked his right hand with his wife's left. "Form a circle. The power of us all together will conquer Patton's—eventually. Just don't expect miracles."

The group clasped hands. At the touch to Brent's and Ethan's, River felt the energy intensify. Even if it didn't get her anywhere near Luke, there was strength with this family, a support she hadn't had.

"Mother Earth, Father Sky, hear us. We know the relationship of mother to her children is special, a bond that must not be broken. But tonight, River's heart breaks at not being able to see her child for such a long time. She longs to hold him again, to get a chance to form that strong connection. Oh Mother Earth and Father Sky, we ask that you give us the vision that will guide us to young Luke Patton, to help us to help his mother reunite with her son. Once that bond is strong again, we ask you to help River secure her future as a mother and teacher to the one so young. What do you see, Ethan?"

"Cold weather. Snow. Mountains. The color red, a lot of red. Blood maybe."

"Brent?"

Brent squeezed River's hand. "A confrontation. Chaos. A man with a beard."

"Good. Good. Now I'll try." Marcus closed his eyes and went through the images his sons had described in more detail with one additional feature. "The child is safe, River. In the end, the child will be okay."

She wanted to believe. She wanted it all to somehow lead to where they might find Luke.

After the ceremony was done, River followed Marcus into the kitchen. "Thanks for that in there. I know you thought I was holding back, keeping secrets but surely—"

Marcus held up a hand. "Not to worry. We're starting again today. Fresh. New. Let me know if we hit a home run in there."

"I will. One thing though. Is there any way you could tell me who's trying to hurt Brent?"

Ethan appeared in the doorway about that time to overhear River's question. His brow wrinkled. "You care about him."

"Of course, I do."

"No, I mean you're in love with him."

River sucked in a breath, let it out. "I guess I am."

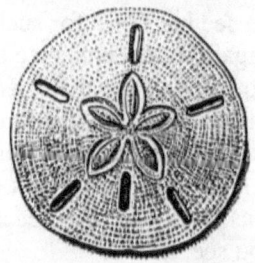

Chapter Eighteen

By the end of the week, the group of parents headed by Nick Harris and Logan Donnelly had called a meeting to address the school issue. The turnout was so good that an overflowing crowd showed up to wedge inside the small community church auditorium. It seemed the entire town had a vested interest in the outcome.

Nick stood at the podium looking out across the room at the gathering. There were more young parents than he realized. Abby and Paul Bonner, Donna and Ricky Oden, newcomers Jill and Ross Campbell, joined Ethan and Hayden, Wally and Lilly Pierce, Kinsey and Logan, in the audience and a slew of others. Even residents with no children on the horizon had decided to make an appearance. Keegan and Cord Bennett sat alongside Murphy and Carla Vargas, Flynn McCready and Janie Pointer.

For the first time Nick realized the future of Pelican Pointe rested in the hands of its parents, those who wanted to contribute to its legacy down the road.

That way of thinking had him kicking off the discussion. And he didn't need a microphone for his voice to carry. "All right, everyone settle down. After years of neglect, this town is beginning to make its way back from an economic depression. Business owners are starting to see a definite upturn. There's no doubt our little town is growing. But those of us who have small children, like

Jordan and I do, are here tonight to address a growing concern, a problem if you will that's old to some of you and new to people like us. If you've been packing your kids off on the school bus for the elementary school over in San Sebastian every day, then this meeting concerns you, too.

"There's no school right now in Pelican Pointe. Unlike some small towns, we don't have one. We're dependent on sending our kids off to another town. Our daughter Hutton starts kindergarten next fall. So does Kyra Pierce, Colleen Bonner and a dozen other children within our city limits. It got us to thinking. If you no longer want to settle for your kids boarding a bus every morning and afternoon heading for the long trip to San Sebastian because it just isn't practical, then hear me out.

"A group of us think we've found a solution. We have a perfectly good former elementary school sitting empty at the corner of Landings Bay and Cape May. With hard work, plenty of volunteers, several fundraisers, we believe we can fund the project. At least, we'll give it our best shot.

"As I look around here tonight, some of you like the Fergusons, the Sullivans, the Boedeckers, the Stovalls, sent your kids there. Even Drea Jennings sitting in the front row attended that elementary before they closed it down. Everyone here either sent their kids there at one time or another or knows someone who did. Now, we need your help to bring the school back for future generations. I shouldn't have to list how every merchant here benefits if the project succeeds. If the town grows, all the local businesses grow with it. In the long run, it's a win-win."

Nick decided to put the hardware store owner, Joe Ferguson, widely known as a notorious tightwad, on the hot seat first in front of everyone. "What about you, Ferguson? Your kids went to Pelican Pointe Elementary years ago before the state closed it down. Starting this project will be huge. If you'll agree to donate a portion of the materials, not all of course, but enough to bring the cost down, Logan Donnelly and I will personally match it. We'll hire a crew to do the work."

"What do you say, Ferguson," Logan said, standing up beside Nick. "Both Nick and I have made it a point to order our materials strictly local and that means from you. We've spent a great deal of money inside your store. Now we're asking for you to step up and return that goodwill, that karma."

Ferguson, a balding, overweight man who had turned fifty last August, shrugged, crossed his arms over his chest. "But I don't have small kids. My kids are grown. In fact, I plan to have my oldest, Tucker, take over the family business next year so I can retire. Donations have their place but a business can't survive for long like that."

Nick had expected that kind of answer and glared at the guy. "Really? Then how would you like it if the majority of the town started going over to San Sebastian for all their hardware and lumber needs? Houses around here need sprucing up. You'd be on the losing end of that, Ferguson, and feel the pinch almost immediately."

Considering that, Ferguson paled. "Okay. Okay. I'll donate materials like sheetrock and hardware. But lumber is another matter. I'll expect you to pay five percent above cost, plus any shipping and handling involved."

Nick and Logan exchanged glances. It was Nick who replied, "If that's the best you can do, then we'll take it."

"How in the hell do you intend to raise money for what has to be a multi-million dollar project?" Ferguson wanted to know. "We're not all rolling in dough, you know."

Logan took over for Nick at the lectern. He stared directly at Ferguson. "Several of our local business owners, like Nick, Murphy and Perry Altman, have agreed to obtain donations and grants from private sources. If you ask me, it's a very generous gesture. We'd be silly to turn down any offers."

Nick spoke up, "As soon as Logan gets the permits in place, renovations will begin immediately. The plan is to open by next fall. The town council voted unanimously to kick off a fundraiser in the next few weeks. We just have to figure out what it will be. Something big that will bring in dollars."

Wally's wife, Lilly, stood up. "The spring street fair has always been a huge moneymaker for the town. How about we put together an additional one before Thanksgiving? We might be able to get the carnival people to set up during that time because folks don't usually think of celebrating Thanksgiving and Christmas by offering carnivals. They've become widely popular around the area."

"Now see, that's the kind of involvement we're talking about. Lilly, will you take care of checking into the carnival vendors for us?" Logan asked. "Anyone else have any fundraising ideas to put forth after the holidays, make sure to see Lilly. Because before this is done, we'll need to meet and finalize several in order for this to work."

"Which brings up a major point," Nick said. "Having been a part of the street fair now for several years, it takes an incredible amount of work. What we'll need from everyone here is participation, commitment. If you've ever wanted to sell your wares, now is the perfect time to do it. We'll also take donations for services and possibly we'll need volunteers to man the booths. No volunteer will be turned away. We'll put everyone to work. This is the time to dig deep, people, to set aside your time and effort, to come up with some creative ways to help Pelican Pointe's kids in the most direct way possible. Contribute anyway you can. Bake cookies, cupcakes, whatever it takes. And remember, we're all in this together."

When half the room enthusiastically held up their hands, Nick smiled over at his wife.

Jordan grinned back and said, "Just think, we might just pull this thing off after all."

Two days later Promise Cove became the gathering place for the meeting where they could further organize the street fair. Since they were getting a late start, they needed everyone to pitch in and hit the ground running.

Crammed into the living room they were elbow to elbow. River felt a little out of place. After all, she wasn't a local, didn't even have a stake in the project. But somehow she and her crew had gotten caught up in the excitement along with the residents as they went about the plan to bring life back to a relic of a school.

She'd taken a run by there already, seen for herself the amount of work it needed. Because her heart went out to the parents, she along with Laura and Julian had chipped in all the extra dollars they could afford. They'd even showed early to help Jordan prepare the snacks tonight.

River looked around at the sea of faces she'd come to know over the past several weeks. Tonight though, she was looking for one in particular.

According to Brent, the only lawyer in town was Kinsey Wyatt, now Kinsey Donnelly. Brent had described the attorney but wasn't here to point her out because he'd gotten tied up with tribal business. Of those River recognized, she zeroed in on Hayden. She asked the bookstore owner for help.

Hayden spotted the pregnant woman standing next to Jordan at the buffet table. "There she is. Go on over and say hi. She's as nice as can be and a first-rate lawyer. The town's lucky to have her."

River crossed the room, extended her hand to Kinsey and introduced herself. "Hi, I'm River Amandez."

"The archaeologist," Kinsey added between mouthfuls of hummus and chips. "So nice to finally meet you. Kinsey Donnelly."

"I know. You come highly recommended."

Kinsey got a kick out of that. "No kidding? When you're the only game in town, I guess people tend to endorse with great fanfare. But look at you. Such a fascinating life you've lived. The places all around the world you've seen. It's hard to imagine that with all the globe-trotting you've done—it's a simple mudslide that reveals an ancient canoe in the ground—to bring you all the way to Pelican Pointe. Life is full of surprises, isn't it?"

She thought of Luke and wondered where he was at that moment. But this wasn't the time or the place to go into her problems. Instead, River agreed, "It definitely is. And that canoe is the one thing we're having trouble getting out of the ground."

"I'd imagine so. You'd want it intact if possible. Listen to me going on. You must have a legal problem, don't you? I can help. Hmm, maybe I'll turn that into my slogan. Every good lawyer has one. Just kidding."

Jordan piped up, "If you want to sue someone Kinsey's the one to do it. She's our resident legal eagle."

"See. Fanfare." Kinsey smiled, rubbed a hand over her slightly protruding stomach. "I try to be. You want to sue someone? I can take care of that. I'm not really a trial lawyer though. So I'll admit that upfront. What I try to do is 'negotiate' things before it gets to that. But I do like to think I'll go to the mat for my clients when necessary, figuratively, of course. As long as I don't have to get down on the floor on a routine basis before the babies get here."

"Babies?" River asked, gaping.

"Twins. We found out yesterday. That's why I look farther along than four months. I'm gonna get huge by the time March gets here."

"Congratulations."

Kinsey laughed. "Thanks. We're both still freaking out a little. Come to think of it, we've both been doing our share of freaking out since July." She tilted her head, studied River. "Enough about me, you *do* have a legal problem? It's weighing on you, I can tell."

"I do. But I realize I should stop by your office tomorrow. I just wanted to get to know you a little tonight first."

"Absolutely. Stop by anytime. I have a clear docket most of the day. I'll be looking for you."

About that time Logan walked up, planted a kiss on his wife's lips even as his hand covered hers, lingering on her belly. "This woman is the reason I get up in the morning."

"Aw, I love you, too," Kinsey said, touching her lips to his. Turning into her husband's arms she said, "When do you plan to announce the good news?"

"I thought I might wait. Shouldn't you be sitting down, getting off your feet?"

"Sweetie, I've been sitting all day. I need to move around while I'm not the size of a beached whale, which is in the immediate future for me," Kinsey answered. "I don't think you should wait to tell them the news though. Look around at this crowd. You can feel their enthusiasm, the upbeat energy in the room. Everyone's pumped about this school project. I think you should go with it. Come on, River, let's find a seat, the meeting's about to start and I want to get my two cents in about encouraging everyone to participate in some way no matter how much money they have or don't have."

With that, Nick got things rolling. "Logan is chomping at the bit to share some news with us so why not get us started, Logan."

The sculptor walked over to where Nick stood in front of the fireplace. "As most of you know, I've been on a sabbatical ever since coming here as far as starting any of my own projects. But I have a client in New York, a very wealthy heiress who comes from old money. Phyllis Milburn is a patron of the arts. She's been pestering me for years now to do a sculpture, a specific subject. I've managed to dodge her requests up to this point because I don't exactly like others suggesting a particular focus. But in this case, I'm making an exception because Phyllis has agreed to purchase it and donate the art to the school once it opens. All we have to do when it's finished is erect it out front with a plaque that says this work was donated by Phyllis Milburn."

"But your sculptures go for millions?" Lilly pointed out. "They're in front of zoos and symphony halls."

Logan smiled at the cute brunette. "They are. But this one will be special because creating it for Phyllis means it will go a long way in paying the bills for the renovation."

"What exactly does she want you to create?" Jordan wanted to know.

"A dolphin of all things," Logan answered. "And yeah, I once thought that was beneath me. But I'm planning to make it my own creation using a pod with mother and babies." He glanced over at his wife, his lips curved up again. "It seems appropriate since we're doing this project for the children and all the future kids of Pelican Pointe."

"That's perfect," Ethan said. "We're a coastal town. Having a dolphin pod out front represents the sea, the community as a whole, and the children inside that school."

"Exactly," Logan agreed while the entire room erupted to life in a flurry of conversation, all of them talking at once, the eagerness growing in each person's voice.

Nick let the buzz go on for a minute or two before taking charge again. "While Mrs. Milburn's generosity is extraordinary and appreciated, it still leaves a lot of work for us to do. We aren't off the hook with cost, not at all. And we won't shy away from any of it because we're going to keep in mind that the beneficiaries of this project are the kids. Priority one is that we want a state-of-the-art educational facility for our children. As parents we want the best.

"So here's the deal. If the state doesn't see fit to sanction our school, possibly because our low enrollment won't meet the guidelines, which is a risk we take, we won't take no for an answer. By that I mean Pelican Pointe Elementary will open next fall on schedule whether or not it's deemed public or has to open as a private facility. But private doesn't equate to charging tuition. Let me be clear on that. The objective is open enrollment for everyone. Because of that we'll still need approaches to making money. And I'll be upfront with all of you. It won't end when the doors open either. Funding teachers, getting staff members, doesn't come cheap. So I'm opening the floor up to suggestions."

Caught up, River got to her feet. "How about an auction? That way people could donate specific items, anything from antiques to their services."

"Excellent. That's one option. Anyone else?"

Several hands shot up.

About that time Brent let himself in the front door and ran right into Murphy, mayor and owner of Murphy's Market. The five-foot tall man grabbed Brent's arm and said, "Just the guy I want to see. I have a proposition for you. Come into the kitchen so we can talk. The noise out here is deafening. But that's a good thing."

Brent frowned. "I'm not sure I like the sound of that."

"You will. How's the PT coming?"

"Almost done with the whole thing."

"And yet the county hasn't seen fit to give you your job back. Why is that?"

Brent remained stoic. "I'm not sure how that pertains to anything."

"Oh but it does. Rumor has it politics has you on the outs with your own department."

He should've known everyone would already have heard rumors about Richardson and his tactics. People liked to talk and especially when it pertained to anything personal. Such was small-town living. "I'm an elected official. Politics is part of the process."

"How would you like to put the county politics behind you for good?"

"And just how would I do that?"

"By becoming Pelican Pointe's chief of police."

Brent couldn't help it, his jaw dropped open. "You're serious?"

"I am. We had one a long time ago. But with declining funds in the city coffers, we had to let him go. That was right after I got here. Our police protection became a matter for the county. I don't have to tell you that when anything major happens here, the response time can be up to half an hour or longer to get an officer on the scene."

Because he knew for a fact residents living here could be at risk for long delays, especially during emergencies like they'd seen recently when it took Garver longer than it should have to arrive, Brent grew curious. "How would that work exactly?"

"You would no longer be an elected official but a municipal employee. Your allegiance would be to the citizens. You'd have to report to the town council every month but then it wouldn't be anything as formal as a typewritten report, less paperwork for you. At first, you'd be the only cop we'd have. Maybe after a year, we'd re-evaluate the situation and you could hire some help. Pelican Pointe isn't exactly a hotbed of crime."

Brent cocked a brow at the shorter man. "Other than the serial killer who called this town home for most of his life, you mean? Or the arsonist Kent Springer who did the same until said serial killer made Kent one of his victims? Or maybe the fact that the Russian mob targeted one of our own citizens in broad daylight? Or—"

Murphy grinned, held up a staying hand. "Okay, okay, I get the picture. That's definitely coming from a cop's viewpoint."

"And not the mayor putting a pretty spin on things," Brent said with humor.

"I know you're over-qualified for the position. But give it some thought. Think about serving the town in an official capacity, okay?"

"Sure. But you should know I'm hoping to get my job back."

"I understand that. But at least now you have a backup plan."

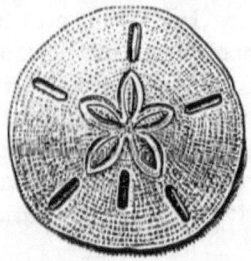

Chapter Nineteen

The law office of Kinsey Wyatt Donnelly was located inside a Tudor-style house on Landings Bay, which according to Hayden Cody would be less than a ten-minute walk.

Because it was a gorgeous autumn day, River decided to forego starting up her gas guzzler and make the trip on foot. She strolled past pretty little cottages lining Ocean Street and small children playing in the front yards.

It looked like any small town in the country where families raised kids, where they went to PTA meetings on Monday nights and little league games on the weekends.

Before she knew what was happening, tears were spilling down her cheeks. Would she ever get a chance to do any of that? What was wrong with her anyway? She'd handled things just fine for two years without getting emotional every time she walked around a town. What was it about this place that had her thinking so much about what might have been? About hearth and home? About settling down in one place?

Which was ridiculous she decided as she went up to the front door, wiping away water from her face with every step.

Since Hayden had mentioned the house acted as both residence and business, she rang the bell.

Kinsey opened the door with a smile on her face. "Look at you, all upset. Get in here and tell me what I can do for you."

River fanned her face. "It's okay, I was just beating myself up for getting so weepy-eyed on the walk over."

"Let's settle into my office. Want something cold to drink?"

"That would be great. Water is fine."

Kinsey led her to a nice-sized home office with a polished mahogany desk and bookshelves to match. She reached into a compact fridge and took out two bottled waters.

"Can you sue a police department, specifically one detective?" River blurted out without prefacing her frustration.

Kinsey eyed River. "That certainly came out of the blue. Sure you can. But usually that sort of thing pertains to having your civil rights violated. Are you by any chance talking about the Santa Cruz Sheriff's Department?"

"What? No. No. Not them. This has nothing to do with them."

More than a little confused, Kinsey suggested, "Okay, why don't you have a seat and tell me what's really going on. Maybe start from the beginning. Wait. Give me a dollar."

"What?"

"Retain my services by giving me a dollar. Until I know what's happening, that is."

River dug in her jeans pocket and came out with a five. "That's all I have on me."

"Perfect. Now give me the deets from the starting point."

River got comfortable in one of the wing chairs in front of the desk. She began by going over the last two years, blow by blow. Once she opened her mouth she didn't seem to be able to stop talking or crying.

When she'd finished with all of it, Kinsey sat back in her chair, rubbed a protective hand over her growing baby mound. "My God, I had no idea. That's the most heart-wrenching story I've heard in quite some time. And you think this Ortega has been taking payments under the table to specifically *not* work his own case file all this time?"

"That's exactly what I think he did. Brent thinks that, too. Each time I call Ortega, which is about once a month, he gives me some lame excuse, some story about why he's having trouble finding time to look into any leads I send his way. I realize proving the Patton family is paying him off might be more than a little difficult but I have to do something."

"If it's true though, that's prosecutable criminal behavior and he would probably need to be charged before proceeding with any civil litigation." When she saw that more tears wanted to leak out along with the disappointment cross River's face at her answer, Kinsey added quickly, "But not a prerequisite to get a financial settlement."

"I'm not doing this for the money. I know it sounds like I am but I'm not. Although I want Ortega to pay for what he's done, I'd sue for a dollar just to get him on record that he's a sleazebag like Wes, maybe get him out of law enforcement entirely. I don't want another mother back in Santa Fe, in Ortega's jurisdiction, to ever have to go through what I have. All this time I thought I had the police on my side, doing everything they could. Now I find out that isn't the case at all. False hope is what it is. And unfair on so many levels. I understand it's difficult to find someone on the run but not impossible. To know the police let me down in locating my child is reprehensible. I might add I have sole custody of Luke legally—and brought the judge's order with me to prove it." River dug out a copy of her paperwork from her back pocket.

Kinsey unfolded it, smoothed out the creases. After reading the document from top to bottom, she said, "Okay, that is a major legal hurdle right there. But it would have to be proved in some way that this detective's bank account increased during these past twenty-four months.

There are lawful means to go about that but we would need to prepare a case, subpoena for records, hire a private investigator and—"

"Sounds like what you're saying is it would involve a great deal of money."

Kinsey nodded in agreement. "It would take money and patience to wind through the court system, perhaps years. You might even be better off hiring an attorney from the Santa Fe area."

River shook her head. "No, if I did that I'd be butting up against the same problem. Wes and his parents are well-off. They know a long list of influential people back there."

"Okay. I certainly see your frustration in the system. I'm appalled that this Ortega did that to you. I'm willing to help any way that I can, mother to mother, well almost a mother."

"Pregnancy counts."

Kinsey smiled. "You bet it does. Bottom line is I won't discourage you from going the civil route. You've had your heart ripped out. I'm right there with you, as I might point out, any jury in the country would more than likely side with a mother in this particular instance. I haven't even held my babies yet, but if someone dared take mine, I'd fight whatever way I could, with whatever tools were at my disposal to get satisfaction, especially knowing the police were protecting the abductor in some way."

"Thank you."

"Well, I haven't done anything…yet. Look, why not come to the house tonight. We're having a birthday party for Troy Dayton. It's a chance to hear some music, do a little mingling. For all I know the entire town will turn out." Kinsey looked at her watch. "I'm not exactly certain how many people will be in this house in six hours."

River frowned and looked around. "You can throw a party together in six hours?"

"Not me. Jordan is catering it. She'll be here in an hour to set up, a buffet-type thing."

"Anything I can do?"

"You can stop crying. I know that's lame but I'm ready to kick some ass on your behalf. How's that?"

"Thank you," River said again. "Do you think we could keep what I just told you between the two of us without everyone in town knowing about Luke?"

"Honey, it's the law. You've retained me now, remember? Lawyer-client confidentiality rocks," she explained with a wink and a grin. "I can't tell another person your woes if that's what you're afraid of."

"Even for five dollars?"

"Yep. I've got to do some research though to get this going. Then the fee will go up. Are you prepared for that?"

"I have some money my grandmother left me. It isn't much but it's been sitting in an account drawing interest for six years. I also pay a private detective back in Santa Fe to work the case. Believe it or not, I lived rather cheaply going from dig to dig until I got to Pelican Pointe, that is. I'm a little in love with Promise Cove. I don't seem to want to leave."

"Everyone falls in love with the B & B. Can your PI be trusted or is he like this Ortega guy?"

"So far, I think he's on the level. Anyway, just getting all this off my chest and ranting makes me feel somewhat better."

"I assume Brent knows all this though since he feels Ortega is a dirty cop."

"Yes."

"Does he have any leads whatsoever?"

"I don't know. He's been pretty tight-lipped lately about a lot of things. He's on the phone a lot making inquiries, checking with the FBI on a routine basis."

"There's hope then. But ain't that just like a man," Kinsey teased. "And we all know Brent Cody is the king of reserved."

"Don't I know it? I'm hoping it's just the cop in him. But I wish he'd open up once in a while."

At that moment, the cop in Brent had just finished preparing River a sack lunch of tuna fish and apple slices. He walked it over to the dig only to see her crew, even the women, sporting baseball caps on their heads and gloves on their hands playing catch on the beach. River was nowhere in sight.

Once Julian spotted him, Brent was forced to send the man a polite nod of the head and the game came to an abrupt stop.

Brent watched as River's lead anthropologist made his way over to where he stood on the strand. He could tell the scientist had something on his mind.

"How's it going?" Julian said amicably enough. A little nervous, he added, "It's a pretty fall day."

"It is that."

"Santa Cruz County is turning out to be one of the most beautiful area's we've ever spent time in." Julian shifted his feet. "Uh, River's not here. She walked over a couple of blocks to meet with the lawyer in town."

"Ah. She mentioned she planned to do that. I wasn't sure when." The two men stood there like that, an awkward silence hanging between them until Brent finally spoke up. "What's on your mind?"

"Am I that obvious?"

"Yeah."

Julian scratched his scruffy beard, shifted his feet yet again. "I don't want to intrude but... How's it going with River?"

"Is that really your question? Don't you really want to know what exactly my intentions are?"

Julian chuckled and scratched his chin again, clearly uncomfortable. "I'm sort of her only family right now. I won't stand around and watch her get hurt, not again. I didn't say anything when she got involved with that bastard Patton and I regretted keeping my mouth shut.

Back then, she used to cry at work all the time. Then this thing with Luke… She doesn't cry so much where people can see her anymore but I know she's still hurting."

"I appreciate your concern for her. I really do. Known her a long time, have you?"

"Fifteen years. We met in freshman year of college. She's a good person. She deserves better than what she's gotten."

"On that we agree."

"Do you think she'll ever find Luke?"

"There are a lot of people working on it."

"But what does that mean."

"It means, I'm doing all that I can."

That night, Logan and Kinsey opened their home to the town in an open house type atmosphere for the guest of honor, Troy Dayton, who was now officially legal.

Troy had helped the couple paint and remodel their two-thousand-square-foot house. So it seemed fitting to celebrate his twenty-first birthday surrounded by the bright colors he'd slapped on the walls, the modern appliances he'd helped install.

Troy looked around at the stylish furniture, the former home of Aaron Hartley, and realized Logan and Kinsey had upgraded it to a warm, inviting place to raise children, something he knew they both were excited about. Tonight the Donnelly residence was jam-packed with wall-to-wall people from every corner of Pelican Pointe.

Troy scanned the room again, this time inching toward the table where the fancy hors d'oeuvres had been set out. He perused the array of gooey finger sandwiches, the spicy empanadas, rolled up taquitos, an array of dips and chips and realized Jordan had, once again, gone to a great deal of trouble just for him. It reminded him of last summer the day he'd been released from county.

He couldn't believe the mayor had shown up. To think that Murphy, and his main squeeze, the county social worker, Carla Vargas, had taken the time to come to his party was only one indication his life had taken an upward turn since the day he'd gotten his freedom back.

For a kid who had scrounged around for scraps to make ends meet—for someone who had once aspired to making jewelry boxes for a living in hopes of getting a business off the ground so he could pay the rent—Troy considered himself the luckiest guy in town.

He'd been raised by a single mother who'd died of breast cancer when he was fourteen, leaving him without a place to live. If not for his uncle, Derek Stovall, he would've been scuttled off to a foster home.

But now Troy had put his false arrest for murder solidly behind him. He worked full-time for Logan as his construction foreman and rented the little studio apartment over the Harris's garage at Promise Cove. He had a place to call his own with a gorgeous view of the ocean that didn't cost a fortune and a job he loved.

While his life had taken a definite turn for the better, his uncle hadn't been as fortunate. Derek had spent the last few months sitting in jail charged with the sexual assault of Abby Bonner, if found guilty, the man faced a ten-year prison term.

Murphy came over, handed him a beer.

"I'm not much of a drinker."

"And that's an admirable quality in any man. But there are times a taste of Guinness helps a deep thinker sort out his thoughts."

About that time Troy spotted the gorgeous redhead, Bree Dennison, standing by the front door. They'd gone to high school together. He hadn't seen her since her own twenty-first birthday party Labor Day weekend. He couldn't believe she was headed straight for him.

"Hi Troy. Happy birthday!" Bree leaned in, kissed his cheek and put her arms around him for a hug. "Good to see you."

"Hi Bree. What are you doing here?"

Bree sent him a puzzled look. "Silly. I was invited just like everyone else. It happens to be my night off too which means I'm letting my hair down a little bit tonight because I have schoolwork to do when I get back home."

He'd forgotten she was in her second year at the community college. "How's school going?"

"It's tough to go to class and hold down a job. I'm lucky to have found work. So I'd say all and all it's going pretty good. I keep my grades up and that's what matters most. I heard about you and Mona. Sorry it didn't work out."

"Ah well, as it turns out, I don't think we suited one another."

"Sometimes it's like that. I got you a present," Bree stated, reaching into the oversized bag that draped from her shoulder. She pulled out a ten-inch box, smartly gift wrapped in their high school colors.

"What is this?" Troy asked, setting down the beer so he could take the package. He tested the weight. It was heavy, weighing at least a pound.

"Open it and see for yourself. I hope you like it. It's not new or anything. I actually found it at a little used shop in San Sebastian in between my classes."

Troy didn't need a lot of encouragement. The idea that she'd taken the time to buy him anything at all had him ripping off the pretty blue and orange paper. When he got down to the cardboard he eagerly tore into the tape. "It's an engraver tool."

"I saw it and thought you could use it to decorate your jewelry boxes. Abby Bonner showed me the one you made for her. It's a beautiful design, both top and sides."

He didn't want to tell her he'd given up the silly notion of making them. Instead he draped an arm around her shoulder. "This is the nicest present anyone's ever given me. Thank you," he managed to fluster out.

"I doubt that. But I wanted to get you something you could use in your work. I knew you already had your own tools and what you didn't have, you'd surely have access to while working for Logan."

"This is awesome. I don't have one. But you know what? I'll make you a jewelry box first chance I get, put something special on the lid, too. You always did like red flowers, California poppies, as I recall."

Bree blushed. "That would be great. You remembered that?"

He smiled. "Of course. You used to wear a white dress with them all over it."

Her mouth dropped open. "I did. I wore that to school a lot."

"It set off your hair."

"You always did say sweet things like that. I had a crush on you in junior high."

Before Troy could pursue that, his boss walked up, slapped him on the back.

"It's the birthday boy. You should see the cake Jordan baked. It's a work of art," Logan stated, clearly oblivious to the fact he'd interrupted something.

"One of these days I'm going to have enough money to treat myself to a couple of nights at the B & B and have Jordan cook for me," Bree tossed out with a sigh. "That may sound silly but—"

"No, it doesn't," Troy said. "Not at all. You deserve a day off, a weekend would be better. You work too much."

"Not much else I can do about that," Bree said. "Dad left us that old house and it needs fixing up. Zach and I keep meaning to paint the thing but neither one of us have the time. Zach spends his days looking for work. That reminds me, I see Brent's here. I need to thank him for throwing some work Zach's way while those archaeologists are in town."

"If all goes as planned, tell Zach to come see me about more permanent work at the school project we're planning," Logan reiterated. "You heard about bringing the school back to life, right?"

"I did. It's exciting."

"We can use all the local hands we can get," Troy added. "It'll be a huge undertaking. But we're up for it. Zach would be an asset to the crew."

Bree grabbed Troy's arm in delight. "That's wonderful. Save a spot for him, will you? I can't wait to tell him. Oh look, here's Brent now. I have to run, Troy. Now that you're legal, you stop by McCready's and I'll buy you a beer."

After she'd gone over to Brent, Logan turned to Troy. "That woman is interested in you."

"You think so?"

"I know so. If I were you I wouldn't waste a minute heading into McCready's first chance I got. You're crazy if you don't ask her out. Take her somewhere nice, like Perry's place maybe."

"You know I can't afford that."

"Okay. How about this? You make the date and bring her to your place for a nice candlelit dinner, dinner you've fixed yourself. Women love a man who cooks. Works every time. I'll be damned if I know why. Your studio is the perfect little garret with a cozy atmosphere. It has a stove that works and a great view from the bluffs. What more could a single guy want?"

"When did you get to be such a romantic?" Troy wondered.

"Since I met and fell in love with the right woman. You fall in love with the right woman you'll want nothing but the best for her. Trust me on that."

Brent's eyes drifted from the conversation with Bree Dennison to River's arrival at the front door. Since the last time he'd seen her that afternoon she'd taken the time to go back to the B & B to French-braid her long mane. The stylish knot gave her a sophisticated air. She'd changed into a simple black skater dress. The full swingy skirt flared out whenever she moved and the wrap slung over her shoulders hung in a soft creamy shimmer for contrast.

The outfit had him wanting to take her back to his place to get her naked—the sooner the better. Good thing he'd gotten Paul Bonner to replace him at the dig site and no longer had to bother with the swing shift.

River spotted Brent from across the room and sent him a wave. There was something about the pair of dress pants and button-down shirt he wore that had her juices revving.

Over the din and the loud music River sidled up to him and asked, "Read any good books lately?"

Brent started laughing. "Just the one about archaeologists. But it never mentioned they were so hot."

"Aww, aren't you sweet." She linked her arm through his, ran a finger down his cheek, whispered in his ear, "Maybe we should pay our respects to the birthday boy, give him his present and start a few fireworks of our own. I can get a lot hotter."

"I'm already picturing that in my head. That can definitely be arranged. But first I promised Troy a twenty-first birthday party he wouldn't forget." He took her hand, led her over to where Bree had gone back to talk to Troy.

"Then let's not disappoint him. Where's the present you and the town got him?"

"Around the corner. The trick is getting him outside for the big reveal."

"Hmm. Leave that to me. He'll never see it coming if it comes from a virtual stranger." River shifted gears and focused her attention on Troy, holding out her hand. "Hi Troy, I'm River Amandez, the archaeologist over at the dig. Brent tells me you're an excellent carpenter. I was wondering what you'd charge to build us a scaffold, you know, across the street at the dig site."

"You need a scaffold? Built on the beach? What for?" Troy asked with a curious look on his face.

"We need a sort of platform for…"River started forming a shape with her hands, a little perplexed at how to continue. But she quickly recovered to go on with the diversion. "We need it built up to fully excavate the side of the cliff." She actually managed to keep a straight face. "How about looking at the site now and telling me how long it would take to construct it sturdy enough on the soft ground?"

"But it's dark outside," Troy pointed out. And he'd have to leave his party.

"It is," River said with a sly grin. "But we need to move on this ASAP while the weather holds. It's kind of an emergency and you'd really be helping us out if you could give us your expertise along with an estimate."

"Sure. I guess so," Troy said in final agreement not wanting to be rude but clearly not happy about it.

River led Troy out the door and down the steps onto the sidewalk. She saw Logan pull up between two cars driving a gleaming white GMC Canyon pickup right on schedule. From behind her, she realized the party crowd had moved outside with them to the curb to take in Troy's reaction.

They didn't have to wait long. Brent put a hand on Troy's shoulder and held up a key ring with a spare set of keys dangling from it.

At that moment the partygoers all yelled out in unison, "Surprise! Happy twenty-first birthday, Troy!"

Troy's mouth fell open. "What's going on?"

"Meet your new ride, courtesy of the entire town. But I have to say it was Jordan, Hayden, Kinsey, and Keegan who got it all started. All of us kicked in a few bucks after that and before we knew what was happening we had enough to get you a replacement for that sad road menace you commonly refer to as a truck."

"But this is brand-new."

"Not quite. One of those returned leases where the person didn't like the color."

"I love the color," Troy said, rubbing his hand over the waxed sheen of the metal, elated at the idea he had a gorgeous new truck.

"Good," Brent said. "Because it's all yours."

Later back at Brent's house, he and River stretched out in front of a cozy fire.

"The look on Troy's face was priceless."

"He must be a super nice guy to leave his own birthday party thinking he was going across the street to help me measure for a scaffold in the dark."

"Where'd you come up with that idea anyway? For a minute there I didn't think he'd buy it."

"It just came to me. It got him outside, didn't it?"

"Hell, I'd've followed you outside," he said, nibbling his way down her throat. "Right now, I'm pretty sure I'd follow you anywhere."

"That's because you want to get me naked."

"Oh yeah. And then I'd do this." He began to move his fingers back and forth between her legs through the fabric of her panties.

In response, she lifted her hips, so he could slide the tiny scrap of silk off from under her dress. "Then you'd better show me whatcha got, Sheriff."

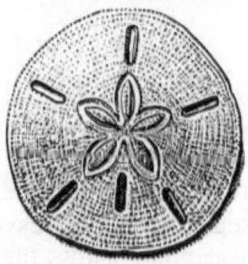

Chapter Twenty

River couldn't have ordered up more perfect weather for the dig if she'd tried. November's days were warm and sunny, the nights cool and crisp.

Confined in the narrow hole, River worked the opposite square of the grid from where Walker and Sandra rubbed elbows. Sitting back on her heels, she beaded the sweat that formed on her brow. She glanced over at the interns as they went through the same steps she did—first brushing the top layer of dirt before using the dental pick to breach another level. Each took turns dumping their take into a bucket for sieving.

Up top, Julian and Laura manned the sieve. No fragment or clod of dirt got past the screen without one of them inspecting the contents.

The process was painstakingly slow and methodical. It required patience and a strong back along with a will to sift through mud to find treasures, like the pipe she'd located in the shape of a fish. River studied the blue and brown quartz piece inlaid with shell beads before taking it into her hands. She ran her fingers over the stone.

The vision came fast and vivid. Planked canoes lined the beach. She saw the village dotted with its dome-shaped huts and their thatched willow roofs.

While plentiful pots of acorn soup simmered over the fire, their main course tonight would be the clams and abalone they'd caught that day.

She watched as the tribe danced in celebration, the occasion, the fall harvest. While the fire blazed and sparks flew up and into the night, River could tell the hierarchy of the tribe by their dress.

The elders, both men and women, had wrapped themselves in fur capes and wore headdresses full of colorful bird feathers. They greeted visitors from neighboring tribes with gifts of turtle shells, carved driftwood, and beads. Their decorated heads bobbed in rhythm as the shamans circled together in song. Like rock stars of their day, their faces and bare chests painted, the medicine men took center stage. They took turns playing their flutes made from deer bones and rattling their clapper sticks for the crowd, the crafters and workers. The male members of the tribe wore narrow slits of bearskin no wider than tool belts around their waists. They one-stepped to the music. The women did the same in their milkweed skirts short as aprons. They'd draped multiple strands of ornate beads around their necks down to their bare breasts. Everyone participated, keeping time to the beat. The throng listened. They cheered. They danced in perfect cadence, stepping to the tune as if moving over hot coals. This fall evening, the village would party well into the early dawn hours.

As River's vision cleared, she lifted her head to take in the ocean breeze—and was surprised to see Brent staring at her from above the hole.

"Where were you just now?"

"Your ancestors were party animals," she said with a wink. But then she tilted her head to study his face and realized he had something on his mind other than his own blood ties. "What's up?"

"The FBI has a new lead."

"What? A lead to Luke?" River dropped the trowel she held. She scrambled up the ladder to look at his face, to stare into his eyes to make sure what she'd heard was real.

He held out a piece of paper for her to look at. "The agent in charge, Matt Swain, faxed me this photo. He wants you to take a look at it and tell him if it looks anything like your ex."

She snatched the picture out of his hand, studied the grainy snapshot. But she was disillusioned to see a man sporting a full beard. "If that's him, he's gone all backwoodsman, which isn't like Wes at all. Unless it's to go skiing and stay in a comfy lodge, he rarely knew how to rough it. He used to give me such a hard time about living out of a tent during a dig. Wes doesn't like to get his hands dirty. This guy looks too…outdoorsy."

"But could it be him? Focus on the eyes or the nose and not the beard."

"Honestly, I don't know. The eyes do look somewhat similar but I've never seen Wes in a beard before. I've never seen him so disheveled. He was always such an immaculate dresser, so put together. This guy looks like the Unabomber."

"River, the man fits Wes's general description, same height and weight. Plus, he had a toddler with him. You said Wes liked to ski. This photo was taken about thirty miles from Jackson Hole, Wyoming, in a little town called Aurora. Aurora's about the size of Pelican Pointe so a stranger can stick out there. Not like Jackson Hole where the tourists generally land. But get this, the ski resorts got a boon a few days ago—their first heavy snowfall of the season."

Chills ran down her arms despite the warmth of the day. Hope soared in her chest so much that she had to sit down where she stood on the dune. Even if it was a long shot, she took a second look, then a third. "It resembles what I remember Wes looking like. But the beard is throwing me."

"To me, the man looks like he's trying to pass for a ski bum."

River grabbed Brent's arm. "Oh my God, you're right. He does, doesn't he?" She so wanted to believe it. "Didn't you say something at your parents' house that night about seeing a man with a beard? I know you did. This certainly doesn't look like his other mug shot though, like the one they took back in New Mexico. It looks like someone snapped it with a camera phone."

"That's exactly what they did. This guy checked into a motel in Aurora, has been seen around town with a little boy he often leaves alone in the motel while he goes across the street to the liquor store."

"Oh no. About how old is the baby?"

"Between two and three."

"Tell me everything Agent Swain told you."

"I told you the FBI sent out alerts using Patton's New Mexico mug shot. That included faxes that went to every police department across the country. This guy's calling himself Steven Patterson. Yesterday morning, he comes into the local dive with the kid, orders breakfast, hits on the married waitress there. Before the child finished his meal, the waitress's husband, who happens to be a cop, comes through the door, catches this Patterson flirting with his wife. The cop is upset. Words are exchanged."

"Then please tell me this guy is sitting in jail."

"Sorry, no, at least not yet. Mainly because before things got out of hand with the cop, Patterson paid his bill in cash and got out of there fast. Since the cop recognizes him as the newcomer in town, he decides to keep an eye on him. In the span of a few hours, the cop tails him back to the motel and snaps this photo with his cell phone of Patterson coming out of the convenience store across the street from the lodge. Later that night, the patrolman starts his shift. He sees the FBI alert, sees the mug shot of Wes Patton and immediately thinks it looks like this Patterson guy. He's keeping the man under surveillance until he hears back from the FBI."

Her heart leapt with faith and hope and the anticipation of it all after such a long time. "Look, I need to catch a flight out of Santa Cruz to Jackson Hole tonight? Or maybe I could drive to San Jose to catch a flight from there? I better check schedules on the Internet and call

Emilio, tell him I'm taking time off. I have lots of vacation built up and I intend to use it."

When she tried to dash past him to get to her iPhone, Brent snaked his arm around her waist. "Baby, is it Wes in the photo? Yes or no?"

She sighed. "I'm not one hundred percent certain but it looks enough like Wes to warrant checking out."

"That's all I needed to know. I'll tell Swain you made a positive ID." Before she could protest, he added, "Swain will handle it."

Her shoulders sagged. "I know what you're going to say. I shouldn't get my hopes up."

"On the contrary, I think this time it is Wes, which means it's the best lead you've had in over two years."

"That's true. If I flew out tonight though, I could be there to ID him and be there to pick up Luke."

Brent kissed her forehead. "Honey, it doesn't work that way. If it's Wes the local cops will detain him, count on it. They'll fingerprint him so there is no mistake. They'll take Luke into protective custody."

He eyed the concern in her eyes and added, "A social worker will be assigned to him for the duration until he gets to you. He'll be okay."

She shook her head. "I can't just sit here, Brent. During all that time, my baby could be with his mother. After all these years of missing him he could be with me right now. He'll be scared with a stranger. He's just a baby, Brent." She rubbed her forehead where a headache began to pound along with stark realization. "But then I'm a stranger, too. Aren't I? He doesn't know his own mommy." The bluster went out of her and she plopped into one of the canvas chairs stationed at the sieve.

Brent sighed and reached for her hand. "Think of it this way. This is nothing more than a tough couple of days ahead until you get to the goal then everything will even out. And it will. Remember that. Swain will notify the nearest FBI field office. They'll take care of IDing the boy and let us know as soon as they have a positive match.

What I'm going to tell you is this. Be patient. I know it's tough and not what you want to hear right now. But let the FBI do their job. The sooner you do that, the sooner you'll get the results you want."

Chapter Twenty-One

Over the next several hours, River did her best to focus on her work and not on the sighting nine-hundred miles away. But it was damned near impossible not hearing back from the FBI and maintaining any kind of center.

When time passed without a word, she convinced herself that the only reason it was taking them so long to call back was that the sighting obviously hadn't been genuine. It hadn't been Wes or Luke and the authorities had neglected to contact her because of it. That's the only thing that made sense.

She was getting her hopes up for nothing.

Once darkness fell and the work came to a stop, her optimism and faith began to dwindle for real. A considerable chunk of doubt crept in. It began to inch its way along her spine wanting to stagnate there. She fought the feeling of giving up and tried to mask it.

But it didn't take long for Brent to sense her temptation to plunge into gloom and doom. He decided he had to do something to offset it.

"Let's play a 'what if' game," he suggested. "What if we get the call over dinner? What if they say they're bringing Luke here? You'll have to shop for a car seat." He bumped her shoulder in a playful gesture at the prospect of going on a spending spree specifically for her son. "Fortunately, you can do that online, you know."

River threw him a grin. "I wouldn't even know the first thing about what kind to get although I do still have the one I used when he was a baby packed away with my stuff in Santa Fe."

"He's no doubt outgrown that one. And it's for that very reason you should grill a seasoned mom like Jordan Harris, get the lowdown on the needs of a two-year-old. If anyone knows about toddlers, it would be Jordan. I'd suggest sitting down with Hayden but Nate isn't even walking yet." Brent also thought the whole idea of chatting with another mom might keep her spirits from drooping into despair at least over the next twenty-four hours.

Her jaw dropped open. "That's brilliant. I think I know how you got to be sheriff at such a young age. That's a great idea. Although you do know I haven't opened up to Jordan about Luke yet. It isn't that I don't want to but I just haven't had the chance. It's tough for me to talk about it and talking to her will mean I have to come clean about all of it."

"Maybe it's time you did though. If not Jordan, how about Hayden?"

"What if I'm greedy? I could use some insight from both about everything kid-related. And the plus side is that Hayden already knows the situation."

Brent took out his cell phone. "Then it's time for a get-together of like-minded moms. How about we needle our way into an invite for supper at Jordan's?"

Two hours later the two of them were still huddled around the kitchen table at Promise Cove with Nick and Jordan and Ethan and Hayden while the kids played on the floor.

It was Brent who took them through the last two years and how in a matter of days, River might possibly be coming back to the B & B with her son.

"That's amazing," Jordan said, wiping tears away. She glanced at Nick. "We knew there was something in your past but had no idea it was anything as serious as having your child taken from you—by your own ex."

Hayden made a similar swipe at her eyes. "I'm so happy for you," she said, removing a Kleenex from her handbag.

"You realize there's a chance I'm jumping to conclusions. What if I'm making a giant leap over a false lead again? After all, there's been no confirmation from the FBI," River pointed out. "I admit I'm getting excited without any proof and Brent's letting me."

Brent rolled his eyes and grinned. "That's because the photo of the man is a dead ringer for Wes Patton." He removed two pictures from his jacket pocket, the mug shot he handed to Ethan, the one from Wyoming he gave to Nick to let each man study a photograph and decide for himself. "Notice the man's eyes and the nose. It isn't just me, is it? That's the same guy as in the New Mexico mug shot."

Nick took the photo from Ethan, stared at the two images side by side. "I see the resemblance. The beard doesn't change the fact that the eyes are the same and the bridge of the nose." Nick handed the copies to Ethan for him to scrutinize.

The former deputy considered the faces of the two men in question and acknowledged, "I'd say you've got yourself a match there, River. Steven Patterson and Wes Patton are one and the same person."

River's heart swelled again. "You really think so?"

Ethan exchanged a glance with Brent before telling her, "Yep. And I think you're reluctant to see the similarity because you've been disappointed in the past and don't want to go through that feeling of sadness again."

"And getting this lead has me anticipating all kinds of possibilities, building up dreams I'd put on hold. Right now, I'm hoping I could get him back before Thanksgiving. That's possible, right?" She sent Brent a pleading look.

He entwined his fingers with hers. "Absolutely."

"If that happens, I need mom-help. Luke was a baby, just six months old, the last time I saw him. He's grown so much," River explained, dabbing at her eyes.

"He used to love his stuffed bear, the one we nicknamed, Mr. Fuzzy Bear, which he had with him the day Wes snatched him out of daycare. Luke used to love listening to *Catch the Moon*. But I always sung *Puff, the Magic Dragon* to him whenever I put him down in his crib. My mother used to sing it to me so… Are those songs even age appropriate now? What about clothes? He won't have anything to wear. Should I pick up outfits for him? I don't know what size to get. I don't even know what he eats." Her shoulders drooped.

"All that will come, River. Trust me, toddlers will let you know when they don't like what's on their plates," Jordan assured her. "You either fix them something else or you play stubborn mom."

"Stubborn mom doesn't usually work for me," Hayden admitted. "And since Nate takes after his father…" she added with a glint in her eye for her husband. "Ethan wrote the book on stubborn. That gets you nothing but cranky pants most of the time. I've found it's better to discover what they love and keep it well stocked. FYI, that works for husbands, too," she tossed in.

"As I recall, Hutton and Scott loved that *Catch the Moon* song," Nick said. "Over and over we played that thing. Still do sometimes so I'd say both are age appropriate."

"*Puff, the Magic Dragon*, huh?" Brent's lips curved up. "I think you should plan on singing that to him again at the first opportunity," he suggested.

"When you're ready, we'll set him up in another room of his own right here," Jordan offered. "You take your time settling in with him. There's no rush. Don't you dare worry about the added expense either, Nick and I won't hear of it."

"Thanks. You guys have been wonderful to me," River said. "If this actually happens and I get Luke back, I think

I'll keep him in my room at first though. In fact, I'll probably stay up all night staring at him making sure it's all real."

Brent squeezed her fingers again. He wanted to prepare her as much as he could for what would take place after she got him here. If it was anything like what he'd seen before, she needed a little heads up to what was coming. "It's real all right. But I imagine the social worker will hang around him for a few days to make sure Luke adjusts."

"She will? I hadn't considered that."

"Most people don't. But that's usually standard procedure with the return of a child, especially in this case when one's so young and—"

"The authorities know he isn't familiar with his mother," River interrupted. "They'll want to make sure he's okay and not just drop him off. I understand that." It hurt but she did see the logic in it.

"When it's been years—like this—they'll want to report to CPS that the child is adjusting well enough in stages. Have you thought about when you'll go back to Santa Fe?" Brent hadn't really wanted to broach the subject but felt he needed to get a better picture so he could prepare himself for the reality of her heading home. But the look on River's face clearly said she hadn't even considered the possibility of leaving yet.

Startled at the question, she said, "One step at a time. I don't want to jerk my baby around right away and put him on another flight so soon after I get to hold him, at least not until we're on firmer ground. What do you think?" She looked around the room for encouragement.

"I'd say that's probably a good idea," Jordan ventured. "You want to give him some stability while at the same time show the social worker you're willing to do whatever it takes to put Luke's concerns first."

"It's better if he settles in with you rather than picking up and changing the scenery right away," Ethan pointed out.

Nick nodded in agreement. "Give him some time to bond with you before a change of scenery."

"My thoughts exactly." But then she turned to Brent. "You think that's the right thing to do, don't you?"

"That's a loaded question since I'm not all that ready for you to leave Pelican Pointe. I'm just being honest."

She grinned and put her free hand over her heart. "I appreciate it. Since I'm not ready to leave just yet, I'd say you guys are in for an interesting few days if this thing really happens. I just wish they'd call and let me know something…anything…one way or the other."

"Don't forget the media blitz you're in for," Brent tossed out, glancing at his brother and then at Nick. "Be prepared. I promise to do what I can to keep the reporters at bay. But any time word gets out that a child's been found safe after a custodial abduction's lasted for such a long time, they'll swarm for sure so they get that 'feel good' story they love so much."

"We'll brace for the onslaught," Nick assured both of them, shaking his head. "You know they'll come from all over, too. They're bound to show up at the airport."

Brent looked at River and took out his cell phone to check it, make sure it was on. "Don't worry. When the time comes I'll take care of that, too."

River scrubbed her hands down her face, a little overwhelmed with it all. "I'm getting ahead of myself. We're all getting ahead of ourselves. I need to step back and take a wait-and-see attitude." For the tenth time in an hour, she glanced at her iPhone which refused to ring.

Sensing they were both waiting for news, Hayden did her best to reassure them. "Nonsense. You've spent years biding your time. Now you're hoping for the return of your son. There's a huge difference. You aren't jumping to a conclusion. You're looking for a positive result and making plans accordingly."

"I'm with Hayden on this," Jordan echoed. "You prepare for the positive outcome and go with it until someone tells you different. At this point the goal is getting him back before the holidays. Thinking negatively right now doesn't enter into the equation."

That confident outlook allowed Brent to talk her back to his place for a bout of lovemaking to keep her relaxed. Afterward though, she listened as he snored softly beside her. A restlessness she couldn't overcome snuck in and despite her best effort she couldn't get it to leave. She got a lump in her throat thinking about the little boy out there she might not be able to identify. And knew he wouldn't recognize her.

Tears welled up. Disheartened at not getting that one phone call, sleep wouldn't come.

That's why when the phone rang on Brent's side of the bed at two-ten, it caused her to sit all the way upright by the second ring. Impatient, she watched as Brent fumbled around the nightstand for the switch on the lamp.

"It has to be news about Luke," River exclaimed. "But it's never good news when they call this time of night, is it?"

Experience might've had him feeling that way too but despite what his brain said, he squeezed her hand and reminded her, "We're keeping the upbeat attitude going here, remember?" He picked up the receiver and said, "Hello."

"Sheriff Cody, this is Matt Swain. I have news about the Patton boy. We followed up on the lead outside Aurora, Wyoming. Using the age-progression photo of Luke Patton as a baby we made what we think is a positive ID. But you should know, earlier this evening there was an incident outside a motel there involving the father or the man calling himself Patterson."

"That's why you didn't call back until now."

"That's correct."

"What's happening?" River demanded. Beside him she put her ear next to the receiver so she could hear. "Did they find my son?"

Brent repeated Swain's news, but held up a hand when he sensed the agent had more to say. "What are you not telling me, Swain? What was the incident?"

"First, Patterson's fingerprints matched to Wes Patton's."

"Then you have Patton in custody?"

"Just let me finish. When the local police showed up at the motel to question Patterson, there was a confrontation. Patton came out of the room pointing a weapon at the officers. He refused to put down his gun."

"Oh my God, is the baby all right?" River interjected.

Brent threw River a look and asked, "Before you go on, is the boy okay?"

"The child is fine, but his father... Patton opened fire on a police officer, Sheriff, the same patrolman he had encountered earlier that day at the diner. Approximately seven hours ago Wes Patton was shot. He died in surgery about three hours later."

"Is Luke all right? What about Luke? When can I see my son? I want to go to him," River demanded.

Agent Swain overheard River in the background and said into Brent's ear, "There has to be a positive ID before the boy goes anywhere. You have to explain that to her and the next steps involved in that process. I need DNA for confirmation before the boy comes home."

River had heard enough. She jerked the receiver out of Brent's hand. "Now you listen to me, Agent Swain. When this first happened two years ago I submitted DNA that I was told at the time would be kept on file for this very purpose. I've been screwed over by Wes, the local cops in Santa Fe in league with his parents, and I'll be damned if you and the FBI will do it to me now. I want my son! Do you hear me? Do you understand? My DNA is on file at the Santa Fe Police Department. It was supposed to be shipped to the FBI. But it's probably still sitting there in storage somewhere. You call them. And you should know I've already retained a lawyer and I'm not afraid to take it to the next level in order to get my son back. Now, I want you to either bring him here or I'm getting on the first plane to Jackson Hole or the nearest city where I can rent a car and go to him. Do you understand?"

She was shaking so badly that when she dropped the receiver, Brent picked it up and said to Swain, "Did you get all that? Because if you didn't I'm bringing her to Wyoming myself one way or another before daylight. She's been through enough."

"I got it. Let me check on where we stand with the DNA. No one told me we had the mother's. I'll call you back."

The click in Brent's ear ended the conversation.

Brent wrapped his arms around her shoulders and let her get rid of two years of pent-up anger. After a few minutes though, she jumped out of bed, pulling on jeans and a shirt.

"I'm flying there anyway. I don't care what Swain says."

"River, you can't do that. They won't let you get anywhere near the child until they confirm you are indeed the boy's mother. You fly there and you'll only piss them off. Trust me on that. You don't want delays in getting the results back at this stage, do you?"

"Of course not." She dropped back down on the bed and covered her face with her hands. "I can't stand this. I want this over and done with. I want Luke."

He drew her close and she curled into him. "Yes, you can stand this. After everything you've been through, this is the last hurdle, the last leg of the marathon. Staying strong like you've done for the past two years is what it'll take now. It's about to go your way. It's about to end, River. I wish you would reconsider and move in here. There's no pressure in the offer. Since you and Luke will need time to bond, I'm happy to bunk with Ethan and Hayden or I'll switch out and stay in your room at the B & B. There's more room for you here."

"That's very generous of you, Brent. And while I appreciate it, I won't be a party to kicking you out of your own home. The ideal situation would be to take him home. But I've decided I'm not taking him anywhere around Wes's family, certainly not back to Santa Fe where I've been duped from the onset. The Patton family is in for a fight if they want visitation rights to see their grandson. If it's proved they were a party to stealing Luke they won't get anywhere near him."

"I think that's wise. All this time, they more than likely have been visiting Luke off and on since Wes was on the run anyway."

"Thinking about that just makes me sick to my stomach so I won't. Think about it, that is. I'm not even certain they'll bother with Luke. It was more all about Wes than you might realize. Now that he's gone…"

"I don't know the Pattons, but if they helped Wes keep Luke a secret, they could be charged with obstruction, same goes for Ortega."

"I just want my son back. Prosecuting the Pattons will be up to the authorities. I'll call Nick and Jordan first thing in the morning and get them to make up the room next to mine, bring in a child's bed or a crib. God, I don't even know what he sleeps in."

"I doubt he's been sleeping in a crib living out of motels along the way to Wyoming," Brent pointed out.

"That's probably true. But it's a temporary fix, right? Just until I decide my next step. I don't know what kind of situations I'll be dealing with or for how long. My baby won't know me, Brent. There's a distinct possibility bonding with him will be a problem. Emilio's already agreed to me taking some time off to deal with that whenever I got Luke back. In the meantime, Julian will take over the dig."

Brent rubbed her shoulders, "I'll keep the offer to move in here open, River. If you should change your mind…"

She picked up his hand, kissed the palm, rubbed it against her cheek. "I'll have to assess Luke before I move him around. More than anything I want stability for him, a home. I want to spend time with him doing things most moms take for granted. I know one thing. I won't be going back to work anytime soon. I have some money saved. I had planned to use it to sue that detective. But now...the money will be much better spent staying with Luke— wherever that is."

"You take whatever time you need with your son. You've earned it. He's been moved around enough. It's time you experienced the same home cooking right here that worked so well for Wes in Santa Fe."

Her forehead creased into lines. "What do you mean?"

"Think about it. You've made friends here, River. There are people who'll be in your corner. You don't have to head back to Santa Fe to rally support. It's right here in California, in Pelican Pointe. We even have our own social worker assigned to the area. I can vouch for the fact that Carla Vargas is a fair-minded woman when it comes to her cases. It's time something or someone worked in your favor. Don't you think?"

Over the next agonizing hours there was no way River could get back to sleep. Instead, she crawled out of bed— grabbed her cell phone just in case—and headed out to make a pot of coffee, leaving Brent sleeping peacefully curled into his pillow.

Standing in his tidy but dated kitchen, looking out into the darkness, she measured beans for the grinder and mulled Brent's words around in her head.

While she waited for the phone call that would hopefully set her life in a brand-new direction, she considered the little town she'd come to love.

The little coastal community had a way about it. She liked the people, the atmosphere, spending time on the dunes working next to the ocean. But she had to admit with all of that, the main draw was her deep feelings for Brent. Thankfully, he didn't have a clue how she felt, unless of course his father and brother had blabbed. She should have sworn them to secrecy and kept that little nugget to herself.

But it was too late now.

Was he right though? She couldn't argue with the prospect of experiencing a little home cooking of her own. She'd certainly made friends here. But was the bond with these people enough to warrant making a home here? Did she have that same connection with anyone other than her mother back in New Mexico?

"You know your mother is the last link you have to Santa Fe. She's the only one there who means anything to you," Scott said, breaking in on her thoughts.

River jumped at the voice. "Honestly, must you do that every single time you decide to have a conversation with someone? It's kinda creepy."

Scott smiled. "It's one of the codes we ghosts live by. I break the code I have to start carrying chains around. You don't want me looking like something out of Scrooge, do you?"

River started laughing. "Thanks. I needed that right now. Luke's coming back to me."

"I know."

"The waiting is awful."

"It's almost over for you, River. Hang in there. You might consider staying in Pelican Pointe. It might be the best thing for you and Luke."

"Even though Mom's there, Santa Fe poses a problem. I don't want to be around the Pattons."

"Don't make the decision because of that. Follow your heart, River."

"I did that once and look how that turned out."

"Don't do that. Don't turn away from what your heart wants this time because of a man like Wes. You know he isn't worth it."

Brent found her in that same contemplative state when he made his way into the kitchen.

While he filled a coffee cup, he noted her tired eyes, the bags underneath and the slump of her shoulders. Her overall body language told him she needed a good night's sleep. "You should come back to bed."

"No way can I close my eyes."

"What were you thinking just now?" he asked as he took the first soothing sip of caffeine.

"That the only thing for me in New Mexico is my mom. And these days she doesn't even know her own daughter."

"You could always move her closer."

"That's a thought. You didn't have to get up, Brent. You should crawl back into bed."

"I will if you will. You look like shit, River. Going without sleep won't change a thing. You get Luke back, you need to be on top of your game."

Because she knew that was true she said, "Then why are we standing here drinking coffee at four in the morning?"

Later that morning at seven-thirty, the phone rang a second time. It was River who reached across Brent's body to answer it. Noting the number on the display, she didn't hesitate or mince words. "I want my son, Swain."

"And you'll get him. The DNA was a match. Luke and the social worker will be on the first flight out to Santa Cruz. Meet us at the airport."

Chapter Twenty-Two

At two-thirty that afternoon Brent walked River into a special room inside the Santa Cruz airport that had been set up especially for the reunion, away from the prying eyes of the press.

During several subsequent phone calls, Swain had revealed to Brent that Luke had been hiding in the bathroom when Wes had inexplicably left the motel room to open the door and confront the police. Wes had walked outside pointing a Luger automatic at the band of police yelling at him to drop the weapon. When Wes had refused, one of the cops opened fire.

"I don't get it. Why would an anthropology professor make that kind of stand when he'd finally been caught with his son? It makes no sense," River pointed out.

"None of this makes any sense at all since Wes wasn't even present at Luke's birth and hadn't bonded in the first six months of his life. Why would he risk getting shot like that when all he had to do was give himself up?" Brent asked, clearly perplexed by the turn of events.

"It's weird, I'll grant you that. Why was he armed at all? Who was he planning to shoot?" Chill bumps crawled up River's arms. "It makes me wonder… You don't suppose…"

They locked eyes. "Don't even think like that. Luke is safe and that's all that matters right now. Are you sure there wasn't something else in his past Wes wanted to keep secret, something he was hiding?"

"I have no idea. I'm just glad Luke wasn't hurt. Wonder if Wes put him in the bathroom or Luke went in there on his own?"

"We'll probably never know. But Luke obviously heard the gunshots. We're lucky he didn't witness the actual shooting," Brent told her.

"Thank God for that," River breathed out as she paced like a caged tiger inside the twelve-by-twelve enclosed space waiting for word that Luke's plane had touched down. "What's taking them so long?"

Brent decided she needed to get her mind off the wait. "I knew we shouldn't have arrived so early. You're gonna wear out a hole in the carpet before they walk through the door."

"I can't remember being this nervous before about anything. I'm shaking." She held out both hands for him to see. "I feel like I might have a heart attack or something before he even gets here."

Brent couldn't take it anymore from his seat in the comfy chair. He stood up, went to her, blocking her in stride by snaking his arm around her waist. He covered her mouth, kissing her until she took a calming breath.

"I needed that."

"I know you did."

At the knock on the door, they broke apart. River smoothed out her top, wiped her hands on her jeans. "Do I look okay?"

"You look beautiful," he said as he went to the door and threw it open.

The social worker turned out to be a fifty-something woman with stylish shoulder-length auburn hair who came in carrying a toddler. The little boy clutched a worn-out, brown, stuffed bear in a tight death grip. He wore a look of absolute uncertainty at what he didn't understand. His big brown eyes were huge as saucers.

Brent decided Luke was the spitting image of his mother. He knew that for certain because he'd stared enough at Wes's mug shot. With the child's bronze skin, Luke looked nothing like the man who'd kidnapped him.

Brent watched as River did her best not to rush over to the frightened child who obviously needed some reassurance that things were going to get a whole lot better.

"Go on," Brent finally whispered in her ear, nudging her toward the baby. "It'll be okay."

"He doesn't know me. I don't want to frighten him," River said with tears streaming down her face.

But the social worker surprised them both and took care of that. River heard her tell Luke, "Sweetie, do you remember what we did on the plane ride here?"

The little guy bobbed his head up and down. "But my mommy's dead. Daddy said so."

"No, sweetie, I showed you the photo of your mommy and what she looked like, remember that? While the plane flew here we looked at pictures of your mommy. And guess what? Mommy's here now to see her big boy. Look over there. Who is that? Is that your mommy? That's your mommy, Luke. Doesn't she look like the photo I showed you on the plane?"

The toddler's eyes got even bigger when they landed on River. Luke stuck his finger in his mouth, not sure how to answer. Confused, overwhelmed, Luke simply stared.

But the social worker persisted and went on, "Your mommy's missed you so very much. And she's right here now waiting for you. Do you want to say hi?"

He shook his head no.

Not to be dissuaded, River had a hard time getting her feet to move. Once she did though, she crossed to where the two of them stood. She tried for calm to get her thudding heart to slow to a natural rhythm so she could get one single word to come out. She went on instinct first, running her fingers through his thick dark hair. "Oh baby, Mommy's right here." She placed his small hand over her heart and cooed in her calmest voice, "It'll be okay now. It will all be okay."

She touched his cheek, rubbed his back up and down. When he didn't draw away she took that as a good sign. Keeping her words simple but not in baby-speak she added, "Luke, I'm so glad to see you. It's been so long. I've been looking for you for a very long time, waiting for you to come back to me."

She picked up Luke's other hand, held it to hers, palm to palm. Hoping to use what she had inside her to trigger some long buried memory—some sort of recognition from those early months she'd spent with him as an infant—she put all her energy into reconnecting. Eager to spark a sliver of awareness from the past, she said, "I'm your mommy, baby. Your mommy loves you and she never stopped looking for you, not once. She hoped you'd come back to her one day. And now you're here."

Another wave of inspiration hit her then. Softly, River began to sing the lyrics to *Puff, the Magic Dragon*. But then Luke broke in, "Why did you go 'way?"

A sob squeaked out of her throat. For a brief moment she locked eyes with Brent in a pleading way. "This is so difficult for him to understand."

"Sing to him again, River," Brent prodded.

River went through the refrain again from the beginning. When she got to the second verse, all of a sudden—as if finally deciding to trust this adult—Luke took his finger out of his mouth. He held up his hand to hers again, palm to palm. River saw father and son on the run. She saw turmoil. She saw Wes get frustrated at changing dirty diapers, losing his temper at the little boy when he wouldn't cooperate.

"My mommy."

At the words, River sucked in a breath. "Yes, baby, I'm your mommy." When he abruptly held out his arms for River, she made a sobbing sound from deep in her throat.

As soon as the social worker relinquished him into River's chest, River dropped down on the carpeted floor to her knees, wrapping up the baby. The last thing she ever wanted to do was scare him by crying uncontrollably so she gutted it out, bit her lip, and rocked him gently back and forth instead of bawling her eyes out.

"It's okay, baby. It will be okay now. Mommy's here now and she won't ever let anything bad happen to you."

"Will you sing me da song again?"

Her eyes filled with tears but she rested her head on Luke's and said, "You bet, sweetie. You bet I will. I'll sing it as many times as you want."

Luke fell asleep in his car seat on the ride from the airport to the B & B. River couldn't stop staring at the miracle in the backseat.

"Look at him," she said, glowing. "I feel like this is a dream, that I'll wake up any minute and he'll be gone again." Her eyes misted over. "I don't seem to be able to stop crying."

"It's an adjustment, both emotionally and physically for anyone, a rollercoaster ride for you in particular that yields a big-time gain in the long run. Who knew Ferguson's carried a car seat."

"It's a good one, too. I looked it up on my phone to check out the safety features before I bought it."

"Look, promise me something." Brent picked up her hand, squeezed the fingers. "Promise me, you'll give yourself some time and won't be so hard on yourself during these first couple of days with Luke."

"I'll try. I'm a mom again." She sighed and it filled the cab of the pickup. "My little guy is alive and well and he's all mine."

"It's amazing how he took to you right away. The social worker said she'd only seen it happen twice before but neither time had been after being away for two years and especially when a baby had been taken so young."

"Because of Luke's reaction to me she handed the case off to Carla Vargas. You were right. Carla is a jewel to have in my corner. Was it my imagination or did it look to you like Luke felt something when he touched my hand? A glimmer of memory from babyhood maybe?"

"You know the answer to that as well as I do."

"Okay, so our Native culture believes in that sort of thing happening from birth. We know our ancestors retold stories about the link a child makes in the womb."

"It's one of the more popular legends for a reason," Brent finished. "Maybe Luke remembered the song."

She glanced over and smiled. "I thought the same thing. Personally, I don't care how anyone explains it because even twenty-first-century research backs up the claim that newborns develop a memory of what they experience early on. The idea that a baby is anything but a blank canvas has been studied from a scientific angle."

About that time River spotted the news vans lined up on the roadway and the reporters waiting outside their vehicles for a chance to pounce even before the truck made the turn into Promise Cove. "Oh no."

Brent drove past the tenacious Tamara Davis and several others he recognized. They'd managed to dodge the press in Santa Cruz but it looked as though that would be impossible now.

"For goodness sakes, look at this mob," River groaned. "Don't people have better things to do than to stick a microphone and a camera into someone's face during what amounts to a very private moment?"

"I'll handle this," Brent assured her. He raised a hand to wave at Nick and Jordan who were standing on the front porch. "You take Luke into the house. Even though you've held one press conference, I'm used to dealing with these particular vultures on a regular basis. I recognize most of them. And I particularly want to get another shot at Tamara," he said with a grin.

She grinned back. "Be my guest."

By this time, Luke's head had popped up. River hopped down out of the truck and hustled to open the back door to get Luke out of his car seat. Still groggy from his nap, he blinked in River's direction, certainly not as wide-eyed as before.

River snatched up Mr. Fuzzy Bear and wiggled it in front of him. For a moment she thought he might pucker up and cry but when she picked him up, he simply rested his head on her shoulder, weary.

"That's my big boy," River said, patting him on the back. "Let's go inside and get you settled."

While River took care of Luke, Brent ambled down to the roadway wanting very much to take his time. He knew they were not supposed to cross over onto private property. Didn't mean they wouldn't but if they did, he'd arrest their asses. Once he reached the throng, he made sure he waited for the cameras to focus on him and not the scene unfolding behind him.

As expected, Tamara kicked things off, wasting no time getting to the heart of the matter. "I understand from the FBI the baby's father was shot and killed in a confrontation in Wyoming with local police."

Brent glowered in her direction. "I'm not here to take questions. But I will make a statement on behalf of the Amandez family."

"But the baby's name is Patton," Tamara insisted.

"Actually, Ms. Davis, you didn't do your homework this time around. Your facts are incorrect. Two years earlier, a Santa Fe judge gave sole custody of the child known as Luke, to his mother, River Amandez. During that court proceeding, the baby's surname was legally changed to the mother's last name, Amandez. At the time, the birth father, Wes Patton, didn't care enough about that event to bother showing up for the custody hearing nor did he do anything to protest the judge's ruling. For whatever reason, for whatever purpose, perhaps to get back at his ex-wife for a reason known only to him, Wes Patton abducted the child from his daycare facility and went on the run. We may never know why Patton did what he did. But it's over now and the family has a request. At this critical time for mother and child to reunite, the Amandez family asks that you respect their privacy and refrain from following them around. What was obviously a tragic event for Ms. Amandez at the time has now turned into a joyous return of her son. She'd like your cooperation in keeping it positive for the child by allowing both of them to have this time to heal. That's it guys. Now, I'm asking nicely for you to move along."

Having said what he'd come to say, Brent walked back up the driveway leaving Tamara with a scowl on her face. It was the closest thing to a public snit he'd seen in years. Let the audience deal with that side of her, Brent thought as he calmly walked back up to the house.

So the big, bad sheriff had a new girlfriend and the girlfriend had a little kid. It made Cody vulnerable, a new angle to consider, new targets. He wasn't as smart as he thought. There were ways to get to him. There had to be other options. It would take persistence and patience to find them.

But the resolve was there, deep within.

Inside the house, once Luke conquered his initial shyness, he discovered a toy box full of Legos and kids willing to show him how to put them together. Between Hutton and Scott, Luke wasn't shy about exploring their trucks and stuffed animals. When Luke didn't seem interested in the frilly assortment of dolls Hutton offered, she decided to force the issue on him by pushing it into his chest, almost knocking him down.

Although Luke didn't cry, in the way of kids, he did shove Hutton back.

And that's the scene Brent stepped into as the living room took on a noisy jumble where three kids tried out their boundaries and put the parents to the test. It reminded him what he'd missed out on over the years. Fatherhood had managed to slip through his fingers. Good thing he hadn't seriously considered it. But there were times a man wanted something and didn't even realize what it was until it happened right in front of him. This was one of those times.

"Hutton, that's no way to offer Luke your doll," Jordan chided her daughter. If he doesn't want to play with Barbie, there's no need shoving it at him."

"I wanted Luke to see how pretty she is," Hutton said in defense. "That's all."

"He sees that, just like Scott sees it sometimes and doesn't want to play with Barbie either. Okay?"

"'K." Eyeing a sympathetic male standing in the entryway, Hutton abandoned the incident with Luke and rushed up to Brent holding up her doll. "Hi. Um, wanna see my Mermaid Barbie?"

"Sure," Brent returned, leaning down to boost her up. "Wow, look at her shiny fins. She doesn't really get those fins wet, does she?"

Hutton shook her head. "I don't want her to get wet. Her sparkles might fall off."

"That's probably a good idea."

River watched the byplay between Brent and Hutton and how easily he adapted to the chaos of the room. Pretty impressive for a single guy, River decided. About that time Luke left the building blocks behind to wander over to where his mother stood. Nothing could have pleased her more. Brushing his hair off his face, she lifted him up onto her hip. "Luke, are you hungry?" She'd learned from the social worker that Luke loved peanut butter and strawberry jelly sandwiches and macaroni and cheese. Since he'd lived on those kinds of meals for months, she'd have to take it slow when it came to incorporating new foods into his diet. But for the time being, it gave her a place to start.

When Luke's head bobbed up and down in response, she walked over to Brent. "Fancy meeting you here. I see you have a pretty girl there. Look what I've got. I found a great big handsome boy who claims he's hungry."

"Luke looks like you," Hutton said from her perch in Brent's arms.

"She's right, he does," Brent agreed, looking at the little tyke River had bundled in her arms. "How would both of you like some pasta?"

"I like pasghetti," Hutton said.

"I wanna hotdog," Luke piped up.

"Then what do you say we go scrounge us up some grub," Brent offered, beaming at River the entire time.

"What do you say, Luke?"

"Hotdog," he repeated with a stubborn bent.

Brent laughed and rubbed a gentle hand over Luke's head. "No sense in arguing with a man who knows what he wants."

Chapter Twenty-Three

The city council couldn't swing getting the carnival dealer to set up any earlier than Thanksgiving weekend. So along with holiday preparations, most of the eager townspeople had to mix their festive plans with prepping and putting together vendor booths.

It was a major undertaking. The community church became a staging area where people could register for whatever craft they planned to offer. The Crawford sisters took care of arranging each table while Drea Jennings kept a chart as where each would be on Main Street.

But by six o'clock Wednesday night, workers began to head for home to get ready for their own celebration with family or friends.

At Promise Cove, Nick and Jordan welcomed a full house. Newcomers mingled with an assortment of ragtag people with no place else to go. Even though she'd been invited to the Cody house in Santa Cruz for tomorrow's Thanksgiving feast, tonight belonged to her crew. River stood at the island inside Jordan's kitchen beside Laura and Julian who were lending a hand at making cornbread stuffing.

While Luke and Brent sat on the floor erecting a tower with colorful blocks, River kept up a steady chatter on toddlers.

"He fell asleep last night next to me. It was wonderful." A lump formed in River's throat. At the sight of Luke and

Brent playing together, she sucked in a breath. "I didn't think this was possible. It just goes to show how Brent's involvement knowing exactly who to contact and how to get the word out turned this case completely around. If not for that one thing—" Her voice trailed off. Fighting back happy tears, she went on, "Scott was right."

River saw Julian and Laura both turn to stare at her.

"You actually talk to him?" Julian wanted to know. "Laura mentioned what's become the local legend."

"Yeah. I know it sounds crazy. But Scott has this way of being right so there's just no way to ignore it."

"Don't I know it," Cord said from the other side of the counter as he nibbled on chips and dip. "In my case, the guy refused to shut up. But look at me now. I'd say between Keegan and Scott, I got my life back on track, a life I never thought I'd have."

"All I know is that I owe Scott and Brent big time. Not only that, if not for that cop who thought Wes acted strange enough to keep an eye on, Wes would likely have gotten out of Dodge again and gone on the run."

"What will you tell Luke about his father?" Nick wanted to know as he set out more appetizers.

"The only thing I can," River said. "His father was a very flawed man."

Bright and early Saturday morning a little before eight a.m., a chilly overcast November day couldn't dampen the town's spirits as they kicked off the very first fundraiser for the elementary school project.

Brent and Ethan along with Cord and Logan had spent the morning closing off Main to Ocean Streets, putting up barricades, and setting out traffic cones directing where fairgoers should park.

While the town came alive, the men stood surveying the scene as people began to mill around the vendor tents, a mishmash of crafts and wares and services donated by its eager citizens willing to contribute to the cause.

This early, the scent of freshly brewed coffee blended with the smell of warm doughnuts fresh from Max Bingham's oven at the Diner. Other scents like fresh cinnamon rolls and bacon wafted from the food court, set up in the common area between the bank and Murphy's Market.

"These fairs keep getting more and more involved. One of the food sellers is a lady Keegan roped into making the trip from San Sebastian who makes the most delicious sandwiches using waffles," Cord commented. "She'll even throw turkey and cheese between two waffles if you want her to."

"Sounds a bit strange and something I might have to try since I haven't had breakfast yet," Brent moaned. He glanced around as pedestrian traffic coming down from Ocean Street picked up. "Just look at all the loyal residents involved in putting this thing together. And how many of the townspeople have booths this time around? They're adamant about supporting the renovation. Our grandmother would be proud of this."

"And they all showed up early just like they promised," Ethan added. "Not one of the volunteers wimped out. I don't think I've ever seen Pelican Pointe come together as a town like this before. Autumn would definitely be as proud as I am right now."

"When you guys started all this everyone certainly stepped up in a big way, more than I thought they would. Do you suppose their excitement will wane after the fourth or fifth fundraiser?" Brent wanted to know.

"Not if we mix things up, start off with the street fair now, hold an auction the first of the year after we get the holidays behind us, then go with a huge community sale at the church in March or so. Get the neighboring towns involved with as many people as possible," Logan declared. Turning to Brent, he added, "You've got a stake in this now, too."

"Me? How so? I don't have kids."

Logan rolled his eyes. "You're dating a woman with a kid," he pointed out.

"Who might end up putting down roots here if she has enough incentive to stay," Ethan tossed in. "I've yet to see a woman who doesn't put a good school at the top of her list when it comes to her kids."

"Think about it. Come time for the boy to go to school, the little guy will be attending the one *we* bring back from the ashes, so to speak," Logan said.

Ethan nodded in agreement. "Speaking of kids, sleep late now because when your twins get here, sleep becomes a fantasy," Ethan cracked. "Babies are a relationship-changer." He eyed his brother's face and noted the look of sheer terror he saw reflected there. "Don't worry. Luke is well past waking up every two hours to eat." Just for emphasis, he slapped Brent on the back.

It was a sobering thought, Brent realized, and more than a little scary. Was he ready to take on a ready-made family like that? How deep did his feelings for River really go anyway? When he realized Ethan was talking to him, he snapped back from those doubts.

"Any word yet from forensics about the DNA on that burger wrapper we found at the lighthouse?" Ethan asked. "Any hits in CODIS yet?"

"No hits in CODIS. But the DNA came back female. No surprise there," Brent replied. "We already figured what with the small footprints that might be the case."

"You mean the person trying to kill Brent is a woman?" Cord asked, cocking a brow.

"The person who made the bomb is female?" Logan repeated.

Brent rolled his eyes. "We don't know for certain the wrapper was even from our shooter. The wind could've blown it there."

"I suppose," Ethan said, scratching his head. "But what females have stood around up there on the cliffs eating a burger from a particular fast food chain?"

"Good point," Brent stated.

"So the one who shot at you on the beach is female? That's a little odd." But then Logan frowned remembering how crazy his first wife had been and added, "You get a pissed off female who's even slightly nuts and you have unpredictability in spades."

"You're telling me. You sound like you speak from experience."

"Oh believe me, I do. I was married to crazy. But then one day I woke up and found the good sense to divorce her ass. But not before she attacked me. You be careful out here, Brent. We'll try to have your back should you need it."

"Appreciate it," Brent uttered.

"But why would this woman have it in for you so bad that she'd resort to bomb-making? I mean that's extreme. She has to be linked in some way to your past," Cord reasoned.

Brent scratched his head a little embarrassed. "If she is, I'm not aware of it. I did my best to stay away from breakups that resulted in hard feelings."

Ethan sent Brent his best sarcastic grin. "Except for the newswoman."

"Yeah, Tamara was the exception."

"You sure about her?" Cord put in. "I mean some women refuse to let go of a grudge."

"I don't see Tamara putting together an explosive device," Brent returned. "She's too concerned about chipping a nail."

"Hayden is expecting huge crowds in town over the next two days. And look around you. So many people already we'll probably run out of parking places on the side streets before nine a.m. We're off to a great start, which means the turnout makes for a lot of strangers in town. We need to get the word out to—"

Brent didn't let him finish. "To what? We can't go around following every person we don't recognize who comes into Pelican Pointe this weekend. It isn't practical."

"I know, but it wouldn't hurt to keep a close watch out for anyone acting suspicious either. How are things going between River and Luke?"

"It's been a stellar three days. We plan to treat Luke to all of the rides as soon as she gets to town beginning with the carousel."

Ethan thumped his brother on the back. "Face it. You're in jeopardy of becoming domesticated, brother, just like the rest of us. How does it feel?"

"Remind me to put out a press release when I figure it all out."

River might've borrowed a stroller from Jordan but when it came to Luke's clothes, she'd insisted on new. She'd spent hours online ordering him jeans, pants, a string of T-shirts and sweat tops, a fleece-lined coat for higher altitudes, a hoodie, a jacket for chilly days like today, several pairs of pajamas with various patterns on them decorated with boy stuff like dogs or trains.

Even the supply of pull-ups she'd chosen had bright red cars on them. After ordering him three pairs of sneakers, she knew she'd gone slightly nuts in the clothes department. She knew he'd outgrow the stuff in a matter of months. But she didn't care. She hadn't shopped for her baby in two years so she'd enjoyed every minute making each selection and adding it to her cart.

Today she'd dressed her little guy in jeans and a long sleeve sweatshirt. She'd brought his jacket along in case the temperature dropped. Okay, she knew she might be obsessing over warm clothes, but wasn't she entitled? One glimpse at the child in the backseat, she decided whatever it took to keep him safe or warm from now on, she would do.

"You like your new clothes, don't you, Luke?"

He patted his chest and said with pride, "Like my bike shirt."

Behind the wheel, she grinned. His sweatshirt had a bicycle painted on it. "Jordan said we could use one of their bikes tomorrow to go for a ride. How would that be?"

He clapped his hands. "Bike ride. Hutton can come, too."

That confirmed her suspicions. She was sure her son had a little crush on Hutton. And now as she circled the block hunting down a parking place near Brent's house, she wondered if she could leave behind the kinds of friends she'd come to love here. People like Jordan and Hayden and Kinsey. River wasn't sure she could do it. They'd bonded over kid talk and various theories about potty training.

After the third time around, River finally spotted a place the Wagoneer would fit into. She eased it to a stop at the curb and hopped out.

As she unloaded the stroller out of the back, she spotted Brent heading their way. If she was honest, she'd missed spending her nights in his bed. But because she was a responsible mother again, lustful thoughts like that had to be shelved for now.

"How's it going?" Scanning the rear luggage area of the vehicle, Brent realized things had changed quite a bit. A slew of toddler gear had replaced all of River's archaeological tools she usually lugged around. One glance at Luke as she settled him into the roller thing and he realized the boy looked different—happier than the scene at the airport.

"We're ready for a ride on the carousel," River said.

"I think we can do a little better than that. According to the firsthand information I obtained by scouting the vendors this morning, one of the rides has race cars like a merry-go-round. How does that sound, Luke?"

Luke clapped his hands. "Race cars go fast!"

It had taken several days for Luke to warm up to Brent. But this morning it seemed as though the little boy knew he was in for a day of excitement and fun.

Once they reached the kiddie rides, Luke wasn't sure about all the other kids around. No doubt the idea of auto racing though sucked him in, as did the frog hopper and helicopter. Too much of a lure for the wide-eyed tot, Luke put aside the noise and the music and wanted to get out of the confinement of the stroller.

Brent recognized that Luke couldn't wait to climb aboard—anything—he just had to make a decision which one he wanted to ride first.

River unbuckled Luke, swung him up to her hip. She did her best to convince him that crawling into the red race car was a good idea. But then Brent put his big booted foot on the metal rim of the ride and stepped up. He held out his hands to Luke.

Hesitant for a good twenty seconds or so, Luke finally decided Brent was worth a chance if it got him into the ride.

But there was only room for two so when the merry-go-round started up River realized she'd have to watch from the ground. While her boy experienced his first lap around a track, River took out her cell phone to capture the moment.

She did the same thing at the carousel where they stood on either side of a huge brown palomino horse while Luke enjoyed his first "pony" ride.

Before noon, Luke had thrilled to riding frogs, dinosaurs, a ladybug, inside an airplane, a chopper, and a pirate ship.

"I'm starving," River admitted. "We need to get some food into Luke before he drops off for his nap."

"How about a waffle sandwich?"

"I wanna hotdog!" Luke said, making his choice clear.

"He really has this thing for hotdogs," River explained. "I'm not crazy about his food choice but…he does know what he wants."

"Nick told me Scott's stuck in a rut where he'll only eat macaroni and cheese."

"They get like that I suppose. This morning for breakfast all Luke wanted was peanut butter and jelly on his toast. I looked it up. He's a little young to be eating foods with peanuts in them but at least I know he isn't allergic. He seemed to have eaten it plenty of times before now."

"There's a lot to keep up with when kids are involved."

River smiled. "It's okay to run the other way, Brent. I wouldn't blame you if you did. I'm well aware adding a child into the mix is a lot to digest. We haven't known each other that long. We were dating and enjoying each other. That's all. We weren't picking out place settings. It's a lot to take on."

"I didn't mean that at all. I just meant this is very new to me."

River laughed. "This part of it is definitely new to me, too."

After Luke got his 'dog, they settled in at one of the tables to try the waffle sandwiches. "Who'd've thought to take waffles and slap ham and cheese in the middle."

"It actually tastes pretty good," Brent said, turning to Luke. "Wanna try a bite of waffle?" No one was more surprised when Luke reached out and took a bite.

"Well, look at that. Maybe we'll break through the hotdog barrier. I really hope we have time to browse through the booths."

"Absolutely. What else is on the agenda?"

"First, I thought I'd stop in and say hi to my crew, show off Luke." She glanced over as the boy's eyelids began to droop and his head dropped to his chin. "Even if it looks like he'll sleep through the visit."

"Has he mentioned you-know-who?"

"It's weird, Brent. He hasn't said a thing about his d-a-d, not since that first night when he asked and I told him his d-a-d-d-y got into trouble. That's the last time. I didn't know what else to say to him or how to handle it exactly."

"I may not know anything about kids but at his young age it's best to keep it simple. You did the right thing. Luke's way too young to understand any of this."

"On top of that, I'm trying to get him to settle in, to feel completely comfortable with me."

"From what I've seen, that's not a problem. Luke looks happy." When he noticed she was tapping the table with her fingers as if she wanted to add something, he prodded, "What else?"

"He has nightmares, wakes up frightened. When I asked him about it, he begged me not to leave him alone. It broke my heart. Why would Wes want to steal a baby he had no intentions of ever truly caring for?"

At that same moment, River noticed Brent's eyes look away at the question. "You know something, don't you?"

"Let's say I followed up on a few things with Swain."

"And?"

"In the two years he'd been on the run Wes had taken on a few personality traits that were beginning to set off alarms. The FBI found some interesting stuff in his gear."

"Like what?"

"For one, detailed papers written on conspiracy theories that would make the Unabomber proud."

"You're kidding? Wes? Are you sure we're talking about Professor Wes Patton? I thought you were going to say they found porn."

"They found plenty of that, too. But it seems among all the nude photos there was one underlying theme. The once revered teacher thought a shadow arm of the CIA was out to get him."

"What? Why on earth would the CIA be interested in Wes Patton?"

"It seems Wes started an online journal a month before he kidnapped Luke about the agency's spying on its private citizens. That's why he had to stay alert and keep on the move so often that they couldn't find him. Swain says that night at the motel Patton probably thought they'd finally caught up with him. The mother now claims she did her best to get him to settle down in one spot to no avail. Because of his belief that this branch of the CIA wanted him dead, Wes decided they would eventually come after his son. Instead of letting that happen, he went on the run with him. According to his mother she says that's why he abducted Luke in the first place. Hilda Patton believes her son exhibited signs of paranoid schizophrenia, which apparently runs in the family."

"So she helped him maintain his life on the run with her grandson and admitted it? Uh uh. That makes no sense to me. Still not buying it. First and foremost, I never saw Wes show any type of behavior that even resembled mental illness. Narcissistic? Absolutely, but not schizophrenic. And I'm having a hard time believing it as fact. Luke was never that high on Wes's list of priorities. And now she wants me to believe Wes snatched him out of daycare that day because he was mentally ill and concerned about his son? No way. Something else is at play. Did you check the porn angle?"

"River, the FBI found essays about shadow governments, listening devices, orbiting satellites spying on private citizens and the like in the trunk of his car. It seems Wes covered it all."

"Well, I have my own crazy theory. I think all that was just a cover so Wes could be the asshole I know him to be. By the way, I'd like to meet the police officer who got curious enough about Wes to follow him around and break this case wide open. You and that man are responsible for me getting Luke back. You, I can find ways to thank," she said with a wink. "The cop needs to know that what he did is highly appreciated. I'd like to thank him personally if that's possible."

Brent nodded. "I'll set it up where you can meet him."

"Thanks," she said as they both began to clean off their table so a family of four could have their spot. "Come on let's drop all this talk about Wes. As far as I'm concerned, the man is history. While Luke's still napping, what do you say we cruise through the tents? I heard from Hayden and Jordan there's a wealth of cool homemade stuff to be found."

"Just about everyone in town has a booth, from grandmas to teenagers, everyone wants a shot at participating."

"I love that about Pelican Pointe. Seems like your town is taking this whole school project very seriously."

Was it his town? Brent wondered as they started down the first aisle. But they didn't get very far before River stopped to admire what she saw in the first booth.

"Oh look at all these!" She reached out to run her hand along the bubble ridges of a handmade quilt done in squares of pale blue and yellow. "This would look great on Luke's bed."

"That's from the Crawford sisters. Marabelle from the looks of that one," Brent went on, earning a smile from Cora Webb, the fifty-something daughter of Ina, Marabelle's sister.

Standing across the display in charge of the booth, Cora said, "You've got a good eye there, Sheriff. Anyone who knows Aunt Marabelle knows she does her creations in different shades of blues and yellows while Mom's fond of using purple or red with white." Cora turned her attention to Luke. "Look at that sleeping baby. What a pretty child he is."

"Thank you," River said, beaming at her son. Instinctively she reached down to touch the soft down of his hair.

"Looks like his mama," Cora continued. When she saw River admiring the one in a soft lilac color, trimmed in creamy white, Cora added, "Uh oh," Cora said smiling at Brent. "This one has that look in her eye. That quilt is my mom's favorite because of the color. But she figures parting with it is for a good cause. We love the idea of bringing the school back to its glory days. You know, I went to school there. We were called the Warriors back then." Cora shook her head at the memory. "The Pelican Pointe Warriors."

Brent wasn't sure Pelican Pointe Elementary had ever had its own "glory days" but to bump River toward buying the quilt, which she obviously wanted, he threw out an enticement. "Remember, it is for a good cause."

"But where on earth would I put it?" River pointed out. "I don't even have my own place yet." Even as she tried to talk herself out of it, she reached for her bag and wallet. "I do love the color though. Will you hold it for me? I'll have to circle back because it won't fit in the stroller."

"No problem. You take your time."

They continued to the next vendor, this one belonging to Emma Colter, the dressmaker. River feasted her eyes on a collection of elegant beaded dresses, ones that were suitable to wear for special occasions or for a night out on the town.

There were booths filled with paintings on canvas done by Lilly Pierce, tablecloths crocheted by Myrtle Pettibone, and jewelry designed by Abby Bonner.

Fresh arrangements from Drea's Flowers shared a space with her family's landscaping nursery, the Plant Habitat. Tempted to load up on easy-to-grow cuttings of rosemary and basil in little starter containers, River had to remind herself she lived in a B & B. Now was not the time to start buying up nonessential items she had no room for.

She came to one stall manned by the guy she recognized, the one she'd pulled outside at his own birthday party. Even Troy Dayton had thrown together a display for his line of carved wooden jewelry boxes and the furniture he'd made out of old wooden pallets and crates.

"How's that new truck?" she asked the carpenter with a grin.

The lanky man smiled back. "It's awesome. You really had me going there that night."

"That was the idea," River said. "Did you make all this stuff?" she asked, scanning the bookcases and coffee tables. "You're a talented carpenter, Mr. Dayton."

"Call me Troy. Thanks. Just some things I used to tinker with when I didn't have all that much money for materials. I used what I found at the Dumpsters. Had all this stuff just sitting around the storage shed at my old place south of town. I figured the street fair would be a good way to try and get rid of it and put what I earned toward the school."

"I'll take one of your jewelry boxes," Brent said from beside her.

River bumped his shoulder. "Aw, thank you."

"Oh, did you want one, too?" Brent said with a twinkle in his eyes. He looked over at the now wide-awake Luke. "Looks like nap time is over."

"Well hello, sweetie. Want to get out of that thing and stretch your legs."

When Luke nodded, she unsnapped the buckle, set him down on the concrete and handed him a bottle of water. "You look thirsty. Why don't we check out the rest of the vendors and you hold my hand." The trio strolled along the row of booths, all the while Luke walked between them gripping their hands in both of his.

"I can't believe these vendors put their wares together in such a short amount of time," River stated. "Oh look, the Fanning Marine Rescue Center has a petting zoo."

Walking through the open gate, they were greeted by the sounds of noisy seals, a couple of sea lions and several playful otters. In the middle of the common area, Cord and Keegan had set up a fenced off area that held lambs, goats, cottontail bunnies, an assortment of ducks, and a honey-colored Shetland pony.

River and Brent grinned when they both noticed Luke couldn't take his eyes off the little horse.

They finally were able to persuade Luke to inch his way over a little at a time until Brent sat the boy astride the animal. Again, to capture the moment, River took out her cell phone making sure she got plenty of pictures from every angle—all the while realizing she'd never been happier than at that very moment.

On a rare day off, Cord took in the crowd streaming through the gates with his former California Guard buddy, Ryder McLachlan, at his side.

He slapped Ryder on the back and said, "It's good to see you again. I might not be able to spend the majority of time with you because I've started the core of my classes, but you're welcome to crash in the guest house at the farm for as long as you need it."

"I'm happy to work for my keep," Ryder offered. "I appreciate all you've done for me, Cord."

"Good to know. And hey, I had plenty of help getting back on my feet. I know what it's like to struggle with a variety of issues. I wouldn't be standing here if it weren't for Nick and Jordan and Keegan. And I believe in paying it forward."

"You know I'll do any kind of work to help out, anything at all."

"Since there's always something to do on a farm, there's a lot of ways you can help us out. You should know my offer isn't entirely altruistic. Taggert Organic is a busy place and getting busier every year, especially the October and November months. Harvesting the seasonal crops is part of it. But this is California where the growing season is year-round. As I told you in my email, I'm well into my fall semester with my classes. Because of that I just don't have the time to devote to the farm *and* keep up my grades. I don't want to let Nick down but at the same time, I can't afford to risk failing any of my courses. I'm committed to becoming a veterinarian before I'm an old man."

"You aren't that old."

"Don't kid yourself, I am for a student, oldest one in all of my classes. Anyway, there's enough to keep you busy there, you'll get a paycheck and a place to stay. Remember though, farm work might not be your cup of tea, so to speak. And if it isn't, don't hesitate to say something. It isn't for everyone. That's why you should tell me if it doesn't work for you. Jobs are starting to open up around town. There's a renovation in the works to bring the elementary school back. With your construction experience, you'd have no trouble hiring on. The only thing is I'm not exactly sure when it will start. But as soon as it does, Nick and Logan could use dependable men like you. Those two are heading up the project. And they are good guys. Make sure you go see Nick or Logan first thing tomorrow morning. And if you do get on, we'll manage just fine out at the farm. We always do, somehow, some way it always gets done."

"I'm not opposed to working both jobs, Cord. Seriously. I could use the dough."

In the way of buddies, Cord slapped Ryder on the back. "Believe me, that's music to my ears. And it's appreciated."

"Hey, what else have I got to do? You know though you'll have to show me the ropes around the farm. I'm a city boy but a quick learner."

"You like animals, right?"

"Love them but I've mostly been around the domestics, dogs, cats, that sort of thing. Never milked cows before."

"It's all state-of-the art stuff, no trick to it at all. I'll show you everything you need to know. And if I happen to miss a step, there's always Silas or Sammy or half a dozen others around to ask. Don't be shy either. Taggert Organic is a great place to work. There's a benefits package. Plus, you get the cottage thrown in as a place to crash. It isn't much—"

"Are you kidding? It's better than what I had back in Philadelphia."

"Sorry about your girlfriend, Ryder. Some women can really do a number on us with all the drama and head games they like to play."

"Looks like you put that behind you for good. It doesn't seem like you have to worry about that with Keegan."

"Keegan and I definitely had our challenges, but she's nothing like Cassie. Keegan's the other half of my heart."

"You're a lucky man."

"I am indeed."

"You really gonna be a vet?"

Cord sighed. "If I ever get through the med science and physics courses I will."

"Knowing you, I thought interning would be your problem."

"Nope. Turns out, that part's a piece of cake. Between the farm, Bran's vet practice here in town and the Rescue Center, I'm getting all the hands-on experience I can handle. Plus I get credit for all of it."

"I hope you realize how much you're helping me out."

"Same goes. Right now, you're a lifesaver. Oh look, here comes Keegan with Brent and River. Come on, Ryder, I'll introduce you to some more great folks."

Chapter Twenty-Four

There was something to be said for small towns, especially when you experienced what seemed like every square inch of it on foot.

Luke exhausted himself chasing around every animal inside the petting zoo. If it hopped, grunted, barked or mewed, Luke had been all over it. River had taken no less than four dozen photos for her newly created digital folder to prove it.

The sun was tipping into the horizon as River and Brent walked along the sidewalk on Ocean Street side by side as they headed to the Wagoneer with Brent carrying a worn-out Luke. River pushed the empty stroller, gliding along carried by love and happiness—the depth of which she hadn't felt in two years.

"I got some great shots today. Those big dark eyes of his were front and center in all of them. It's a great beginning to adding to the album I have from when he was born. I didn't have that many. I should've taken more. Had I known—"

Brent loved to see her excited, loved it when she got that gleam in her eye, or simply watching her watch her son. What he didn't like was to see her fade back into those days without Luke—and so many regrets. Maybe he understood better now spending time dwelling on those things that "might have been" just wasn't worth it.

"You'll make up for it now by taking out your camera more often," he proposed, glancing over at the boy he held in his arms. "He'll probably conk out any minute now. Instead of packing him up in the car and you heading back to the inn, how about we get takeout from the Diner. We'll go back to my place. I'll call in the order there, maybe talk Mona into delivery with an extra tip."

"Sounds like a plan. But you know I can't spend the night. I don't want Luke waking up in another strange place he isn't used to. He's had enough of that to last a lifetime."

"I know. Instead of hot and sweaty s-e-x, we'll order Max Bingham's Saturday night special, and stuff ourselves with southern-fried chicken and mashed potatoes. Then I'll follow you out to the B & B. How's that sound?"

She giggled. "The food sounds delicious but I'd prefer the s-e-x."

They crossed the street, their minds on how they'd spend the evening—when River waved to a passing couple with two kids in tow, a boy and a girl, heading south toward the Rescue Center—and probably the petting zoo before Cord closed the gates for the night. If the foursome hurried they'd just barely have time for the kids to give the rabbits a hug and take a ride on the pony.

She followed Brent as he led the way up to his front door. Reaching into his jeans pocket to pull out his keys, he turned to River. "Hold him for a sec, will you, while I jiggle the lock. It's a little tricky."

Just as he was about to stick the key in the door, Brent felt chills go up his spine first, and then Scott's presence surround him. Without thinking, Brent grabbed River and Luke and dove into the flower bed. Two shots in rapid succession rang out striking the door dead center where they'd just been standing only seconds earlier.

He motioned for her to stay down as a third shot whooshed over their heads. It was then he noted the sheer terror in River's eyes as she clung tight to Luke.

Brent crawled to the end of the dirt, purposely away from River and the boy and took out his cell phone, punched in nine-one-one. "This is Brent Cody. Get your asses over to my place now. I have shots fired again by an unknown assailant." As he relayed the info, more bullets pinged off the house.

"River, look at me." He saw the panic and did his best to ignore it. "I want you to remain here, stay down, as low to the ground as possible."

"Where…where…are you…going?" she stuttered.

"I need my weapon." He'd been so distracted by setting up the barricades for the street fair that morning he'd forgotten to strap on his gun. Pinned down now, without disconnecting the call, he inched his way back up and onto the porch, ducking around bullets the entire time.

Using his elbow, he smashed the pane of glass out of the front window of the living room and dove through the opening. Once inside, he hurried over to where he kept his loaded .45. He then moved to the hall closet to retrieve his Colt rifle.

Ramming the handgun into the waist of his jeans, he crossed to the front door. Even though he heard sirens in the distance and knew backup was on the way, he was on his own until they arrived.

Throwing open the door, he shouldered the firearm and went into sniper-mode. Walking out onto the porch, he used the scope to scan the street and the surrounding area.

Brent hunkered down at the end of the porch steps where River still crouched in fear with Luke. With his hand he signaled for her to move forward through the bushes and behind him into the house. "I've got you covered. Come on, River, move toward me."

All the while he continued to look for the shooter. But when he looked down at River again, he saw her shake her head and discovered she was too scared to budge.

"River, look at me. Look at me, honey," he repeated. "I have to get you and Luke inside and out of the line of fire," he whispered. "You need to scoot through the dirt on your belly if you have to and move toward me. Now, honey! Do it now! I'll see that you make it inside I promise. Come on, honey, you can do it."

He watched as she finally started to slink her way through the hydrangeas on her hands and knees with Luke creeping along under her, terrified. As soon as she got within arm's reach he protected Luke, shielding him with his own body while pushing him through the front door. He did the same with River.

By this time the first patrol car careened to a halt. Brent watched as two of his deputies jumped out with guns drawn. They crept behind the car looking for anything that moved.

"Where did the shots come from, Sheriff?" one officer yelled.

"Across the street somewhere near the pier."

A second patrol car pulled to a stop, then another and another until there were half a dozen cars each carrying two officers.

"Fan out, do a search." Brent yelled as he stepped back inside to check on River. He found her hiding behind the couch, clutching Luke in her arms. He went over, pulled both of them into his chest. "It's okay, you're safe now."

"Could Wes's parents have had anything to do with this?" River said in between quick breaths.

Brent shook his head. "No, don't think like that. This was meant for me, not you." They stayed like that for several minutes longer until an officer stepped through the doorway.

"Whoever it was is gone now. We did find a lot of shell casings."

"Bag 'em as evidence. Make sure you don't miss any. Cover every inch of the area. Canvass the neighbors to see if anyone saw anything. I want a description, detailed if you can manage it. Get a sketch artist out here."

"Will do," the deputy said, retreating back outside, leaving them alone.

"Look, I'll have an officer drive you back to Promise Cove," Brent assured her, not wanting to let her go.

"I…we want to stay with you."

He shook his head. "I need to find this person and until I do, you and Luke aren't safe being anywhere near me. You've already been with one asshole You don't need to put up with being with me and all that entails right now."

"You're breaking up with me?"

He squeezed her shoulders. "It isn't healthy for you and Luke to be around me right now. Don't you understand that? Until I find who's responsible for this, until I find who wants me dead, I need to put the brakes on my personal relationships."

Her temper flared. "And just how many personal relationships do you have going on right now?" she snapped.

"You know what I mean."

"No. I think you need to spell it out for me. You can't exactly shove people away just because things get tough."

"Tough? River, someone shot at me just now and they almost took you and Luke right along with it. You were so frightened you couldn't move out there and Luke was terrified. That's the third time they've made an attempt on my life. If they were a better shot…"

"Or if you hadn't felt Scott's presence…if that hadn't warned you in some way. I felt it too right before the shots rang out."

Brent ran a hand through his mass of hair. "Okay, if Scott hadn't warned me the first and second times, I might not be standing here talking to you."

"And if not for you I wouldn't have my son back. Do you think I'm that weak? That I won't stand with you like you stood with me these past months? What kind of a person do you think I am anyway?"

"I want you safe, River."

She ran a hand down his cheek. "How much safer could I be than with someone who cares about me and Luke."

"I love you, River. I'm not sure when it happened but I love you and Luke. All the way."

"Then we're exactly where we're meant to be."

Chapter Twenty-Five

The next day Brent walked into the Sheriff's Office unannounced to confront Jim Richardson face to face. If the man was behind all the attempts on his life, Brent wanted him to come clean about it, man to man.

He blitzed past an administrative assistant he didn't recognize because his own had been let go during his absence and replaced by Jim's personal aide.

Brent didn't bother to knock. Instead he threw back the door and stared at the balding, middle-aged gasbag who'd been a thorn in his side from the moment he'd taken office. Brent stated point blank, "I want you to tell me straight if you're the one responsible for all the chaos in my life, if you're the one who wants me dead. The least you could do is face me with the truth."

"What? Why would you think that?" Richardson asked, stupefied at the open accusation.

"Why? Because you haven't exactly been secretive about wanting my job. You've made it clear from day one you thought you were the better man. Ever since I got elected and you didn't, you've done everything you could at every opportunity to sabotage any changes I wanted to make. You made sure you poisoned people against me, making sure they saw things your way. For the most part, I didn't address the problems between us, a mistake I think. But I'm addressing it now. You've gone behind my back slinging a lot of shit. Up to now, I've taken it, but no more. Put up or shut up."

Brent could tell by the expression on Jim's face the man wasn't sure whether to admit it or try to bluff. After several long seconds, Brent was surprised when Jim decided to play it upfront. "I...all right...I admit I tried to damage your administration. But you have to believe me when I say I had nothing to do with all these shootings. I don't know anything about that."

"What about your flunkies? Maybe one night during a poker game you decide to put a subtle word out that you wouldn't be completely opposed to the idea if someone took me out."

"I didn't do that. I talked about mounting another campaign against you in the spring. That's it. I confess I wanted to throw up as many roadblocks as I could during the meantime because you have such limited experience. I've been in this department since I started as a rookie deputy some thirty years ago. You, you come along after a measly seven years and get elected because of your stint in the military."

"I know that's what you think, but believe it or not, the people elected me because they wanted change. They wanted me to clean up the department. I did or tried to. But you backstabbed me at every turn. You never could accept the difference in opinion." Brent shifted gears. "Are you the one keeping me on medical disability?"

Jim sent him a sheepish look. "Yes. But that was because I figured if I could keep you sidelined for as long as I could, it would give me the advantage in the spring. I'd be able to show my detractors I'm better at the job than you ever were."

"What you've done, Richardson, is split the department in half. And if I decide to fight you on this, I'm taking you down. Are we clear?"

Jim swallowed hard and nodded. "You wouldn't."

"Hey, you might've split the department, but I'm about to turn it on its head."

To Brent's surprise when he got outside to his truck, he found his brother leaning against the hood with his arms folded across his chest.

"What are you doing here?"

"River told Hayden where you were headed. I thought I'd better wait out here to see if they had to bring you out on a stretcher or in handcuffs. Either way, I figured you might need bail money."

Brent grinned. "So little faith in your big brother. That asshole is pulling strings from the inside to keep me out of action."

"I figured as much. But he isn't responsible for the shootings and the bomb, is he?"

"He's a slime-ball backstabber asshole, but he wouldn't go that far."

"You're sure?"

"I've confronted and interrogated suspects over the years. From what I could tell Richardson was on the level about that one thing."

"What are you gonna do? Fight to get your job back?"

Brent blew out a sigh. "Honestly, Ethan, I'm not sure I want the job back. When I got here this morning, I thought I did, had convinced myself I'd do anything. But right now, I'm not sure it's worth the aggravation. I don't mind a good fight but my heart just isn't in it. Did you know Murphy offered me the chief of police job?"

"I wasn't sure he'd mentioned it yet. But he asked me to recommend someone back in September, Labor Day weekend to be exact. I told him he should approach you."

"But that was before I got to Pelican Pointe, before my house exploded."

"Yep."

"Why? Did you have some premonition about this mess?"

"I wouldn't call it a premonition. After all, I had no way of knowing someone would try to kill you in such a drastic way. But I sensed you were unhappy for months before it happened, maybe as far back as last Christmas. Dad felt it, too. We talked about it, thought maybe it was a personal issue, you know, that maybe you didn't have anyone in your life and you weren't exactly thrilled about it."

"I was spending too much time at work that's all."

"If you say so."

"You don't think it was eighteen-hour days?"

Ethan shrugged. "I know how it was with me before meeting Hayden. It felt like something was missing in my life. And when I fell for her it was like a punch to the gut."

"Don't make it sound so thrilling."

"I must not be the great writer I thought I was because what I'm trying to tell you is that taking the fall changes your whole perspective on things. I gave up law enforcement because Hayden showed me that following a dream is what's important. I'm not sure I'd ever taken the plunge into writing full-time if it wasn't for the support I got from her."

"And what if I don't have a dream?"

"Everyone has something they want to do but might be stymied for whatever reason."

"Law enforcement is all I know."

"So is being single."

"I'm thinking about ending that."

"Brother, admit it. You've been headed that way ever since you met her."

"I guess I have."

Over the next couple of days things got more intense. With the street fair behind them, the entire town went on high alert making sure they looked out for Brent, River, and Luke. Every man took a turn at sentry duty outside Brent's house. In addition to that, off-duty deputies volunteered their time to stake out the area, courtesy of Jim Richardson. His way of showing Brent he'd had no part in the attacks.

River refused to hide, even though Brent wanted to send her and Luke out of town. She also wouldn't let him sit around brooding. So in spite of the circumstances, the newly-minted little family spent as much time doing normal things as they could.

But when they weren't shopping for groceries, eating out, or spending time with Luke at the beach, they tried figuring out the puzzle. Who hated Brent enough to kill him? There was plenty of input from friends and family. Even her crew stopped by to put in their two cents. Everyone seemed to have a theory.

They all had no problem digging into Brent's past with all the enthusiasm of amateur detectives.

"What about the ex-wife?" Julian asked. "The DNA came back female so, it's gotta be the ex-wife, right?"

"I checked Cindy's alibi, checked her current husband's. It isn't either one of them," Brent explained. "Besides, Cindy's moved on. Our marriage ended and neither one of us has any lingering hostility toward the other. There's no motive there."

"And you've gone through the list of people you've put behind bars?" Ethan wanted to know.

"Several times over," Brent said. "I've even gone back in time to when I was in the army. An MP makes a fair share of enemies."

River jumped on that. "Wait. You think someone from your unit could do something like this?"

"Not in my unit maybe but I did more than access control in Iraq."

"What's access control?" Laura asked.

"Checking IDs at the gate, making sure that only authorized personnel get on base, write speeding tickets when warranted, the usual cop stuff. But all that changed once I got to Baghdad."

"How so?"

"Other than patrolling and dodging IEDs you mean? When I wasn't doing convoy security for senior officers or detainee detail, I broke up fights, arrested soldiers if the situation warranted it, tried to keep the peace among units experiencing heavy conflict. Sometimes tempers flared."

"So with all that you could've royally pissed someone off, right?" Ethan prompted.

"Sure, it comes with the territory," Brent returned with a shrug.

Ethan thought about that for longer than he needed to. "You know, I think you might be onto something. This is a connection to someone in Iraq."

"Intuition?"

"Some, but more like deduction. The bomb should've been the giveaway."

While Brent ran down that avenue until he hit a dead end, he utilized every tactic he had at his disposal to track down the culprit. From his laptop he did online searches, checking on possible names that he'd stuck at the top of the likely suspect list—those he could remember anyway.

After everyone had left and they'd gotten Luke to sleep, River sat curled on the sofa studying the man from across the room. Intense concentration in those deep brown eyes had her staring at them until he finally looked up and made eye contact.

"Should I be concerned that Julianne Dickinson has decided to relocate to Pelican Pointe?" she asked with a glint in her eye.

Brent scowled in her direction. "Not a bit. Where did you hear that?"

"From your mom. Seems Nick offered Julianne a position as principal at the elementary school when it opens next fall. Julianne accepted."

"Good for her." His brow creased in irritation though at the implication. "So you think I'd be tempted to cheat with Julianne just because she's handy?"

River sighed. "It was a joke, Brent, nothing more. Where did you put your sense of humor?" But then she took in the look on his face. "I understand why you're so edgy tonight but don't read anything into my comment. I was trying to get your mind off this mess."

"Sorry. But after having been on the receiving end of cheating, never would I ever do that to another person. And I mean that. I would never put anyone else through the heartbreak and anguish of something like that. Ever."

"Just so you know, same goes for me."

He sat back in his chair and said, "What would you say if I told you I didn't want to be sheriff anymore?"

"I'd say do whatever makes you happy."

"Why aren't you trying to talk me out of law enforcement? If any situation called for anxiety, anyone else would see the danger I'm in and try to talk me into quitting."

"Is that what you think I should be doing? Talking you out of a career you obviously love? First of all, I'm not that sort of person, Brent. I agree this is a bad situation. Two days ago I was hiding in your front flower bed scared to death for me, for my son, for the man I love. But you handled it, Brent. That's part of who you are. The only time I'd ever try to talk you out of quitting is if it didn't make you happy."

"No, I still like the idea of law enforcement. I don't want to be sheriff anymore though." He felt good to voice it out loud. He told her about Murphy's offer.

She tilted her head and grinned. "It's a shame I might never get to see you in a uniform. Come to think of it, I like you a whole lot better out of one."

"That can be arranged. Are you sure Luke is sleeping?"

"Uh huh. He was so tired he almost fell asleep before he took the last bite of his hotdog."

Brent went to her then, lifted her feet to put them in his lap. His hands roamed under her top so he could explore the mounds of her breasts. They each began to shed their clothes. T-shirts came off, jeans dropped to the floor.

Rocking her back on the cushions, his body stretched out over hers. "If Luke's asleep, let's make this count then."

"It always does."

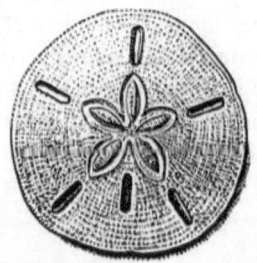

Chapter Twenty-Six

The next morning before breakfast Brent answered the door to a man holding up a government badge. "Sheriff Cody, I'm Mike Baker, ATF. Can I come in?"

"Sure." He led the way into the kitchen as Luke came out of the bedroom still wearing his pajamas carrying his Mr. Fuzzy Bear. A still sleepy Luke stretched his free arm out for Brent to lift him up. Scooping the tot off the floor, Brent asked, "Did the doorbell wake you up?"

Luke bobbed his head.

"What do you say we get our guest some coffee and get a bowl of Cheerios into you?"

"Cute kid. Yours?" Baker asked.

Brent grinned into Luke's dark eyes. "He is now."

About that time River came through the back door with a fistful of flowers in her hand she'd picked in the yard. "Look at these gorgeous yellow daisies—I hope you have a nice vase to do them justice..." But her words came to a sudden stop when she heard Brent's declaration and then took in the obvious stranger standing in the kitchen. Just as alarm tickled her throat, Brent introduced her.

Relief let her finally take a breath. "Here, give me Luke. I'll get him settled with his breakfast and bring you guys out some coffee," she said, wanting to avoid any chance Luke might overhear talk about bombs and suspects.

The two men backtracked to the living room where Brent took a seat on the sofa. "I guess if ATF shows up at my doorstep it means you've finally got a lead on my bomber."

"We do indeed. We have reason to believe the bomb that exploded inside your garage was a sophisticated device we'd only seen used in Iraq and Afghanistan. That is until we saw it earlier this year."

"The person who blew up my house has ties to the Middle East? I'd already come to that basic conclusion. But there's just one problem with my theory. The DNA I collected at the cliffs came back female. I did my damnedest last night but I never could think of a single female soldier I'd put in jail in Iraq."

"You were military police during your stint in the army, correct?"

Brent narrowed his eyes. "You already know I was. Why don't you just shelve the games and come out with it? Tell me what you've got."

"Okay. When you were in Iraq you arrested a man by the name of Allandale, Curtis, went by the name Rick. One night he got drunk, beat and raped one of his fellow soldiers, a woman by the name of Connie Hoffman."

"I remember that case. What does Curtis Allandale have to do with me? Last I heard he was serving twenty years in Leavenworth."

"Quite a lot. We think his sister, Jamie Allandale, has been on a tear this entire year, ever since Curtis committed suicide in Leavenworth last Christmas. She told friends, or anyone else who would listen, she'd make everyone pay who she feels was responsible for locking up her brother. You're on her short list of people she wants dead. I'd put her on the top of your suspect pile."

"How did this woman learn how to make the same kind of bomb we saw in Iraq?"

"Easy. She dated a soldier, one of her brother's army buddies. We've already interviewed him. He shared that info with her never suspecting for a moment she'd put it to general practice."

"I know for a fact it was Allandale who beat the crap out of the Hoffman woman before he raped her. Turns out, Corporal Hoffman wasn't his only victim either. Records show he was a serial rapist even before he joined the military. Although this sister would explain the female DNA we found where she'd parked up on the cliffs before taking a potshot at me."

"I know all about Curtis Allandale. I went through the case file. He and his sister grew up in the foster care system in St. Louis. For siblings, they were especially close because they were the only family each other had. Neither was ever adopted out. Both had drug problems off and on. My guess is when you made the arrest and testified against Curtis at his trial, Jamie took it personally. We think it sent her over the edge. We're pretty sure Jamie is the one who tried to kill the judge who sentenced Curtis to twenty years along with two other murders we've managed to link her to."

"Busy girl. She sounds like a psycho."

"That's not the worst of it. The sophisticated timing device used in your garage matched to the same kind of material, same construction, as the one used to try to kill the judge. Like you, the judge survived his injuries. Ten days later she went after her brother's attorney, a man by the name of Don Ellis in Kansas City, Missouri. Ellis wasn't as lucky. And neither was his wife. They both died in the blast. Arson investigators have tied Jamie to that bomb from the fingerprint she left on some of the material she used to put it together. We've had an arrest warrant out for her since last March. But Jamie's been clever. She's been on the run now for eight months. She did get picked up in a little town outside Denver last August for public intoxication. Apparently she spent twenty-four hours in their jail and they ended up letting her go without fingerprinting her or running any kind of check for warrants. No doubt about it. We missed an opportunity there because she's been one step ahead of us ever since."

"I hate to say this but that doesn't speak too highly of your tracking skills. If this Jamie Allandale is the one who set the bomb in my house, she's been a pain in the ass for months now. I'm tired of it."

"With three attempts on your life, you've been lucky."

Brent studied the agent's face. "Okay, you know more than you're saying. Tell me how I can help put this person where she belongs."

"I have agents crawling all over this place. If we play this right, I don't think Allandale will be able to stay away."

"Okay. But I need to take care of my family first."

The heavy dew peppered Jamie Allandale's boots and left wet spots on her camouflage pants as she surveyed her quarry from the knee-high grass on the dunes. She knew she had to wait for the right opportunity. She'd blown too many chances already to mess up again.

She shouldered the AR-15 and let the soft rolling mounds of sand hide her presence. Keeping to a low crouch, she eyed the people milling around at the site. For some stupid reason they were fond of digging in the mud.

Knowing she wasn't the best shot, she'd switched rifles, hoping that would solve the problem with her aim. She'd even spent time at the gun range, practicing with targets. She figured with the right weapon she could take a couple of the diggers out before anyone called the cops.

She tapped the handle of her brother's nine millimeter she'd tucked into her jacket pocket. The feel of metal gave her comfort. Absently she fingered the medallion she wore around her neck, the one Rick had given her for Christmas the last year before he'd gone overseas. It helped bring the focus back on Cody.

But the voices told her she needed to stay out of sight until that perfect window of opportunity—and made a vow to Rick she wouldn't miss again.

Chapter Twenty-Seven

For days River had resisted leaving Brent alone. But in the end she agreed to take Luke and spend a couple of days at Promise Cove. The B & B wasn't as far as Brent wanted to send her but it was as far as she was willing to go.

It wasn't until that afternoon when she was helping Jordan with kitchen duty peeling potatoes for dinner that it came to her. "Oh my God. He's acting as bait. That's why he sent me out here."

"What are you talking about?" Jordan asked. "You mean Brent?"

"Oh yeah, the sneaky so and so. He and that Agent Baker want to lure this woman out in the open. I'm sure of it." She turned her attention to Luke, albeit briefly, to make sure her little guy was oblivious to the conversation and lowered her voice. "Brent got me to take Luke out of town so he'd be free to draw this crazy woman out without worrying about us. Ever since that ATF agent came to see him, they've been cooking up this scheme to end this once and for all. I'm sure that's exactly what's happening." River untied the apron she'd put on and tossed it on the counter. "Will you watch Luke for me?"

"River, you can't go diving into Brent's stakeout. It isn't safe."

"I promise not to do anything stupid. I wouldn't do that. I have Luke to think about now."

"Then where are you going?"

"I just need to make sure Brent's okay."

"River this isn't a good idea."

"Maybe not. But Brent was there for me at a time when things looked bleak for me, for Luke. He got my son back to me, Jordan. I intend to make sure he knows how I feel about him."

"I'm sure he knows that."

"Look, it's a feeling I have. I need to be there…for Brent."

By the time River reached her Jeep though, that feeling became an urgent knot in the pit of her stomach. That's when she heard Scott's voice and knew for certain Brent was in deep shit.

She gunned the engine, threw the vehicle into reverse and headed south back into Pelican Pointe.

"Just calm down. Don't go charging in there with your head up your ass. He's a cop, River. He knows what he's doing."

River rolled her eyes at Scott sitting next to her in the front seat. "And he's a damned good one, too. That's why it's a stupid thing to do. Just wait until I see that Baker guy. This all started with him. It's his fault. I plan to give him a piece of my mind for dragging Brent into this screwball idea."

"If you think Cody can be dragged into anything he doesn't want to participate in, you don't know him half as well as you think you do," Scott reasoned.

"Men," River grumbled. "Hardheaded, never willing to listen to reason."

"From a male's point of view, let me just say, right back atcha."

"Oh, shut up."

Once she reached Beach Street, Scott did his best to offer input. "Approach the house from the rear. Park on Landings Bay and make your way between the houses. Down that way there's an alley where you can park. Leave your car there then go through Myrtle Pettibone's backyard along the side."

"Thanks," she muttered as she crawled out of the truck.

"You don't even have a weapon," Scott pointed out. "What's your plan?"

She blew out a breath. "Then be of some use and provide a distraction because I don't have a plan."

"What kind of distraction?"

"You're a damned ghost. Think of something. Rattle a chain or something."

"Too clichéd."

"Then get creative. Whatever you do, do it now 'cause that's his house right there."

Silent as she could, she moved along the side of the fence until she reached the corner of the stucco where she could peer around to take in the street.

A series of shots rang out. She heard voices, one calm, one agitated and growing more so.

"Put the gun down, Jamie!" Brent demanded.

River stuck her head out, saw three bodies lying across Ocean Street beside a black SUV. None were moving. River turned her eyes on the disturbed female, a blonde dressed in camouflage with her face painted up with what looked like war paint. That's when River spotted the cannon Jamie held in her right hand. The barrel glinted in the dwindling sunlight as Jamie approached the porch where Brent stood—inching her way with every step—aiming the large caliber weapon at Brent's chest.

Her words turned sharper and angrier. "You son of a bitch, you killed my brother," Jamie screamed at Brent. "You were the MP who arrested him then testified against him, you saw to it he was locked up in that horrible place. You might as well have killed him yourself when he took his own life. You did that to him."

Brent stared into Jamie's dull blue eyes and saw insanity. "I arrested your brother because he was accused of raping a fellow soldier, a corporal in his own unit," Brent pointed out calmly. Using all the patience he'd honed in law enforcement over the years, he made sure his voice stayed level when he added, "I practically caught him in the act, Jamie. Although by the time I got there it was too late to stop the actual attack from taking place."

"But Rick didn't do it," Jamie argued. "You arrested an innocent man."

"Didn't you hear what I said? I walked in on Rick after he'd beaten the victim so badly she had a concussion. Rick's own unit heard the victim's screams and called the MPs. It wasn't just me who testified against him but at least fifteen members of his own unit, the ones there that night. Do you intend to go after all of them?"

"If I have to."

"I did my job that night, Ms. Allandale, and if I had it to do over again, I wouldn't change a thing. I'd do exactly what I did. I arrested Rick while my partner took the victim to the hospital where they took more than a dozen photos of her that showed the bruises and bite marks Rick put there. The DNA and the bite marks matched your brother's. There's no mistake about who hurt Connie Hoffman."

"No, no, it wasn't Rick. He was a good person," Jamie said stubbornly. "He wasn't even there that night."

"Was that what he told you, Jamie? Because if it is your brother lied. I'm sorry but he did. Rick had violent rape in his past. He was charged with raping a sixteen-year-old when he was a senior in high school. That's what prompted him to join the army in the first place. When he left town, the teenager's parents decided to let it drop. Rick got lucky then. Reading your file from back then, you couldn't have been more than sixteen yourself at the time. That's young for a sister to deal with the fact her brother is a rapist. But this is about more than your brother's past. At his court-martial a seven-panel military court weighed all the evidence. My testimony was merely part of it. I told them what I'd seen the night I walked into the compound, described the condition of the woman. They considered all that. Rick was found guilty and got twenty years."

"My brother got beaten up in that God-awful prison almost every single day he was there. He couldn't take the abuse anymore. That's why he took his own life. One morning the guards found him dead. He'd hung himself. That's on you! It's your fault!"

"I'm sorry about your brother. I am. I know he was your only family. But I can't help what happened to him once he got to Leavenworth."

"You're a cold-hearted bastard, aren't you? My brother suffered every day because you locked him up in that hellhole. You sent him there."

"I arrested him. I testified against him in court. But I didn't send him there. The judge sentenced him. That's the system."

As River continued looking on from the corner of the house, she noted Brent kept trying to reason with the woman even to the point of stepping back with each verbal volley. But River didn't think Jamie was inclined to listen to reason. The blonde kept creeping toward him, getting closer with that big cannon of a gun pointed at his chest with each step she took until she was almost in his face.

"Now, River! Move now," Scott instructed. "Take her down!"

River took off running. "Don't!" she shouted. But about that time Jamie pulled the trigger as Brent ducked and reached for the .38 he'd strapped to his ankle.

The move saved him from taking a slug straight to the armor vest he wore.

Out of the corner of her eye, River caught Brent stagger backward until he hit the wall at the end of the narrow porch.

Heart pounding, as soon as she reached the steps, River leaped onto the shorter blonde's back. The tackle knocked Jamie down. The woman's chin hit the porch with a thud.

The jolt caused her to drop the weapon, skidding across the concrete.

Unarmed now, River took full advantage of her height and weight. Sitting on Jamie's back, she knocked her head a couple of times into the cement for good measure. River rolled her over, pinned the still struggling woman's arms back.

Brent righted himself enough to wobble over and pick up the weapon.

"What the hell were you thinking!" River shouted at Brent. "You could've been killed."

"I'm wearing a bullet-proof vest."

"And that makes it okay? I don't think so. That stuff dripping down onto the porch is blood. Yours."

"She was supposed to aim for the chest. What's taking Garver so long to get here?"

"You're armed and you let her get too damned close. Why? Why did you let her get that close to you?" River said, her voice still shaky, her hands still trembling in fear.

But about that time, cop cars began pulling to a stop along with the EMTs, she glanced around looking for Baker. When she didn't see the agent in charge she groaned, "Don't tell me he's one of the guys lying over there in the street?"

"I'm afraid so." Holding his right arm, he leaned up against the side of the house, tried to ignore the searing pain. He stared across the street at the ATF agents. As the paramedics rolled one over, he was relieved to see a thumbs-up sign from one of Baker's men.

"Baker better be all right because I can't wait to tell him what I think about his lousy idea."

Brent grinned, decided to make light of the situation. "You would, too. Did I mention that I haven't seen moves like that since last Thursday night's NFL game when a defensive back took down a quarterback with the game on the line?"

"Don't you dare try to make me laugh, Brent Cody. What you and Baker cooked up was downright ridiculous. Look at the body count."

"And what you did just now was nothing short of amazing. You'll probably get a medal."

"Don't try to butter me up. That won't work."

"Okay, then marry me."

When the blonde tried to move again and bump River off, River banged her head again on the cement one more time for good measure. "I'd say that's an excellent idea. Maybe then I can keep you out of trouble."

About that time, Brian Driscoll, one of the med techs dashed up the steps. "What've we got here?"

"Treat those guys first," Brent directed, bobbing his head across the street. "Those guys are in worse shape than I am. This is just a little scratch."

Brian shook his head. "Yeah. Right. Then you won't mind if I stick a Band-Aid on it."

Brent reached around behind his back, took out a pair of handcuffs with his left hand. He dangled them in front of River. "Since you took her down, I'll let you do the honors."

"Gladly," River said, snapping the metal in place around Jamie's wrists. River yanked Jamie to her feet and yelled at Garver, "Take this worthless excuse for a human being out of my sight."

All business, young Garver trotted over. "I think we can find a slew of charges to put her away for good. The least of which is possession of a firearm during the commission of a felony. But the feds get first dibs. According to them, she's looking at two counts of first degree murder."

"As long as there's no chance for her to resurface, I don't care which agency locks her up," Brent said.

It wasn't until later that night they learned that all of the agents who had been shot had successfully come through surgery. The most severely injured had been Baker. He'd been transported to Doc Prescott's office for immediate treatment before being life-flighted over to a larger facility in Santa Cruz. They were all expected to make a full recovery.

"I wanted to yell at Baker," River said as they got ready for bed. "I suppose now I'll have to let him off the hook."

"It wasn't Baker's idea, River."

"What?"

"River, I had to get this behind me, behind you. We couldn't move forward having this nutcase skulking around town, hanging around right across the street every time we left the house. Not now, not with Luke. This woman wasn't going to give up until she'd forced the issue." Brent shifted to put his arms around River. "How do you feel about sleeping with the chief of police tonight?"

"Right this second?"

"Yep. Effective immediately. To hell with waiting for the county to make a decision about giving me my job back. I called Murphy while you were giving Luke his bath. He agreed I could start immediately. So, it's official."

"There's a lawsuit in there somewhere."

Brent grinned. "You're just itching to throw business Kinsey's way, aren't you?"

"Nah, not really, not anymore. I have Luke back. And I have you. That's all that matters."

"Will you continue to head out to digs? It's okay with me if you do. I know how important your work is to you."

"Are you serious? I wouldn't leave my kid now if someone paid me fifty million bucks. Not to mention I recently have this hot guy in my life. Looks like you're stuck with me. My roving days are over."

"From where I am that's not such a bad deal." He kissed her hair, ran his good hand down to knead a breast.

"Besides, your dad had this idea about opening a museum in one of those old buildings across from the Marine Rescue Center. We'd take the artifacts we find out of the ground and put them on display to share with tourists, school groups, and anyone else interested in the history of the area. And you know what? It sounds crazy, but I think to keep Marcus happy, Emilio would go for it. And I'd be the curator of the whole thing, in charge of cataloguing the items, tours, that sort of thing."

"Is that something you'd be interested in doing?"

"You bet, right up my alley."

"You do realize Marcus suggested this because he doesn't want you globetrotting around, right? My dad is great and all but he has this distorted sense that my woman shouldn't go traipsing all over the world."

She giggled. "I got that. But Marcus has nothing to worry about on that score and neither do you. I'm not going anywhere. Try to picture that big-ass canoe on display in the foyer of the newly remodeled Pelican Pointe Museum. I know I have."

"Do we have to talk about canoes right this second?"

"I don't know. That canoe gets me all hot and bothered, especially if I imagine you paddling your way to shore in it, coming in from a catch all hot and sweaty wearing nothing but a loin cloth and skin."

"Then by all means, continue with that image," he muttered, nipping at her bottom lip.

"Oh I plan to do just that," she said as she pushed him back into the pillows to show him she meant it.

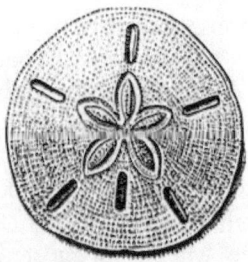

Epilogue

Four weeks later
Christmas Eve Night
Pelican Pointe, California

River stood at the kitchen table rolling out the last of the cookie dough while Luke swung his legs back and forth as he sat next to her, coloring with his crayons.

Thanks to her grandmother's recipe that promised to make four dozen, she thought she'd have plenty on hand for any guests that might drop by. But between what Luke and Brent had already packed away, she doubted she'd have enough to share with Hayden and Ethan when they got here for the pot-luck supper they'd planned together.

She and Luke already slathered icing on two dozen assorted reindeer, Santas, Christmas trees, and snowmen and were waiting for another batch to come out of the oven. That's why sugar, vanilla and butter smells wafted through the house in waves.

Brent walked through the back door with an armload of wood for the fire.

"You know we won't be able to build a fire tonight, right? Rumor has it Santa won't be able to get down the chimney if there's smoke coming out of the top."

"Santa!" Luke yelled out, clapping his hands together.

"With the breeze blowing in off the ocean the wind chill makes it feel like forty degrees out there. A fire will make things nice and cozy. I promise it'll go out long before Santa ever lands on the roof though," he told Luke with a wink. He couldn't believe how easy it had been to accept the child as his own.

As Brent moved past the table, he snaked out a hand from under the firewood hoping to score another cookie. But River slapped it away. "You eat any more and they'll have to wheel you into Doc Prescott's treatment room in a sugar coma."

"I'll take my chances. They're too good to pass up. Aren't they, Luke?"

"I want anover snowman, a red one dis time," Luke prompted.

"See what you started," River said. "We'll be eating supper in less than an hour."

"I wanna hotdog."

"Not tonight, young man. We're eating healthy. There's yummy homemade sweet potato chips and goldfish pizzas and broccoli cheese bites for you."

Brent rolled his eyes. "I'm taking bets on whether or not you get him to eat any of that stuff. Whaddya bet?"

"You're probably right. Come on, Luke. Let's go into the living room and finish putting the ornaments on the tree. Then we'll wrap the rest of the presents before Hayden and Ethan get here. That should take your mind off cookies."

"Why?" Luke asked.

"Because mommy's running out of time. Help me listen for the oven timer, will you?" she asked, picking up Luke and swinging him onto her hip as she followed Brent into the living room.

"Luke, come help me hang your stocking," Brent offered.

Setting him down, River went to retrieve the rest of the decorations from the hall closet, a roll of gift wrap, bows and tape and took it all over and dumped it near the bottom of the tree so she could spread out on the floor.

On bended knees, she handed a stocking to Brent for him to hang on the mantel. As she scooted a few of the packages out of the way to make more room, she leaned over to rearrange the boxes and spotted a gift box she didn't recognize underneath. Picking it up, she gave it a light shake. "Brent, did you get Luke a present and not tell me?"

"Nope. You know what we agreed on." He lowered his voice so Luke wouldn't hear. "The little tool bench and the Tonka truck he asked for. Why?" But he was beginning to get a strange feeling in his gut as he eyed the package. "You didn't buy that? How did it get in here then?"

"No. It was behind the tree. Look at the wrapping. It looks like old-fashioned Christmas paper from another era. See, it's got that yellowish tint to it. And the holly wreath and berries and those candles with the crystal tops make it look vintage. There's a card addressed to Luke."

Brent stared at the rectangular box in her hand covered in the dated paper. "I didn't buy that, River. That better not be ticking."

She left her hand on the package long enough to get a more measured glimpse—from the past—and smiled at the image. "It's okay. Wait. Luke, would you like to open an early present?"

"Is it from Santa?" Luke piped up.

"In a way it is."

"You're sure it's okay?" Brent asked before helping Luke with the box. "You know who sent this?"

"I do and I'm sure it's okay." She watched as her son and the man she loved ripped off the old decorative wrap. Cringing a little as the pretty paper shredded into bits and pieces. She watched as it drifted down in strips on the floor around Luke's feet.

It was Brent who first looked inside. As soon as his eyes landed on the toy, his lips curved up. He let Luke take it out of the box.

"It's a twuck!" Luke said, immediately kneeling down to test out the wheels and run it along the hardwood in a circle.

Built from sturdy maple, painted red, white, and blue, the heirloom fire truck had been designed to be passed down from generation to generation, from father to son.

"Who did this?" Brent asked. "What does the card say?"

Unable to speak, unbelievably moved, tears streaming down her face, River handed it off to Brent to read.

From one guy to another, this truck was once mine. It was my favorite toy when I was your age. I spent many hours putting out fires with it. I hope you have as much fun as I did. Merry Christmas, Luke, you've earned it. Your mom and new dad have, too. Much love from your Uncle Scott. P.S. Be sure to leave out plenty of cookies and milk for Santa because he gets hungry making his rounds in the California cold.

Dear Reader:

If you enjoyed *Starlight Dunes*, please take the time to leave a review.
A review shows others how you feel about my work.
By recommending it to your friends and family it helps spread the word.
If you have the time let me know via Facebook or my website.
I'd love to hear from you!

For a complete list of my other books visit my website.
www.vickiemckeehan.com

Want to connect with me to leave a comment?
Go to Facebook
www.facebook.com/VickieMcKeehan

Don't miss these other exciting titles by bestselling author

Vickie McKeehan

The Pelican Pointe Series
PROMISE COVE
HIDDEN MOON BAY
DANCING TIDES
LIGHTHOUSE REEF
STARLIGHT DUNES
LAST CHANCE HARBOR
SEA GLASS COTTAGE
LAVENDER BEACH
SANDCASTLES UNDER THE CHRISTMAS MOON
BENEATH WINTER SAND
KEEPING CAPE SUMMER (2018)

The Evil Secrets Trilogy
JUST EVIL Book One
DEEPER EVIL Book Two
ENDING EVIL Book Three
EVIL SECRETS TRILOGY BOXED SET

The Skye Cree Novels
THE BONES OF OTHERS
THE BONES WILL TELL
THE BOX OF BONES
HIS GARDEN OF BONES
TRUTH IN THE BONES
SEA OF BONES (2018)

The Indigo Brothers Trilogy
INDIGO FIRE
INDIGO HEAT
INDIGO JUSTICE
INDIGO BROTHERS TRILOGY BOXED SET

Coyote Wells Mysteries
MYSTIC FALLS
SHADOW CANYON
SPIRIT LAKE (2018)

ABOUT THE AUTHOR

Vickie McKeehan's novels have consistently appeared on Amazon's Top 100 lists in Contemporary Romance, Romantic Suspense and Mystery / Thriller. She writes what she loves to read—heartwarming romance laced with suspense, heart-pounding thrillers, and riveting mysteries. Vickie loves to write about compelling and down-to-earth characters in settings that stay with her readers long after they've finished her books. She makes her home in Southern California.

Find Vickie online at
https://www.facebook.com/VickieMcKeehan
http://www.vickiemckeehan.com/
https://vickiemckeehan.wordpress.com